CHASING SUNSETS

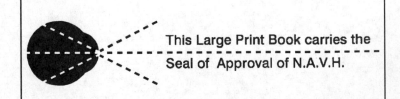

This Large Print Book carries the
Seal of Approval of N.A.V.H.

CHASING SUNSETS

KAREN KINGSBURY

THORNDIKE PRESS

A part of Gale, Cengage Learning

GALE
CENGAGE Learning·

Farmington Hills, Mich • San Francisco • New York • Waterville, Maine
Meriden, Conn • Mason, Ohio • Chicago

LIBRARY OF CONGRESS CATALOGING-IN-PUBLICATION DATA

Kingsbury, Karen.
    Chasing sunsets / by Karen Kingsbury. — Large print edition.
      pages cm. — (Thorndike Press large print basic) (Angels walking ; book 2)
    ISBN 978-1-4104-7499-5 (hardcover) — ISBN 1-4104-7499-2 (hardcover)
    1. Miracles—Fiction. 2. Life change events—Fiction. 3. Large type books. I. Title.
PS3561.I4873C48 2015b
813'.54—dc23   2015000501

Published in 2015 by arrangement with Howard Books, a division of Simon & Schuster, Inc.

To Donald:

Well, my love, the nest isn't empty just yet, but it's getting there. The years have picked up speed and now most of our boys are out of the house and caught up in the wonder of college at Liberty University. Kelsey has been married to her wonderful Kyle for nearly three years and Tyler is about to graduate from college. Where in the world has the time gone? Wasn't it just yesterday that we were taking the kids to the zoo for a Super Surprise Saturday? Or bringing home three wide-eyed orphans from Haiti? So much laughter, so much fun, and always you at the center, leading the way. I remember once writing down the ages the kids would be as the years ahead unfolded. The years sounded almost futuristic — 2014, 2015, 2016. A million miles away from my comfortable place at the turn of the century. I would try to imagine life without the noise and homework and music and childlike laughter. Life without six sports and theater and dance schedules to somehow balance. I couldn't picture it. But now that we're here I can see something I didn't see back then. I see you, my love, ever so much more clearly. You and me, holding hands and having more and more time together, the two of us rejoicing over the goodness of God, the faithfulness of Him. The lesson we're learning is this: It's all wonderful. Every amazing season back then and now and yet to come. It's been said the best is yet to be. And so it is, especially with you by my side. Let's play and laugh and sing and dance, and together we'll watch our children take wing. The ride is breathtakingly wondrous. I pray it lasts far into our twilight years. Until then, I'll enjoy not always knowing where I end and you begin. I love you always and forever.

To Kyle:

Kyle, our newest son, who so beautifully leads and loves our only daughter. I think of Don and me, standing on the beach in Mexico on the last day of our honeymoon, praying for the next generation — kids that God might bless us with and their future spouses. That day as we prayed on the beach, thousands of miles away, you were born. While we were praying. Amazing how God works out His plan and how faithful He is to answer prayers. Kyle, your heart is beautiful in every way. You cherish simple moments and are kind beyond words. You see the good in people and situations and you find a way to give God glory always. Your music is taking wing and now everyone knows about Kyle Kupecky and your gift of singing for Jesus. God is doing such great things with you and Kelsey and your ministries, your love for people. I thank God for you and look forward to the beautiful seasons ahead. Love you always!

To Kelsey:

My precious daughter, how wonderful that our dream of making a mother-daughter card and gift line has come true. Possibilities by DaySpring/Hallmark is now in stores everywhere . . . and we are hearing such beautiful things about how this line is bringing people closer. It's all just a dream come true — something I couldn't have seen coming. But God did . . . and He continues to surprise us, doesn't He? Also, I'm so happy for you and Kyle. Your first book comes out soon and girls everywhere will want to read *The Chase: When God Writes Your Fairytale.* I pray it will change the hearts of this generation. I've never known you to be so happy, and time and again I point to you and Kyle as proof of God's faithfulness. Now, as you two move into the future God has for you, as you follow your dreams and shine brightly for Him in all you do, we will be here for you both, praying for you, believing in you, and supporting you however we best can. In the meantime, you'll be in my heart every moment. I love you, sweetheart.

To Tyler:

It's hard to believe you're so close to college graduation. The time has moved along faster every year and now here we are . . . knocking on the door of all that is ahead. All that God is still revealing to you. I'm so proud of the lead roles you've had in your college musicals. To think your papa told you he could see you as Tony from *West Side Story* one day . . . and that this past year you were Tony — it's further proof of God's love. But most of all I am proud of the example you have been to your friends — day in, day out. People around you are stronger because of you, and they are closer to God because of your example. I love that most of all about you, Ty. I'm so excited about your future. You are such a talented screenwriter, songwriter, director. One day the whole world will know! However your dreams unfold, we'll be in the front row cheering. Hold on to Jesus, son. Keep shining for Him! I love you.

To Sean:

You're finishing your first year at Liberty University with the dream of playing football. No one has worked for it harder than you, and we're so proud of your effort. But more than that, we are proud you want to be at a school that puts God first. In every sense of the word. He has such great plans for you. Sean, you've always had the best attitude, and now even when there are hard days — you've kept that great attitude. Be joyful, God tells us. Be honest. Be a man of character. Keep working, keep pushing, keep believing. Go to bed every night knowing you did all you could to prepare yourself for the doors God will open in the days ahead. You're a precious gift, son. I love you. Keep smiling and keep seeking God's best.

To Josh:

What changes you've gone through in the last year. You're at Liberty University now, working on becoming a champion for Christ! Whether on the football field or soccer field, you play with everything in you, leaving everything you have in the moments between the whistles. I'm so proud of you! This we know: there remains a very real possibility that you'll play competitive sports at the next level. God is going to use you for great things, and I believe He will put you on a public platform to do it. Stay strong in Him, and listen to His quiet whispers so you'll know which direction to turn. I'm so proud of you, son. I'll forever be cheering on the sidelines. Keep God first in your life. I love you always.

To EJ:

EJ, it's hard to believe you're finishing up your first year at Liberty University! As you continue to walk into this new season, I'm so glad you know just how much we love you and how deeply we believe in the great plans God has for you. With new opportunities spread out before you, keep your eyes on Jesus and you'll always be as full of possibility as you are today. I expect great things from you, and I know the Lord expects that, too. I'm so glad you're in our family — always and forever. Thanks for your giving heart, EJ. I love you more than you know.

To Austin:

Austin, what changes God has brought about in your life this past year. First the devastating blow that you could no longer play football, that you would never suit up for your junior year or ever again, for that matter. The heart defect you were born with finally caught up with you in ways we didn't see coming. And though you are so very healthy, as the doctor told you that very sad day, his job is to keep you alive. And so we have watched you cry and call out to God, but also we have watched you embrace this next stage of life like a quarterback, fourth and twelve. Like every-thing about tomorrow depends on it. We've always known there's no quit in you, and now we can see that happening. God has great plans for you still, son. What they are? Well, that's still taking shape and it has all of us more excited than ever! God saved you at birth and again when you gave your life to Jesus. Now He has saved you a third time by taking you off that field before the unthinkable might've happened.

Whatever He has ahead, I pray you will change the world for the better. I am completely convinced. But through it all I pray you remember you are only as strong as your dependence on Jesus. Only as brave as your tenacious grip on His truth. Your story is a series of miracles and this next chapter will be more of the same. Along the way, your dad and I will be in the front row cheering you on — whatever you play. Whatever you do. Sky's the limit, Aus. The dream is yours to take. I thank God for you, for the miracle of your life. I love you, Austin.

And to God Almighty, the Author of Life, who has — for now — blessed me with these.

PROLOGUE

Town Meeting — Heaven

Jag was going to volunteer.

He had decided long before he walked into the meeting. It had only been a matter of convincing his still-broken heart. He moved into the room as the others took their seats. A spot at the back was still open. He slipped in and waited.

At the front, Orlon rose to face them. "You know why we're here." His voice sounded somber. "It's time for the next part of our mission." He set his shoulders back, strong, determined. "This time the task ahead is very serious. Life or death."

Jag closed his eyes. The feel of the moment, the electricity and sense of expectation — all of it was familiar. Just like last time. *Am I wrong? Wrong to think I can make this journey when I failed last time?*

No answer whispered to him, but Jag knew what God would say. The Father had already told him after his last Angels Walking mission. What had happened, the tragedy of it all — it wasn't Jag's fault. Earth belonged to the ruler of the kingdom of the air. Darkness would often prevail among men.

Until the trumpets sounded. And the Father would defeat evil for all eternity.

But that truth didn't lessen the weight of Jag's decision this time around. He had been told he would work again, that the day would come when another Angels Walking mission would require his skills. The time was now. Jag was convinced.

He opened his eyes.

Orlon was explaining the situation. "This time our mission involves Marcus Dillinger, the pro baseball pitcher."

Around the room the angels nodded. They had all shared a window to the work of the last Angels Walking team. The way Marcus Dillinger was used by God to bring his childhood friend Tyler Ames to Los Angeles.

"Marcus was MVP for the World Series win a few months ago." Orlon smiled. "On earth this is a big deal." His smile faded. "But now more than ever, Marcus is searching for meaning. Not only in life, but in love."

Of course he is, Jag thought. *Man's trophies*

and titles, his fortune and fame, could never satisfy. Deep in the depths of any human heart that much was understood. Chasing after such meaningless things resulted in emptiness every time.

Orlon went on. "Marcus is a good man. He will not let darkness satisfy the longing in his soul. He wants the plans of God. This will work in our favor." His voice fell. "Even when everything else in Marcus Dillinger's world will seem to work against us."

He explained that Tyler Ames and his longtime love, Sami Dawson, would be part of this mission, as would Mary Catherine — Sami's friend and roommate. "The success of this mission will come down to Mary Catherine." Orlon narrowed his eyes, his shoulders set. "Our team will work in the inner city of Los Angeles, where survival is key. I'll be clear with you. The enemy wants to cut short several lives — especially the lives of Marcus and Mary Catherine."

Orlon hesitated. "You remember the ultimate goal." It wasn't a question. Of course they remembered. All of heaven was mindful of the near-impossible goal for this angel team, the way each mission would require victory before the next could begin. How only at the end of these missions would they know if they were ultimately successful.

That success would come with the birth of a baby named Dallas Garner.

"As I've told you" — Orlon moved along the front of the room — "if the child is born, he will grow to be a very great evangelist, a teacher who will help turn the sons and daughters of Adam back to knowledge of truth and love. Back to a foundation of Scripture. Dallas will offer a revival, especially for the United States. A nation that once trusted and revered God."

Orlon had never looked more serious. "We have one successful mission behind us. We have several more ahead. But this one . . . this one will be dangerous for everyone involved. Even our team of Angels Walking."

The angels shifted in their places, as if the heaviness in the room had taken up residence on each of their shoulders. Jag felt it most of all. Angels were never in physical danger, of course. They were eternal. But they could lose a battle with man, and certainly they could be detained by the enemy. When Jacob of the Bible wrestled an angel, Jacob won. And when an angel was sent to Daniel in Babylon, the angel was prevented from his mission — blocked — by the prince of darkness.

Orlon checked the notes on his mahogany podium. "Michael tells me the baby has only a two percent chance of being born. The enemy has orchestrated a number of very dangerous circumstances. Health issues, relationship struggles, discouragement." He looked around the room again. "Our Angels Walking team will be very busy."

Jag ran his hand through his wavy blond hair and flexed his muscles. The tension in the room was building. It was time to choose the angels. Everyone could feel it.

"I need experience on this Angels Walking team. Veterans." Orlon searched their faces. "Who would like to go?"

Jag didn't hesitate. He rose to his full height. "I volunteer."

Orlon paused but only for a moment. His eyes spoke volumes, for he knew Jag's history, his heartbreaking past. "Jag." A smile tugged at Orlon's lips. "I was hoping you would consider this. It's time."

Once more Orlon looked around the room. "Who will take this Angels Walking mission with Jag?"

From the front of the room a willowy black angel rose from her seat. Her eyes shone like emeralds as she looked back at Jag and then at Orlon. "I volunteer."

Aspyn.

If Jag could've chosen any angel in the room, he would've chosen her. The two of them had succeeded at a dangerous Angels Walking mission a hundred years ago in Germany. Aspyn was skilled at intervening in battle, practiced at working with people who lived angry, violent lives.

Orlon looked satisfied. He drew a deep breath. "Very well." He motioned to the others. "Our job will be important also. We will watch and we will pray. Beginning now."

In a rush the other angels surrounded them. And with that their voices rose to the Father on behalf of the mission ahead.

Never mind the danger. Jag had a decade of defeat to put to an end.

He was practically desperate to begin.

1

The January sunshine cast an array of shimmering diamonds across the Pacific Ocean that early morning as Mary Catherine kicked off her sandals and headed for the water.

"We'll freeze. Even with our wetsuits." Sami Dawson, her best friend and roommate, was right behind her, laughing at the insanity of their decision.

"Only for a few minutes." Mary Catherine's long golden red hair was caught up in a ponytail and it flew behind her as she ran. She was laughing, too, but more because she loved starting her Saturday like this. "Once we're in we won't feel a thing."

They carried their boogie boards as they ran through the shallow surf and then jumped over the frigid foamy breakers. In no time they were in up to their shoulders, past the foam and ready to ride the next set of waves.

Mary Catherine shook the water from her hair, breathless. "See? It isn't terrible!"

"Sure." Sami shivered. She nodded to the wave headed their way. "Come on. Keep moving."

They caught the first one and rode it all the way to shore. The spray of cool seawater in their faces, the rush of the powerful ocean beneath them. Mary Catherine loved everything about this. She felt alive and whole and connected to God. A thrilling diversion from the news she'd received last week.

The news that her heart didn't have long.

Sometime today she would tell Sami the truth about her health, come clean about the things she'd been hiding. But for now she would enjoy this moment. And she would remember what her mother told her years ago. Life could never be measured in the number of days a person lived, but only by the beautiful, brilliant life that had colored those days.

Mary Catherine paddled back out alongside Sami. Her friend's eyes were wide. "I think I saw a dolphin." She pointed behind the waves. "Like fifteen feet that way."

Mary Catherine scanned the distant water. "I hope it wasn't a shark."

"What?" Sami let out a quiet scream. "Don't say that!"

"I'm kidding." Mary Catherine laughed again. "I saw it, too. A few of them. Definitely dolphins."

Another swell came and again they caught the ride all the way in. They took their boards and sat on the wet sand, trying to catch their breath. Sami shook her shoulder-length dark hair. "Thank you for making me do this. I'm not cold."

"It's perfect out here." Mary Catherine headed back out. "Come on. A few more."

They pushed through the white surf to the smooth area and waited. Sami wiped the water from her face. "I can't wait for tonight. I really think Marcus is onto something with this youth center."

"Me, too. I'm glad we're going early." Mary Catherine felt it, the way she always did at the mention of Marcus's name. A feeling that started in her heart and made its way down her arms and up the back of her neck. She hated the reaction. The last thing she needed was a crush on Marcus Dillinger. "Is he still dating his coach's niece?"

"He is. We're double-dating with them next week." Sami wrinkled her nose. "I don't think they're a good match." She shrugged. "I don't see it."

Between her heart condition and half a

dozen charities she was involved with, Mary Catherine certainly had no time to worry about a professional baseball player. The guy could never be her type.

They rode a few more waves and then Mary Catherine nodded to the shore. "Let's dry off."

"Good idea. I still have to do laundry before we meet up with the guys."

Their towels were ten yards up the beach, and after a few minutes they pulled on sweats and sat on the sand facing the water. Mary Catherine turned her face to the winter sun and savored the way it melted through her. How could anything be wrong with her heart? She felt too good to be sick.

The quiet suited them. Since rooming together a few years ago they'd had the sort of friendship that could erupt into laughter or feel comfortable in complete silence. They were very different, she and Sami. Mary Catherine broke the silence. "Did you and Tyler have fun last night?"

"We did." Sami's smile lit up her face more than the morning sun ever could. "I can't believe how good things are. I think he's going to ask me to be his girlfriend. Officially."

Mary Catherine jumped to her feet. "Really?" She danced around in a circle.

"Yes!" She raised both fists in the air. "Yes, yes, yes!" Then just as quickly she dropped back to the beach. "What in the world is taking so long?"

"Well . . ." Sami shrugged, sheepish. "It's more me. Like I told you." This time her laugh sounded more nervous. "I needed time."

"Come on." Mary Catherine leaned back on her hands and grinned at her friend. "You've been in love with him since you were in high school."

"But I was practically engaged to Arnie." Sami's tone held a mock protest, nothing serious. After a few seconds she burst into the sort of laughter she and Mary Catherine shared so often. "Okay, okay! You're right. I don't need much more time."

"Oh, come on." Mary Catherine leaned forward and crossed her legs. "How long before he'll ask you to marry him?"

"Seriously?" Sami looked shocked. "Let's not rush things!"

"It won't be long." Mary Catherine raised her eyebrows. "You heard it from me first."

"You're crazy."

"But in this case, also right." Mary Catherine let her silliness fade, let the breeze off the ocean frame the moment, the significance of it. "Was it beautiful? Your date?"

"It was. We were at Disneyland, as you know." She looked so much happier than before, back when she was dating Arnie. "When it was dark he took me to the bridge in front of Sleeping Beauty's castle." Sami was sitting cross-legged now, facing Mary Catherine. "He told me he never stopped adoring me, never stopped thinking about me. Even with every bad decision he made back then."

"That's sweet."

Sami's smile held a contentment that hadn't been there in the beginning, back when Tyler first returned to Los Angeles. "He says he has just one regret now. One that still haunts him." She paused and lifted her face toward the sun for a few seconds before looking back at Mary Catherine. "That he ever left me at all."

The story touched Mary Catherine. She couldn't be happier for her friend, for the love she'd found. "I want to be maid of honor." She held up both hands in a teasing surrender. "That's all I'm saying."

"Seriously, though . . . you could be right." Again Sami's joy was tangible. "I love him so much. This new Tyler, the one with lessons learned and a faith that gets stronger every day . . . I just never dreamed we would have a second chance."

"I did." Mary Catherine gave Sami a knowing look. "Remember?"

"True." Sami's laugh mixed with the disbelief she still clearly felt. "You told me I couldn't leave Florida on that business trip, unless I spent a few hours with him."

"Let's just say I'm a very good friend." Mary Catherine grinned.

"Definitely maid of honor status."

The sun was higher in the sky, temperatures heating up. Mary Catherine allowed the silence again. She needed some kind of buffer before she could tell Sami the truth about her health. The one thing they'd never talked about. She checked her phone. Nearly eleven o'clock. They needed to be at the newly renovated youth center by three that afternoon to help with last-minute details for the grand opening.

Finally Mary Catherine shifted on her towel so she was facing Sami. "You ever wonder why I changed my eating habits lately? No more frozen pizza?"

Sami's smile came easily. "The whole no sugar, no gluten, no grain thing?" She uttered a quick laugh. "Because you're amazing and you like feeling good enough to climb walls and jump out of planes?" She laughed again. "That's what I always figured. I sure couldn't eat that clean."

Mary Catherine hated what was coming. She wanted everyone in her world to go on thinking she had switched up her eating because of her zest for life. Nothing more. She hesitated.

Finally Sami's laughter faded. "Isn't that why?"

"No." Mary Catherine's smile remained, but she could feel a sadness filling her eyes. "I'm diabetic. Type two."

"What?" Sami put her elbows on her knees and leaned closer. "Since when? How come you never told me?"

"I only found out last month, and my eating keeps it under control." She angled her head, willing her friend to understand. "I don't like thinking about it. Obviously. And, well, the way I eat I don't need pills or shots. I check my blood sugar every morning. So far, it's controlled."

Sami hesitated. "Okay, good. You scared me for a minute."

"There's more. Diabetes runs in our family." She paused. "Just like congenital heart defects. My uncle died because of his heart disease when he was in his late twenties. My mom never had any problem, but the gene passed on to me."

Again Sami looked beyond confused. She stared at Mary Catherine. "You're saying . . . there's something wrong with your heart?"

Mary Catherine took a slow breath. "I was born with a coarctation of the aorta, and a bicuspid aortic valve. I had emergency surgery when I was a few weeks old and since then I get checkups every year." She forced her smile. "No big deal."

"You should've said that first." Sami looked like she wasn't sure whether to relax or expect more news. "So . . . you're okay? Like long-term?"

"Not really." She hadn't talked about this with anyone. Not even her parents. "I had a checkup last week. My heart's enlarged — which isn't good. And my valves are deteriorating. I'll need a transplant sometime in the next year."

Sami pulled her knees up to her chest and hung her head for several seconds. When she looked up, there was no mistaking the fear in her eyes. "What does that mean?"

"The valve transplant isn't the worst thing. People survive those — though mine will be trickier for a lot of reasons." Mary Catherine looked to the sky; the California sun filled the morning. "It's my enlarged heart that's the real problem. Even with a transplant I may not have more than ten years. Maybe less."

The color left Sami's face and she simply stared, like she couldn't begin to believe the news. "That's . . . awful."

"You're the only one who knows." She reached out and gave Sami's hand a brief squeeze. "You're my best friend, Sami. I've been looking for a way to tell you."

Sami hung her head for a long moment again. When she turned to Mary Catherine, there were tears in her eyes. "There must be something they can do. Your parents know the best doctors, right?"

"They do. But this . . . well, you can't fix an enlarged heart like mine. There are drugs that can slow the process. But that's about it."

"I can't believe this." Sami stared at the sky. A minute passed before she lowered her arms and faced Mary Catherine again. Tears fell down her cheeks. "We have to find another opinion."

"I've done that." She looked straight into Sami's eyes. "Look, the reason I'm telling you is so you'll pray. God can do anything — even with this." Again, she worked to keep discouragement from her voice. "That's why I care so much about living. Why I'm always talking about only living once. Because I don't have as long as most people."

Sami wiped her tears with her fingertips. "It's not fair."

"It is." Mary Catherine sat up straighter. "God's given me all these years of life and probably many more. I still have lots to do — like get that youth center up and running tonight. And maybe move to Africa for a year and work with orphans."

"You always say that."

"I'll do it one of these days." Mary Catherine found her smile again. "Of course, I'll probably skydive another dozen times at least, and look." She turned her face toward the ocean again. "I have mornings like this, with you." She felt a familiar peace fill her soul. "God has been far more than fair with me."

"Are you in pain? I mean . . . like, does it make your chest hurt?"

"Not at all." She raised her hands and dropped them again. "I feel perfect."

"Good." Sami looked off, her expression marked with sorrow. "What about love?"

"What about it?" Mary Catherine felt her heart sink.

Sami stared at her. "You deserve love."

"No." She shook her head. "I won't have time." Mary Catherine felt tears sting her own eyes. "But I'm okay with that."

Sami looked into her eyes again. "You

were going to find someone real, remember? Someone like you, with faith like you and a love for life like you." Sami shook her head. "That was supposed to be the miracle of your life." She exhaled hard. "I can't believe this."

"Sami . . . it's all right." Mary Catherine put her hand on her friend's shoulder. "God's going to give me a different kind of miracle." She stood and reached out her hand. "Come on. Let's go find those dolphins."

Sami waited several seconds before she took Mary Catherine's hand. "Really?" She shaded her eyes so she could see better. "Can you do this? Swimming in the ocean? Is that good for you?"

"It's all good." She slipped back into her wetsuit and ran a few steps ahead. "The more life in my days, the better. Then it doesn't matter how many days I have. Just that I really lived them."

"I hate this." Sami climbed into her wetsuit and caught up to her. "You're probably supposed to be home resting."

"Never." Mary Catherine grabbed her boogie board and ran through the surf. Her laughter mixed with the sound of the waves. "God wants me out here."

Sami paddled alongside her. The moment

they reached the calm area before the swells, they spotted the dolphins. Three of them, playing in the water a few yards away.

"See!" Mary Catherine's joy was as genuine as the sun on the water. "I don't want to miss this."

For the first time in many minutes, Sami smiled again. "I don't know anyone like you, MC."

"I'll take that as a compliment." Mary Catherine looked over her shoulder as the perfect wave came straight for them. "Here we go!"

And with that they both caught the wave and started to ride it in. The moment they did, Mary Catherine spotted two of the dolphins riding alongside them. "Look!" she shouted.

Sami turned her head and saw what was happening just before the dolphins kicked out of the wave and headed back out to sea. "Wow!"

"That never happens!"

"So beautiful." Sami was laughing now, too.

Mary Catherine turned her attention to the shore as the ride continued. Tears filled her eyes and mixed with salt water and a happiness that knew no limits. The heaviness from earlier was gone. No matter how many years she had or where God would lead her from here, one thing would always be true.

As long as she drew breath, she would spend her days living.

2

Dwayne Davis was her life now.

Lexy watched him behind the wheel, his face twisted in an angry look. He was determined . . . this time he was really going to do it. Which was crazy, because a daytime robbery was the stupidest thing ever. They could both get caught and Lexy would wind up in prison just like her mama. How was she going to tell her grandma something like that?

Dwayne jerked the car into the parking lot of the Shell gas station. Lexy couldn't breathe, couldn't talk. What if the guy behind the counter had a gun? What if Dwayne got shot?

"I'm not sure if we should . . ." She couldn't think of anything else to say.

Dwayne slammed the car into park and glared at her. He left the engine running. "Shut up." He looked over his shoulder. "Stay low."

She did as he asked. Her heart pounded against her thin T-shirt. Dwayne was her man. She wasn't ready to lose him. If the store guy had a gun then this could end bad. Really bad. Lexy closed her eyes. She was only sixteen. But they would throw her behind bars. She could already feel the cold metal handcuffs on her wrists.

If he could do it, if Dwayne could pull off the robbery, he'd be leader of the gang. Which would make her the girl everyone wanted to be. That girl. Gang leader's girl. She opened her eyes. Her heart was beating so hard, the noise was all she could hear. Where was he? What was taking so long?

For a quick second she caught her reflection in the mirror. Her dad was black, mom was Hispanic. She had long, straight hair and light brown skin. Guys thought she was pretty. She'd been sleeping around for a year, but the last few months she'd belonged to Dwayne. Him alone.

He made her feel special. Like she was someone.

Lexy peered through the window. She couldn't see the cash register, but she could hear yelling. Probably Dwayne. He was so angry today. Like he could shoot someone without thinking about it. He was actually scaring her.

Suddenly Dwayne burst through the door with a paper bag, probably full of money. He stopped, aimed his gun back toward the store, and fired. At the same time a bullet whizzed past Dwayne's head, barely missing him. "Dwayne! Hurry!" she cried out.

Dwayne turned and ran for the car. He jumped in and sped out of the parking lot. He didn't look at her or say anything. His eyes were like black steel.

Lexy felt like she was going to throw up. The wheels spun as they turned left and peeled down the street. She tried to understand. "Where you going?" Her voice was loud and frantic. She hated this. Why couldn't he talk to her? She could hardly breathe. "Dwayne, where?"

"I'm thinking." He was breathing hard. He looked into the bag as he drove and let out a victory shout. "We did it, Lex . . . we got this thing. Gotta be a couple hundred dollars here."

"Did you . . . did you kill him?"

Dwayne glared at her. "I missed, okay?" He kept one hand on the wheel and lunged at her like he might slap her. Instead he shoved the bag onto the floorboard.

Lexy didn't dare ask where they were going again. Dwayne was eighteen — he would think of a plan.

Sirens sounded in the distance. Dwayne rattled off a bunch of cusswords. He leaned forward, like he was looking for a way out. The car's steering wasn't the greatest, so he took a turn on two wheels and sped halfway down the street before he pulled over.

Dwayne dropped down in the seat and pulled his baseball cap low over his eyes. "Don't talk."

Lexy wanted to yell at him that she wasn't a baby. She could talk if she wanted to. But then Dwayne might tell her to get out and walk home. If she wanted to belong to him, she needed to do what he asked. She crossed her arms and kept her mouth closed. At his house, when they were in bed, he was the nicest guy in the world. One day he'd quit getting so angry. Maybe if he became leader of the gang. That would make him happy.

Dwayne's phone rang. He was shaking, looking at the money and then checking the rearview mirror. He took his phone from his pocket and answered it. "S'up."

It was a guy's voice on the other end. Lexy could hear that much. But she couldn't make out what he was saying.

Dwayne cussed at the guy and then lowered his voice. "You can't keep changing the rules."

Lexy felt sick again. Must've been someone from the committee, the guys who would decide the next leader of the gang. So far Dwayne was only supposed to hit up a convenience store in the middle of the day. Nothing more. But it was never that easy, not with the WestKnights.

Dwayne shook his head and then smacked his hand on the dashboard. He cussed under his breath this time. "Fine. Tonight." He shook his head, angrier than before. "Later."

Lexy knew better than to ask. Instead she looked straight ahead, her arms still pressed against her stomach.

He slammed his hand against the dashboard again. "Gotta kill three EastTown thugs or Marcus Dillinger. Tonight."

"The baseball player?" Lexy stared at him. "You can't kill him."

Dwayne made a fist and then relaxed it. "Marcus is an easy kill." Dwayne laughed, but the sound seemed dark. Almost evil.

Lexy's heart raced faster than before. Dwayne couldn't be for real. He couldn't kill Marcus Dillinger. The guy was a hero. MVP of the Dodgers. The opening of his youth center was tonight. Killing Marcus? Lexy wanted to scream. Marcus was the hottest player on the Dodgers. From everything she'd seen on TV he seemed like a great guy. Why would the committee want Marcus dead? None of it made sense.

Dwayne picked up his phone and made a quick call. The voice on the other end sounded like the same guy. "Yo. I made up my mind. I got Dillinger. Tonight."

Dwayne took off his baseball cap and rubbed his head. He looked over his shoulder behind them. "Police missed us."

This time, Lexy wanted to say.

He tossed the bag of cash at her. "See what your man did for you, baby? This is only the beginning." He peered at her as he pulled the car back onto the street. "Now put it down. You don't touch my money unless I tell you."

He drove down the street and turned right toward the freeway. With every mile he seemed to relax a little more. "Gonna be a bloody night, baby. Gonna make you proud."

"You should get the EastTown guys. That'd be better."

He glared at her again. "Maybe I'll start with you."

"I'm just saying you can't kill a professional —"

"Shut up!" He cussed at her again. "You take orders from me. You got that?"

Lexy felt her anger rise up, but then it fell

38

away. She was here by her own choice.

They drove ten miles south before Dwayne pulled off the freeway and headed north again, toward home. Toward the streets just a few miles from Dodger Stadium.

Lexy felt tears in her eyes. The feeling wasn't something she was used to. Gang girls didn't cry. Too much going on. Still, Lexy wished they could take a week off from stealing and killing and claiming territory. The whole thing was exhausting. And now Dwayne was going to kill the city's favorite baseball player. She should've demanded he pull over so she could get out, demanded to be done with this life, but she couldn't. It was the only life she knew. Besides, she had everything she'd ever wanted.

She was Dwayne Davis's girl.

3

Coach Ollie Wayne walked into the bathroom where his wife, Rhonda, was finishing up her eye shadow. Ollie came to her and kissed her neck. "You look beautiful. Prettiest coach's wife ever."

She cast him a teasing look. "Coach's wife?"

Ollie loved her spunk. He gave his own forehead a light smack. "What? Did I say coach's wife?" He did a humble bow. "Forgive me. I meant you're the prettiest woman in all the world. Wife or not. Forget about just us coaches."

"Thank you." She gave him a flirty grin and returned to the mirror. "Will Tyler be there today?"

"Yes. Tyler and his girlfriend. A few other friends of Marcus and the volunteers from the neighborhood."

Rhonda smiled. "I'm proud of Marcus. What he's done, it's really something."

"He and Tyler have worked on it around the clock." Ollie sat on the edge of the tub. "He requested that the media not be there tonight. Doesn't want it to be a circus."

"See! That's what I love about him." Rhonda was putting on her lipstick. "This isn't about getting another headline."

"The exact opposite." Ollie stood. "I'll bring the car up."

"Okay." She grinned at him and returned to the eye shadow. "Five minutes tops."

Ollie chuckled as he left the bathroom and walked downstairs to the garage. They lived in Silver Lake, in the shadow of Dodger Stadium, an area recently voted the number one most hipster neighborhood in the country. Of course, that wasn't why Ollie and Rhonda and their family lived there. They'd moved to Silver Lake fifteen years ago when Ollie was hired by the Dodgers. He'd been the head pitching coach for the last decade. They didn't plan on going anywhere.

Besides, the neighborhood suited them. Organic food and farmer's markets and the new Whole Foods down the street. People were friendly and the coffee was the best in all of Los Angeles. Ollie and Rhonda loved being with their neighbors and sharing their faith whenever possible.

Ollie climbed in the family's Suburban and pulled it up the driveway and around to the front of the house. As he waited, Ollie thought about the goodness of God. He and Rhonda were about to celebrate twenty years of marriage. Their three kids were healthy and finding their way through life with a faith that was increasingly their own. Shane was eighteen, a senior shortstop at nearby La Mirada Academy, and at eleven, Tucker was finishing up fifth grade and excited about middle school next year.

The only one Ollie worried about was Sierra. Their pretty brunette was sixteen, a sophomore at La Mirada. All her life Sierra had been close to Rhonda. The two of them shopped and shared coffee dates and spent Saturday mornings hiking around Silver Lake. But this year things had changed. Sierra had started to hang out with a rougher crowd, and before Christmas break a school monitor caught her in the parking lot with a group of shady kids, ditching class.

More prayer, Ollie told himself. They wouldn't lose Sierra without doing everything in their power to keep her from straying. She was inside now, up in her bedroom studying for a biology test. Ollie almost wished she was coming with them to the youth center instead. Serving someone else might help Sierra remember who she was and the family she belonged to.

Part of the problem was his niece, Shelly. She was nineteen, a fashion design major at USC. Shelly didn't share the same faith as the rest of the family, but Sierra looked up to her. The two would go for coffee or shopping every few weeks. Shelly figured herself too smart to need Jesus, too gifted and financially secure to need redemption. That attitude was rubbing off on Sierra.

Her father — Ollie's brother — was a neurosurgeon. He'd lost control of Shelly long ago. Even before her freshman year at USC, when she moved in with a grad student she was dating at the time, she'd told her parents she didn't share their beliefs or their values.

And now Shelly was dating Marcus Dillinger.

Rhonda came hurrying out and jumped in the passenger side. "Let's do this." She smiled at him as she set her purse on the floor.

"We're picking up Shelly?" Ollie assumed as much.

"Yes." Rhonda gave a careful nod. "Your niece wouldn't miss this."

"Amazing. She's found this sudden desire

to help others."

Rhonda gave Ollie a polite smile. "She would pick up trash in the gutter if it meant being close to Marcus."

"I know." Ollie sighed. "What does Marcus see in her?"

This time Rhonda cast Ollie a wary glance. "Really?"

Ollie thought about his niece for a long moment. Tanned, bleach blond, with a body that bore the proof of her twice-daily yoga. She had confidence, a career ahead of her, and money. She was the kind of girl Ollie was used to seeing on the arms of his ballplayers.

But Marcus Dillinger?

His star pitcher had changed so much in the past year. Ever since Tyler Ames arrived, the two of them had shared a quest to change life in the inner city. He had watched Marcus's faith in God grow every week in every area except one: Marcus's decision to date Shelly.

Ollie could only pray that in the next six weeks before spring training, Marcus would see the light about Shelly. Sooner than later. Before things got more serious. He'd seen some very good men brought down by the wrong women.

Marcus was a great guy, but he wasn't bulletproof.

4

Marcus pulled his Hummer off the freeway and turned right toward the brand new Chairos Youth Center. The afternoon sun was even warmer than expected. Marcus had the windows down and now he turned the radio off and breathed. Just breathed.

God, you did this. You gave me a dream to change things on the streets and now, well . . . here we are. It's all You, Lord.

My son, you will do even greater things in My name. I have chosen you for such a time as this.

The words came like the softest whisper, so real and clear Marcus jerked around to make sure no one was in the backseat. Chills ran down his arms and legs. Was it his imagination or was that really God? Talking to him right here in his SUV?

He felt the adrenaline begin to subside. God was with him. There was no question about that. The whispered words echoed in his head. Marcus wanted to do great things for God. It was the reason he was excited to get up in the morning. This new adventure of faith.

But the idea that he might've been chosen for such a time as this? That thought had never occurred to him until now.

Marcus took a deep breath and focused on the streets ahead. Tyler Ames liked to say he'd spent his life chasing sunsets across the country for baseball. Always heading into the sunset but never really finding it. The elusive happy ending.

Now Tyler agreed with Marcus. The happy ending wasn't in baseball. It was right here — helping other people.

Marcus was five minutes from the center. All he could think about was that early morning when he ran the stairs at Dodger Stadium after Baldy Williams died of a drug overdose.

That morning everything had felt meaningless. The pitching, the fame, the money. All of it. What did a life in pro baseball matter if it could all end in a cold hotel room with a needle in your arm?

So he'd made God a deal. He would believe in Him, if only God would give Marcus's life meaning. Days later Marcus heard from a woman he had once rented a room from, a woman who was calling looking for help for Tyler Ames.

The same Tyler Ames that Marcus had grown up with.

Marcus remembered picking up Tyler at the airport and bringing him back to the stadium. Tyler needed shoulder surgery, and Marcus wanted to pay for it. But Tyler struggled to accept the gift. *This isn't your problem to fix,* he had told Marcus.

But Marcus had only smiled, his heart full. "No. It isn't my problem, Ames. It's my miracle."

And so it was. The answer Marcus had asked for, the meaning he had wanted, started with finding Tyler Ames again and helping him with that surgery. Since then the two of them had worked together to convert an old warehouse into a youth center. A center they believed would make a difference for lost kids in the inner city.

The World Series win and the MVP trophy sitting back home on his bookshelf meant nothing compared to this day. The grand opening of the youth center. A crew of contractors had worked practically around the clock to meet today's deadline.

Marcus pulled his Hummer into the back parking lot. Inside he met up with Officers Joe West and Charlie Kent, along with the mayor. One of the parent volunteers made the introductions, and Marcus thanked them for being part of the celebration. "A year from now," he told the officers, "I hope we can celebrate a drop in crime around here. Kids staying in school. Drug dealers leaving the area. Gangs broken up."

The officers exchanged a look and the older of the two, Officer Kent, stepped forward. "We'd love that." He looked back at his fellow officer and at the mayor. "But, Marcus . . . we're not there yet."

Marcus recognized a heaviness in the man's words. "Did something happen?"

"If you have a minute, we'd like to talk to you in private before things get started."

"Sure." Marcus followed them into a small room. Every part of the building was freshly painted. Three new basketball courts had been built at the front of the center.

When they sat down, Officer Kent took the lead. "You live in Silver Lake, not far from Coach Ollie Wayne's family, right?"

"Yes." Marcus felt his heart drop to his knees. He had no idea where this was going.

"You obviously know things are bad in this part of town." He hesitated. "I'm not sure you understand just how bad."

Marcus felt himself begin to relax. This

was a warning speech. He could handle that. He leaned back in the chair and listened while Officer Kent explained the statistics here in the projects.

"Few of these kids survive. Half of them don't make it to their twenty-first birthday. The gang activity here is at an all-time high."

He told Marcus about the WestKnights and the EastTown Boyz — rival gangs that would kill for status and recognition. "We've got kids turning tricks, dealing drugs, and killing rival gang members because that's what their dads and granddads have done for years."

The weight of the situation settled in around Marcus's shoulders. "We need to change that."

"Yes, well, first you need to know something. We've gotten reports of some gang activity planned for tonight. Probably right here on this block." The officer went on to explain that the leader of the WestKnights had been shot and killed last week. "A new leader has to be chosen by committee."

"Committee? They're organized?" Marcus had no idea.

"Definitely. They set up challenges for guys trying to lead."

The other officer nodded. "The challenges

usually involve killing. Rival gang members, or innocent people walking by or sitting on their front porch."

Anger began to build in Marcus. He had been raised in the suburbs of Los Angeles, in Simi Valley, where gang activity was rare. It was impossible to live in Southern California and be ignorant of the gangs in their midst. But Marcus hated that things in this very neighborhood were so bad. He looked from one officer to the other and then to the mayor. "What can we do about it?"

"Not a lot. We arrest them, of course, but they don't care. There're six young boys ready to join the gang for every one that gets killed or locked up."

Marcus didn't want to feel defeated. "What about educating the kids, helping them find a different way to live?"

"That's possible. It takes money and time. A lot of commitment. There will be set-backs." The mayor straightened his tie. "It's very dangerous trying to make a difference down here. Tough to find volunteers."

Marcus thought about Tyler and Sami and Mary Catherine. The Wayne family and his girlfriend, Shelly. They were committed to the youth center. "Maybe no one's ever really tried."

The three men nodded, but none of them

looked encouraged. Officer Kent studied Marcus. "We're just saying be careful. It's not easy coming into an area like this and trying to change things."

Marcus thought for a moment. "What about the Scared Straight program?"

"We used to have it." The other officer nodded. "It didn't work as well as people thought. The recidivism rate was actually higher than for kids not involved in the program."

Images filled Marcus's mind, scenes from the TV show *Beyond Scared Straight*. "I thought it always worked."

"That's just for TV." Officer Kent's expression remained serious. "These kids might not like the idea of prison, but they don't know anything different. In most cases they have a parent there."

A heaviness hung over the small room. Marcus thanked the men for their time and warning. "No matter the danger, I'm supposed to be here. I believe that. We already have local volunteers willing to staff the center around the clock. So that kids will always have a place to get away from the crime and gang activity."

"Yes." Officer Kent smiled, but it didn't reach his eyes. "I'd love to see a change." He looked at the other men. "We all would."

Marcus stood first. "My friends will be here soon." He shook each of their hands. "Will you stick around?"

"Absolutely." Officer Kent rose to his feet and the others joined him. "We plan to keep a few patrol cars circling the center. Gangs like to take over a place like this. If that happens, every bit of money and work has been wasted."

"That's why the patrol cars. So that won't happen this time, right?" Marcus waited. He wanted more than hope here. He wanted a promise.

"You have our word." The mayor nodded. "This center will be for kids looking for a way out."

"Great." Marcus led the way to the door. He couldn't get out of this meeting fast enough. Yes, of course, he knew the streets were tough. They were dangerous to anyone in this part of town. But if someone didn't offer these kids hope, then nothing would ever change.

So maybe that's what the whispered response meant while he was driving in. Maybe this was exactly what God had chosen him to do — to give kids hope where currently they had none. If things had never been worse, like the officers said, then the rest of the whisper made sense, too.

He had been chosen for such a time as this.

Jag and Aspyn stood in the corner of the room, invisible to human eyes. The news was troubling but not surprising. They had been told from the beginning that this mission would be dangerous. And so it would be. The officers had no idea how serious the gang activity would be that night.

But Jag and Aspyn knew.

They knew about Dwayne Davis and his plan to kill Marcus Dillinger. They knew about the trap Lexy was in and the desperation that filled every home along the streets of this neighborhood. That's why they were here.

It was time to decide where they would take their stands.

"I'll be a police officer." Jag spoke first.

"Good." Aspyn looked serious, her mind working. "I'll be a volunteer. A local parent."

Jag liked the idea.

"We need to break up the gang activity tonight. EastTown plans to kill Dwayne. They know he's pushing to be the leader of the WestKnights."

"Such a waste." Aspyn stayed in place. "Why do they want to kill each other?"

"Sons and daughters of Adam have strange ways of finding identity and power." Jag watched the two police officers, the mayor, and Marcus Dillinger. "The offer of love and salvation is available for any of them." He felt the pain of earth. "But they choose this."

They needed a plan for tonight. Aspyn was small but capable. Jag believed in her. He steadied himself. "The biggest danger tonight is Dwayne Davis. One of us has to stay here at the center. Distract Marcus. Keep him from going out front. No way Dwayne's coming inside the center tonight. Not with the police here."

"I'll stay. I can distract him." Aspyn's confidence was unwavering. "All of heaven will be praying. Don't forget that."

"Exactly." Jag thought for a moment. "I'll deal with the EastTown gang . . . and keep watch over Dwayne."

Aspyn must've seen the look in his eyes. She put her hand on his shoulder. "You have nothing to avenge, Jag. Nothing to prove." Her smile was weighted with understanding. "This is a new mission."

"I know." New mission or not, Jag had a score to settle with the enemy. He needed to succeed at this Angels Walking mission. "I'll be fine."

"Okay." Aspyn knew Jag's past, the reasons he hadn't been on a mission in ten years. "Remember how this works. You can't have the assistance of heaven unless you follow the rules."

"Of course." He reached out to her. "Let's pray."

They held hands and asked God to guide them, to give them wisdom and vision, and to help them prevent any loss of life — one of the directives of those angels who walked among the sons of Adam.

Jag turned to Aspyn. "Godspeed."

"You, too."

And with that they were gone.

5

Jag had no trouble finding the alley where the EastTown Boyz hunkered down, waiting for nightfall. He could see the enemy gathered in the shadows up and down the passageway. He could feel the presence of darkness.

You're not winning this one, he thought to himself. "Jesus has already defeated you." He uttered the words out loud and smiled when the demons in the shadows cringed, when they shrank back in fear.

The name of Jesus. Scripture was clear about the power of that one name. At the mention of Jesus the demons had no choice but to obey. Every time.

But that didn't mean the enemy would run from a fight.

As soon as they gathered themselves, the dark beings lunged toward Jag, hissing at him, trying to scare him from their gathering. "This is our territory."

But Jag wasn't about to move. "I'm here in the name of Jesus."

Again they twisted, writhing in pain at the sound of the name of the Savior.

Jag felt a holy satisfaction. How dare the enemy send his evil army to destroy the sons and daughters of God, His chosen ones, His creation? Moments like this made Jag impatient for the time when all angels would be unleashed and the enemy would be overthrown once and for all. When time ended and eternity began.

Until then, Jag wasn't backing down. The scene about to play out tonight was all too familiar. He'd already failed on a day like this one.

While the demons hissed and spat at him, Jag remembered. The years faded and Jag was there again. That Angels Walking mission had also been in Los Angeles. Jag had been assigned to protect a man of great faith, a police officer. Terrance Williams was his name. He had been called to testify against one of the city's most notorious drug dealers.

There had been only two days left in the trial when Jag failed.

Up until that point Jag had kept Terrance Williams safe at every turn. Two hit men had been assigned the job of killing the officer. In the weeks that led up to that fateful day, Jag had found ways to distract Williams, ways that had saved his life. Jag had also created obstacles for the killers, delays that had kept the men from carrying out the murder.

The whole time Jag knew the situation. The murder was the bad guys' only hope to avoid a guilty verdict. If the trial reached a guilty verdict before the hired guns could kill Williams, then the deal was off. No hit, no payment. No point. With only two days left in the trial, Jag was hovering behind Officer Williams's car when the man stopped at his son's school.

This was not part of the plan.

Jag hadn't known that on that day the man's son was in a class play, or that the boy had invited his father to watch. Jag had missed that. Even now, with a host of demons threatening him, Jag could see what had happened that day. Terrance Williams had parked his police car across the street from the school and gone inside. Jag had been nervous, his instincts on high alert. His Angels Walking partner had been across town, working behind the scenes at the courthouse.

So Jag was alone.

He stayed in the auditorium with Officer

Williams for the entire hour-long school program. It was an hour Jag could still remember, every detail. The boy attended a Christian school and that day he sang a solo from the front of the stage. "How Great Thou Art." Halfway through the performance Jag saw Terrance Williams wipe tears from his eyes.

The boy was ten years old and everything to the man.

Which created a problem. What if Terrance decided to take the boy home with him early? For weeks, when Terrance picked his son up, Jag had his Angels Walking partner with him. Together they had been able to protect both father and son.

But that day Jag could feel the demons, same as he could feel them now. Without his partner he would be outnumbered if a battle ensued.

Long before the program was over, Jag knew the hit men would be waiting for Williams, their guns trained on him from the moment he left the school. They had followed him here. Jag knew he would have to appear like one of the parents picking up their child at school.

But he had wondered if his efforts would be enough.

As the program ended, Jag had materialized in a hallway outside the auditorium. He looked like any other parent as he walked into the crowded room. Quickly he found Terrance Williams and his son, Ryan. Jag had walked up and put his hand on Ryan's shoulder. "Hello. You're Ryan Williams, right?"

The child looked startled. Same with his father. Officer Williams stepped forward. "I don't believe we've met."

"I'm Jag. My nephew Billy Goodall is in Ryan's class." Jag smiled. But he could see the confusion on the officer's face.

"How do you know Ryan?" The man pulled his son close.

"Ryan's been a good friend to my nephew." It was true. Information Jag had picked up during the mission. "Billy gets picked on by the other kids, but Ryan . . . hc stands up for Billy."

Ryan smiled and looked at his dad. "Billy's my friend."

Jag remembered feeling desperate. He was out of ideas. He needed time to figure out how to get between Terrance and the hit men. If Jag could delay the officer long enough, the hit men would leave. They needed the cover of a crowd to pull off their deed without getting caught.

"Okay, well . . . thank you for saying so."

Terrance Williams took a step back. "We need to go."

Jag could still feel the way his heart had fallen. If only they could've stayed in that moment. He would've begged God to freeze time so that the father and son might've stayed there, safe in the auditorium.

But freezing time was not something angels could do.

"See you." Terrance Williams waved and then he smiled at his son. "Mom made lasagna!"

"Hold on!" Jag had followed him. For five minutes he tried stalling by asking the officer questions. But in the end, it wasn't enough. As they left the school, Jag stayed behind them. He saw the hit man across the street behind the wheel of his car, saw him lift his gun, aiming for Terrance Williams, and in that split second Jag tried to knock both of them to the ground. "Look out!" Jag had shouted.

But years of police training kept Terrance standing on his feet even as his son hit the grass face first. The bullet was through Terrance's chest before Jag could say another word.

"Daddy!" Ryan screamed, and ran to his father's side. "Daddy, no!"

Demons celebrated in the air above them

as Jag rushed up to Terrance. A crowd gathered quickly, but Jag kept them at bay. "Give us room. I know CPR."

But even as Jag began administering chest compressions, he knew it was too late. The gunman had been too accurate. Ryan stayed near his father's head, patting his hair and crying. "Please, Daddy, wake up! Please, God!"

That afternoon Jag tried for twelve minutes until the paramedics arrived. Only then did he stand up and disappear into the crowd. He watched the rest of the scene from a few feet away, hovering over the fallen officer and his brokenhearted son.

Please, God, he had prayed. *Don't let him die.*

Paramedics finally helped Ryan away from his dying father. Even then the boy stood as close as he could, reaching out both hands and crying for his daddy. It was a scene etched forever in Jag's mind. They didn't officially declare Officer Williams dead until an hour later at the hospital. By then Ryan's mother was with him, along with half the officers from Terrance Williams's precinct.

But none of that changed the truth for Jag.

He had failed.

The loss of Terrance Williams made Jag doubt his very purpose. He had been given one task — protect the life of Terrance Williams. Yes, God knew the number of a man's days. But sometimes that number was small because the enemy had cut it short.

The demons in the alleyway hissed at him again, grabbing for him.

"Jesus will win this battle."

Screeches filled the air, the demons recoiling in painful fear.

Jag remembered what happened after his last failed Angels Walking mission. The other angels had tried to comfort him. Failure was always possible. The enemy would win some battles — but not the war. The other police officers would care for Ryan Williams now. He would never be without the love of a father figure.

Jag had appreciated their efforts. Their words were true.

But none of that would ever give Ryan Williams his daddy back. Jag had failed. He would always believe the failure was his fault. He should've found another way to protect Terrance.

It had taken every one of the past ten years to believe he could be used by God again. When he learned of this mission, of the danger it entailed, he knew it was time.

His chance — not only to find victory in this mission, but to make right the one he'd failed at a decade ago.

The sun was setting. Darkness gathered in the alleyway. The demons continued to hiss and scream. If they had it their way, someone was going to die tonight. Several people, maybe. And somewhere on the other side of the new Chairos Youth Center, Dwayne Davis was feeling the same way. Ready to kill Marcus Dillinger.

Jag wasn't afraid.

This time he had a plan that would work.

6

Mary Catherine and Sami walked into the new youth center just after three o'clock. She felt more like herself again. Now that she had told Sami the truth about her heart. At their apartment earlier Mary Catherine had made Sami promise she wouldn't treat her any differently.

"I'm not dying," Mary Catherine had said. "Not yet."

"But you will . . . too soon."

Mary Catherine had held up her finger and shook her head. "None of us knows how long we have."

Eventually Sami had agreed. "God wants us to live today, that's what you're saying? He'll handle the rest?"

"Yes. Exactly."

Since then they hadn't talked about it. Sami was a little quieter than usual, but nothing the guys would notice. Mary Catherine was only glad the discussion was behind them. As difficult as it was to share the news with Sami, Mary Catherine had wanted her best friend to know.

They headed through the triple gymnasium into the Virginia Hutcheson Hall, the place where tutoring would happen every school day afternoon and evening. Today, though, tables were set up around the perimeter for the grand opening. Marcus was carrying a box of plates to one of the tables.

Mary Catherine felt it again, the way her dying heart came fully alive in his presence. She chided herself to keep tight control over her emotions. Marcus wasn't interested, anyway.

"Sami!" Tyler was at the opposite side of the room setting out plastic cups. She hurried to meet him.

Mary Catherine made eye contact with Marcus. At the same time, the box he was carrying broke open and plates started to fall to the ground a few at a time.

She hurried over and began picking them up. "Perfect timing."

"So you were late on purpose?" Marcus set the box down and helped her gather the plates from the floor.

"Late?" Mary Catherine hoped he couldn't see the heat in her cheeks. "It's not

67

fashionable to be exactly on time. You should know that."

Mary Catherine and Marcus always slipped into this teasing type of banter. Sarcastic and even a little flirty. Nothing too deep. The two of them held the box together long enough to get it to the table.

"Seriously. How can I help?" Mary Catherine kept her tone light. She probably should've gone to the other room and helped Sami and Tyler. It did her no good being around Marcus. Not when he had this magnetic pull on her. Like being in his presence caused the oxygen to leave the room.

"I still have to wash down half a dozen tables in the back." He winked at her. "You can help."

Mary Catherine looked over her shoulder. "I thought the Waynes were coming."

"They are." He grinned. "Even more fashionably late than you and Sami."

Before they could head to the back for the dirty tables, Coach Ollie Wayne, his wife, and his niece entered the room. "We're here!" Rhonda Wayne led the way. "Ready to help!"

Mary Catherine took a step back. As she did, Shelly set her eyes on Marcus and came to him. She looked like a hunter eyeing her prey. Mary Catherine felt her frustration rise. *Don't be catty,* she told herself. *You have no reason to be jealous. Just walk away.*

Shelly reached Marcus and gave him a long hug and a kiss on his lips. Marcus looked surprised, and maybe a little embarrassed. He chuckled. "Well, hey there."

"Help can mean a lot of things, right?" Shelly spoke loud enough for everyone to hear.

Mary Catherine was ready for a new location.

She crossed the room to where Rhonda Wayne was helping Sami with the cups. Rhonda was explaining that they'd brought six flats of water bottles. "I'd like to get them in the fridge."

"That's another project." Tyler was bringing in empty jugs. "Someone donated three additional refrigerators a few hours ago." He made a face. "They work, but they're filthy."

"Perfect." Rhonda clapped her hands and looked at Mary Catherine. "You up for some refrigerator cleaning?"

"Definitely."

On the way back to the kitchen, Rhonda introduced herself. "I've heard of you. Sami can't stop talking about how you taught her how to live." Rhonda smiled. "You're her hero."

"That's sweet." Mary Catherine felt the compliment to the center of her soul. She had no idea Sami talked about her to other people. God was letting her help other people learn how to live — even while she was dying. "I hear a lot about your family, too. I guess yours is the hangout house."

"Marcus lives in the neighborhood, and you probably know Tyler's staying with him for now. They come over for dinner, and then a game of pool breaks out and the two of them stay till midnight. Happens all the time."

Mary Catherine could picture that. Sami had been there many times with Tyler. Apparently, Shelly was usually there, too. "You host a house church, right? That's what Sami told me."

"Yes." They reached the refrigerators and found a few empty buckets. "Our pastor stepped down so our main church is in transition. For the next few months the staff encouraged us to meet in our homes. Invite neighbors, that sort of thing. Tyler and Sami have been joining us for a while now." Rhonda found a few rags and she and Mary Catherine filled the buckets with hot soapy water. "Do you have a church?"

"I do. It's an hour away."

"Well, then join us tomorrow. We'd love to

have you!"

The invitation was tempting. "Thank you. Maybe some other time." Mary Catherine couldn't attend. Not when Shelly would be there fawning over Marcus. In that setting it would be almost impossible to focus on God. Besides, the hour drive each way was good for her. Time to pray and sing and remind herself that true happiness could only come if she busied herself with things that mattered.

Things like this.

She and Rhonda worked for an hour cleaning the refrigerators, until the mold and the mildew were gone. They even found a box of baking soda in the pantry and after a few rinses the shelves actually smelled clean.

The whole time they talked about family and faith, how Rhonda and Ollie liked to think of their home as a church in more ways than one. "We ask God to fill our home, and then He does. Every time." Rhonda's laugh came easily. "Not saying it isn't crazy around the dinner table sometimes, but it's worth it."

Mary Catherine tried not to feel jealous. That was the type of home she had always wanted. Instead she'd been an only child raised by wealthy parents. Parents too busy with their social clubs and charities to notice their daughter's loneliness.

Maybe someday she would take Rhonda up on her offer and attend home church at their house. Whenever Mary Catherine stopped reacting every time she saw Marcus Dillinger. However long that might take.

When they finished, Mary Catherine and Rhonda joined the others in the hall. The place had filled up. Volunteers from the neighborhood had flooded the place and half the tables were full of cookies and cupcakes. In another room, neighbors were helping set up games and filling bowls with candy.

Marcus and Tyler hadn't missed a detail.

Mary Catherine found Sami working on one of the dessert tables. Shelly was helping Coach Wayne at the other end of the room. "Where's Marcus?"

"The police wanted to talk to him and Tyler." Sami didn't sound worried. "Probably just figuring out logistics for tonight. They're expecting a ton of people."

A few minutes later Marcus and Tyler returned, their expressions concerned. Tyler motioned to Sami and Mary Catherine. "We need to talk to you." He pointed across the room. "Mary Catherine, could you get Rhonda and Ollie Wayne? They need to be there, too."

Something was wrong. Mary Catherine could feel it. In this part of town, there was no telling what had happened, but whatever it was the guys were deeply concerned. She found the coach and his wife and they headed to the small room with the others.

Once they were in the small room, Marcus took over. "The police have warned us." He looked alarmed and more than a little frustrated. "The two largest gangs in the area, the WestKnights and EastTown Boyz, are planning a confrontation tonight. Here. In front of the youth center."

For several seconds, no one said anything. Coach Wayne was the first to talk. "They should call in backup. You can't let a bunch of thugs ruin this for everyone else."

"It's their way of resisting change." Marcus pinched his lips together. "That's what the officers said."

"Well, that's not right." Rhonda stood at her husband's side. "I agree with Ollie. Let's get more police out here. Until they figure out that this isn't a place for gangs."

Sami stood next to Tyler. She looked terrified. "Maybe we should call it off. We can do this next week, right? Let the police figure it out and try again when the gangs aren't threatening."

"We can't do that." Mary Catherine's words came before she could stop them. "We need to pray. God will keep us safe. We just have to ask Him."

Marcus looked at her and his eyes softened. "I like it." He held his hands out to the others in the room. "Let's pray. The police will keep a watch out front, and here on the inside we'll just love on whatever kids come through the door."

A quick discussion broke out about whether they should cancel, but in the end everyone agreed on moving forward and praying for protection. God was with them. Who could come against them? As they formed a circle, Mary Catherine realized too late that she was standing closest to Marcus. He reached for her hand. As he did, he whispered, "Thank you."

She smiled and gave him the slightest nod.

Then it happened. His hand was around hers, his fingers warm and strong. Something about the feeling felt familiar and breathtaking all at once. *Dear God, help me think. Help my heart get back in line. Please.*

Coach Ollie was praying, asking God for protection, asking that He place His angels around the building to keep them safe at tonight's open house.

Mary Catherine could barely concentrate.

When the prayer ended, Marcus gave her hand a slight squeeze. He smiled at her. "Seriously. Thank you." He allowed a brief laugh. "I can't believe no one else thought to pray."

"No big deal." She needed to get away from him. Falling into his gravity wasn't going to do her any good. "I'm going to check on the game room."

"Okay." He looked like he might ask her to stay. But instead he hesitated and then he turned to Coach Wayne and his wife.

Moving as quickly as she could, Mary Catherine returned to the game room. A new volunteer had arrived, a willowy young black woman who didn't seem to have come with anyone. Mary Catherine came up to her. "Hi. I'm Mary Catherine."

"Hi." The new woman held out her hand. "I'm a parent in the neighborhood. Aspyn. Thought you could use the help."

"Aspyn. That's pretty." Mary Catherine checked the time. It was close to five o'clock. The pizza would be there in an hour. "Let's work on the corn hole boards."

They walked over to a part of the room where six corn hole games needed to be set up. Someone had left a set of directions, so together she and Aspyn got to work. "How long have you lived in the neighborhood?"

"Not long, actually." Aspyn smiled. She had the greenest eyes. Something about them looked almost otherworldly. "I figured no time like the present to jump in and help."

"Do you know Marcus?"

"Not well." Aspyn smiled. "I know he plays ball."

"Yes. That he does." They both laughed and Mary Catherine was grateful to talk with someone new.

Across the room, Marcus and Shelly set up a small plastic basketball hoop. Mary Catherine tried not to watch, but it was impossible. The girl was hanging all over Marcus.

Aspyn seemed to notice. She looked that way and then turned her eyes back to Mary Catherine. "She's not his type."

"Who?" Mary Catherine wasn't sure what her new friend meant.

"Shelly Wayne. She's too young. Too much growing up to do." Aspyn smiled. "If you ask me, Marcus Dillinger needs a girl like you."

The heat was back in Mary Catherine's cheeks. "How do you know what he —"

"Be right back." Aspyn dusted her hands off on her jeans. "I'll get us some water."

Mary Catherine watched her go, confused.

Aspyn said she didn't really know Marcus, but then . . . how could she have known whether Shelly was right for him? And what would've made her say that last part about Marcus's needing a girl like her? Mary Catherine could've been married for all Aspyn knew.

For a moment she watched Marcus and Shelly across the room. Marcus worked on the hoop and Shelly mostly flirted with him. Truthfully, Marcus didn't really look interested.

After a few seconds, Marcus turned her way and their eyes met. Mary Catherine looked away, embarrassed at having been caught. What was she doing? Even if Marcus had been single, she wasn't interested. He wasn't her type. Besides, she had no time for love. Just as well that God didn't bring along the sort of guy who could really turn her head.

Still, as Aspyn returned with their water, and as they worked on the boards, Mary Catherine couldn't quite shake her new friend's words. The idea that Marcus might actually need a girl like her. Or vice versa. The possibility defied her mind and filled her heart.

More than a couple of times she caught herself looking for him, watching the kind way he had with the volunteers, the humility in his eyes. Finally, she stopped herself and focused on the task at hand. She wasn't going to waste the hours dreaming about a guy she could never have. Life was too short.

Especially hers.

7

Lexy sat in Dwayne's passenger seat, once more slumped down in the shadows. They were parked half a block down from the new youth center.

Any minute Marcus Dillinger was going to walk outside and get the pizza. That was the big draw tonight. Free pizza. Lexy felt sick to her stomach. She wanted to be Dwayne's girl. Wanted her spot beside him. But she didn't want Dwayne to shoot the Dodgers' pitcher. *Don't come outside, Marcus.* Lexy silently begged the baseball star. *Stay inside.*

Beside her Dwayne tugged at his baseball cap. He had one hand on the wheel, the other on his loaded revolver.

Lexy didn't dare say a thing. She looked at her shaking fingers. She looked toward the youth center. If only she could defy Dwayne, take a stand for herself. Find her own way. But she couldn't. Being Dwayne's girl was the biggest thing that had ever happened to her.

Lexy thought about the rest of the guys in the gang. The WestKnights were on a drug run tonight. At least they were supposed to be. Dwayne made a call. His words were short, but Lexy got the idea. The gangs were going to fight in the alley across from the center. Dwayne needed to kill one of them before he could take a shot at Marcus.

Her teeth began to chatter. So many rules. She wanted to open the door and throw up. What if they got caught? And why did Marcus Dillinger have to die? He was only here because he wanted to be nice. She kept her mouth shut and waited.

Dwayne had shaved his head. He didn't look as hot now. His face was meaner. Scarier. Beneath his baseball cap he had a blue bandana around his forehead. He told her he had to look the part. More gang leader than gang boy.

Five minutes passed, then ten. Dwayne made another call. If the EastTown Boyz didn't show, the killing was off. When the call ended, a pizza delivery car pulled up in front of the youth center. Dwayne started the car and pulled out onto the street.

No! Not Marcus. Lexy put her hand over her eyes. This was terrible. She couldn't watch. Through the cracks in her fingers she saw Dwayne drive slowly up to the youth center. So far no one was coming out for the pizza.

Through the windows they could see kids playing basketball and what looked like maybe carnival games. For a moment Lexy wondered what it would be like to be inside. Playing games. Being a kid.

Dwayne laughed, and the sound rumbled deep in his throat.

Lexy stared at him and then looked down at her lap. What was so funny? Had he seen Marcus? Was the baseball player about to come outside? How could he laugh at killing Marcus Dillinger?

Dwayne hit the steering wheel. He looked down the alley, down the street. Suddenly Lexy realized something. The EastTown Boyz were nowhere to be seen. At the last second Dwayne sped up and squealed down the street. If the EastTown Boyz weren't going to show up, the fight would happen another night. She had never been so scared in all her life but now Lexy felt like she could breathe again.

Later, back at her grandmother's house, Lexy sat alone in the dark. Just sat there staring at the picture of Jesus on the wall. She sort of wanted to wake her grandma up and tell her what had almost happened. What was about to happen. Maybe her grandma would have some advice. Some way she could get out of this crazy life.

Last thing Dwayne had told her before she got out still made her feel sick. He told her he was still going to kill Marcus. But more than that, he would kill her if she said anything. If she told anyone what he was about to do.

Lexy clenched her teeth.

For a year all she had wanted was to be Dwayne's girl. But now she was afraid of him. Like for real. She couldn't tell her grandma. The woman was old. She still missed Lexy's mom every day. Her grandma would be so disappointed if she knew Lexy had joined the gang.

No, there was no one to talk to. Nowhere to turn. She needed to go to bed. There was only one reason she could bring herself to walk to her bedroom and fall into her bed.

Marcus Dillinger had not been killed.

Not tonight, anyway.

Jag was a police officer again, all six feet five inches of him. His blond hair framed his face, but it did nothing to lessen the fierce look in his eyes. He had distracted the East-Town Boyz, kept them away from the youth center. Now he shouted just once at them. "Leave!"

The EastTown Boyz — twenty or so of them — sauntered into a cluster. One of them pointed a gun at Jag and laughed. "You talking to us, pig?"

Jag knew how to respond in a situation like this. The kids were just that — kids. They weren't the ones at fault. This was all they knew. It was all their parents knew, and their parents before them. The kids gathered before him were not the enemy.

But all Jag could see was the gun. The same type of gun the hit men had used against Officer Terrance Williams. He felt fire in his veins. Without a single hesitation he walked toward the gang members. "I said leave!" He boomed the words like so many gunshots.

"We ain't 'fraida you, man!" One of the guys flashed a gang sign at Jag, taunting him. Another fired his gun toward the sky.

"Hear that, big guy? That's you if you come another step closer."

Jag kept walking. "You will leave this place in the name of Jesus."

The guy with the gun aimed it at Jag.

"I said leave! In the name of Jesus!"

The one with the gun waved it in the air. "We don't care about your Jesus." He aimed the gun again. "You're dead, pig. Don't come any closer."

Jag had taken enough.

In a fraction of a second he disappeared and reappeared at the opposite side of the alley.

The EastTown Boyz shouted expletives, turning this way and that looking for him. "How'd he do that?"

"You see that, man? He disappeared!"

"Yeah . . . like a ghost."

Jag appeared again, this time a few feet from the guys. With a voice that echoed through the alleyway, Jag shouted, "I . . . said . . . leave!"

The guy with the gun aimed again. "That's messed up, man." His hand was shaking. "No one plays with the EastTown Boyz."

Jag simply put his hands on his hips and stood there, legs a few feet apart. "Go home."

This time his booming voice made the boys back up, slowly at first and then faster until finally they took off running.

Jag felt the deepest sense of satisfaction. He hated violence, hated the way the sons of Adam loved to hurt each other.

They aren't the problem, he told himself. But they felt like the problem. They felt like the enemy, if Jag were honest with himself.

He searched the alleyway. The demons were gone. They had scattered with the gang. Now that he was alone, Jag exhaled. For today, he was successful. He felt the unfamiliar adrenaline rush, the feeling that only came when angels were in human form. And something else, something angels weren't supposed to feel. Something he would have to pray about if he were to be successful in this mission.

The feeling was rage.

8

Marcus looked around the packed youth center and silently thanked God for the success and safety of the night. Everything had gone perfectly. Whatever gang violence was supposed to materialize, it hadn't happened yet. In fact, the whole night had been one unforgettable series of amazing moments.

And it had all started with Mary Catherine's suggestion that they pray.

He hadn't talked to her since then. Of course, Shelly hadn't left his side once, so he didn't blame Mary Catherine for keeping her distance. Still, he had seen her look his way a couple of times throughout the night.

The girl intrigued him.

She didn't care what anyone thought. Her allegiance was to God and her friends and helping others. There wasn't an ounce of pretense or showiness — qualities that practically defined Shelly.

The night was winding down, and he stood in a corner of one of the basketball courts signing autographs for the kids. Across the room, Mary Catherine read to the littler kids. Everything about her was real and genuine. The way she laughed and held the hands of the toddlers.

A woman came up next in line. She had a small boy with her. "Hi." She seemed shy. "My name's Shamika."

"Hi, Shamika." Marcus smiled at her. He was signing press photos of himself pitching. He picked one up and stooped down eye level with the boy. "What's your name?"

"Jalen." The boy grinned. "My mom says you're a hero."

Marcus gave the boy's mother a quick smile. "Well, I think the real hero is your mama. She takes care of you, right?"

"Yeah." The boy giggled. "Seems funny having a mama for a hero."

"Not at all. My mom and dad are my heroes." Marcus held the photo up. "Want me to sign it to you?"

"Yeah." Jalen grinned.

" 'Yes, please.' " His mother put her hand on the boy's shoulder. "Use your manners, Jalen."

"Sorry." He looked down for a beat and then back at Marcus. "Yes, please."

Before they left, Shamika looked deep into Marcus's eyes. "We're about to be kicked out of our apartment." She kept her voice low. "I need another job and no one's hiring." She looked down at Jalen. "I'm all he has. So maybe . . . would you pray for us?"

"Of course." Marcus had never been asked to pray out loud before. He wasn't even sure he could manage it. But he had to try. Coach Wayne prayed out loud all the time. Just talking to Jesus, that's what Coach said. Marcus put one hand on Shamika's shoulder and the other on Jalen's. "Dear God, I know You're here and I know You're listening. Could You please help my friend Shamika? She's up against it pretty bad, and she loves her boy so much. If You could just give them a reason to believe again. The way You did for me. Thanks, God. Amen."

Shamika had tears in her eyes. "That's why I came here tonight. So I could see for myself that someone like you really exists." She looked around. "Thank you. For doing this for all of us. And thanks for praying."

She leaned in and gave Marcus a quick hug. "At least now I know you're real and not some imaginary angel."

Marcus watched Shamika and Jalen head toward the junior basketball hoop. The image of the two stayed with him as he finished signing autographs and as he took the microphone and thanked everyone for coming. More than two hundred people had stayed for this moment. They gathered around, their attention on him. Most of the adults looked despondent. Defiance flashed in the eyes of half the teens.

Marcus understood. They had come out of curiosity, hopeful for free pizza and candy and wondering what sort of difference a pro ballplayer could ever make on streets this rough.

He held up the mic and took a slow breath. "Good evening. Thanks for being here. For sharing in our grand opening." He looked at the back of the room to Tyler and Sami, the Waynes and Mary Catherine. "A special thanks to my friends, who have been here most of the day."

The crowd was quiet, shifty. "You gonna have free pizza next week?" one of the teens yelled out.

"Maybe." Marcus felt himself relax. "In life, you gotta have vision, man. If your vision is free pizza every week, then talk to me after. Maybe we can figure out a way to make it happen. Do a little fundraising."

A nod came from the teen and his eyes showed something he didn't have when he blurted out his question.

Respect.

Marcus looked around the room. "That goes for all of you. We all have to want something better for ourselves. Better than kids joining gangs and dropping out of school. Police tell me half the kids on these streets don't live to be twenty-one. That's insane." He felt the passion in his voice. "You gotta have a bigger vision if you're going to have a different life."

He talked a little about his own vision, how he pictured kids coming to the youth center after school and getting help with their studies. "I'd like to have counselors here, too. You got problems, you should have someone to talk to."

His speech was winding down, and really he had just one thing left. "Six months ago my life didn't have meaning. Sure, I play for the Dodgers. Pro ballplayer with the big contract. But that doesn't give a man meaning."

The kids were listening.

"I gave God a challenge. Told Him I'd believe if He would give my life meaning. Something that lasted. And guess what? God did exactly that. So now I give that challenge to you." Again his tone picked up intensity. "Every one of you. A youth center isn't a reason to live. God's the only one who can give us that. So tonight before you hit your pillow, talk to Him. Ask Him to give your life meaning." Marcus took off his baseball cap. "Pray with me."

Then, for the second time in his life, Marcus Dillinger prayed out loud. He could hardly believe it, but he was getting the hang of this. He asked God to bless the people there that night and to bless the efforts of the youth center. "We need a purpose, God. So give it to us. Make us a community. Thanks for tonight, God. Amen."

When he was finished, the crowd gradually dispersed. Several parents came up and thanked him for his commitment to the center and the community. The teens mostly kept to themselves. Marcus wondered how many of them were already in one of the local gangs.

The volunteers stayed to clean up. Most of the games had been borrowed from a local church, and plates of the leftover food had to be wrapped up and saved for whatever kids would come by the center in the coming week.

Marcus and Tyler were washing down tables when Sami and Mary Catherine found them. "We wiped down the water coolers." Sami brushed her hands together. "You guys must be exhausted."

"Exhausted, but happy." Marcus shot a smile at Mary Catherine. "That idea of yours . . . that we all pray before everyone got here? It was the perfect choice." He looked at Tyler. "Ty was saying he could almost feel the hand of God over this place. Like we had divine protection."

Mary Catherine smiled, but she looked more at Tyler and Sami than at Marcus. "Prayer makes a difference."

Marcus thought about Shamika and little Jalen, and then the talk with the people at the end. He aimed his next words at Mary Catherine again. "You've made me a believer."

She didn't seem to know what to say. Instead of responding to Marcus she turned to Tyler. "Where's the Wayne family? I didn't see them leave."

"They needed to get back to their kids." Marcus looked at Mary Catherine, but she wouldn't make eye contact with him. "They invited us back to the house for coffee whenever we're finished."

"What about Shelly?" Sami looked at Marcus. "She didn't say goodbye."

"She had plans with her friends." Marcus wanted a moment alone with Mary Catherine. Why was she acting like this? Like she didn't want to talk to him? "Anyway, we're almost done here."

He was about to ask her to join them for coffee back at the Waynes' house when Officer Kent walked through the door. He stopped when he saw the group. "Marcus, you got a minute?"

"We can talk here. My friends know about the gang stuff."

"Okay." He came closer. "Something happened tonight I can't really explain. We learned the fight here was supposed to be a big one. We had a few leads that everyone was talking about it. Supposed to have been a few killings, as well."

"That's what I told them." Marcus turned his eyes to Mary Catherine again. "But then my friend MC here, she suggested we pray." He looked back at the officer. "I'd say God answered our prayers."

Officer Kent ran his hand over his dark hair. "Definitely." He paused. "Apparently some officer from another precinct showed up in the alley where the EastTown Boyz were gathered. Just one guy. By himself. No backup. No one knows who he was." He hesitated again. "Anyway, whatever went on between the officer and the gang, the boys came running out of the alley like they were being chased by a pack of Dobermans."

Marcus chuckled. "I like that picture."

93

"He was probably an angel." Mary Catherine looked serious, the light in her eyes brighter than before. "They're real, you know."

Officer Kent shrugged. "After tonight I'd believe anything." He nodded to the group. "Be careful leaving. We'll be outside until you go." He looked around. "I'd say tonight was a huge success. Keep up the good work."

When they finished cleaning, Marcus asked the others back to the Waynes' house for coffee. It was after ten o'clock, but he still wanted to be with them, maybe share stories from the night.

"You coming, too?" Marcus walked next to Mary Catherine as they headed out to their cars.

"I think so. I really liked Rhonda Wayne."

"She's everybody's mama." Marcus grinned and as they reached their cars, he waved once. "See you there."

Tyler drove with Marcus. When they were on the freeway headed to Silver Lake, Marcus looked at his friend. "What do you think of Mary Catherine?"

"Sami's friend?" Tyler turned so he could see Marcus better. "I thought you were into Shelly."

"I was. I mean, I am . . . sort of." He narrowed his eyes, his attention on the freeway ahead of them. "Mary Catherine . . . she's different. You know what I'm saying."

"She's one of a kind. That's for sure."

"Exactly. I got that tonight." He glanced at Tyler. "What do you think of her?"

"Mary Catherine?" Tyler smiled. "She's crazy and fun and full of life."

"She has beautiful hair." Marcus heard the distraction in his voice.

Tyler raised his brow. "Not that you're interested."

"I like her spirit." Marcus could still see her, the way she looked tonight surrounded by the younger children. "The girl loves God more than anything or anyone."

"That she does." Tyler smiled. "Sami says Mary Catherine's the real deal."

"Yeah." Marcus felt his laughter die off. "Maybe that's it."

The conversation switched to spring training and the fact that pitchers, catchers, and pitching coaches had to report earlier than everyone else. Marcus didn't bring up Mary Catherine again the rest of the ride, but he was glad Tyler did most of the talking. It was all Marcus could do to stay partly interested. His mind was too preoccupied with the one thing he couldn't stop thinking about.

The light in Mary Catherine's eyes.

And the fact that in a few minutes he would see her again.

Jag and Aspyn watched from the back of Marcus's Hummer as he headed back to Silver Lake. They were exhausted, but they weren't about to leave Marcus. Not with so much at stake.

Jag felt the strength of God fill him, renew him. "We succeeded tonight."

"Yes." She gave him a concerned look. "You were angry, Jag. I could feel it when we met up at the youth center."

"Of course I was angry." He was calmer now. "Those kids wanted to kill someone. There's enough killing on earth without kids killing each other."

"It was more than that." Aspyn had an uncanny way of reading other angels. Him in particular. The skill made her a great partner, but a meddlesome one at the same time.

There was no getting around the truth. Angels were honest. Period. "One of them pulled a gun on me. Same kind of gun the hit men used when . . ."

"Terrance Williams died." Aspyn's tone was rich with sympathy. "I'm sorry."

"This . . . rage. It came over me." Jag was

completely himself again, full of peace and purpose. "I've only felt that one other time. In the minutes after Officer Williams was shot." He could barely describe it.

"I understand." She touched his shoulder. "Just be careful, Jag. Anger does not bring about the righteousness God desires. You know that."

"Yes."

"This is only the beginning. Things will get rough again on Tuesday night."

"I know. I need to be in control." Jag nodded. He appreciated Aspyn's wisdom.

"Exactly."

Jag pictured the gang gathered in the alley, the way they taunted him and flashed the gun at him. He let the images disappear from his mind. "Thank you, Aspyn. I'll be ready."

He had a feeling Aspyn was right. The worst of the violence was days away.

9

From the moment she walked inside, Mary Catherine loved everything about the Waynes' house. The smell of fresh coffee came from the kitchen, and something else, something warm and rich with cinnamon.

"Come in!" Rhonda welcomed them inside. "I roasted a batch of organic almonds. A little coconut oil and cinnamon and they're delicious."

"Mmmm." Mary Catherine flashed a grin at Sami and then back to Rhonda Wayne. "I knew I liked you."

"We don't do sugar. At least most days." She grabbed a potholder and pulled the pan of fresh roasted almonds from the oven. They smelled delicious. "I whipped up a pint of organic cream."

Rhonda went on about how organic cream from grass-fed cows was actually healthy. "Full of omega-three acids. The good ones."

Mary Catherine knew all about that. She

could've written a book on the foods that healed as opposed to those that caused inflammation. Low carb, high fat. Moderate protein. "I love that kind of cream."

Sami looked lost. "You two are speaking a different language."

"Here." Rhonda put a spoonful of the almonds in a bowl and topped it off with a dollop of whipped cream. She handed it to Sami. "Try this."

From the first bite it was clear Sami loved the dish. "This is amazing. What's in it?"

Rhonda laughed. "Nothing. Pure cream and organic vanilla. I whip it myself so it's just the right kind of creamy."

"I don't think I could ever go back after this. I don't miss the sweet taste at all."

"Sugar fuels illness."

"Exactly." Mary Catherine pulled up a chair and grinned at Rhonda. "I've been telling Sami that. She eats way too much chocolate."

"I'm an addict. What can I say?"

Mary Catherine took a bowl of the almonds and cream as the guys walked in. Tyler led the way. "How'd you beat us?"

"Better driver." Mary Catherine looked over her shoulder, teasing him. "Nah, you got stuck at the light before the freeway."

"I was gonna say . . ." He laughed and

looked back at Marcus. "Also, we took it slow on purpose. Us guys need our bonding time."

"Oh, I'm sure." Sami went to Tyler and the two of them shared a quick kiss. "You have to try Rhonda's almonds and cream."

Ollie had been checking on the kids. He joined them now and smiled at Mary Catherine. "So you're a health nut like my wife?"

"You could say that." She shared a look with her new friend. "We're trying to convert Sami."

The conversation continued, and Mary Catherine held onto every moment. This was what family love should feel like. Fifteen minutes later, Sam came down for water. Rhonda was kind and tender with him, kissing him on the cheek before he returned to bed.

And when Shane came home from a movie with friends, Rhonda and Ollie took time talking to him, hearing details about his night. Only their daughter, Sierra, wasn't home. She had spent the night with a friend. But Mary Catherine had seen enough to know that if God by some miracle blessed her with more time, with a man like the one she used to talk about finding, then this was the sort of family she wanted to have.

A family who lived out their faith as easily

as they breathed.

They talked for a good hour before Sami and Tyler decided to head out. "We'll be here tomorrow for church!"

Mary Catherine had planned on leaving now, too, but as she found her purse Marcus approached her. "Hey . . . why don't you stay? I can take you home in a bit." He grinned at Sami and Tyler. "You know, give them their space."

"Marcus!" Sami sounded disappointed, but she was teasing him. "We don't need our space." She motioned to Mary Catherine. "Come on, MC. We want you to come with us."

"No, really." Marcus seemed like he was trying to keep things casual. "Stay and walk around the block with me. I want to hear your story." He patted his stomach. "Plus I have to walk off these almonds."

Mary Catherine could feel it again, the heat in her cheeks, the way her heart beat faster around him. Was he serious? Did he really want to take a walk with her? In her peripheral vision she thought she saw Tyler give Sami a light elbow. Whatever the signal meant, Sami was suddenly quick to change her mind.

"Actually, it might be nice to have a little time with Tyler." She leaned up and kissed him again. "We have a lot to talk about."

Like that they were gone, and before Mary Catherine could argue, Marcus was ushering her outside for the walk. Never mind that it was nearly midnight or that Mary Catherine had intended to avoid anything even remotely like this. Marcus couldn't help himself. Every time they shared a moment together, the world around him turned to summer. The hillsides and skies of his heart came alive with new life.

They were still in sight of the Waynes' house when Marcus laughed. "Sorry if that felt a little forced."

"Just a little." Mary Catherine had no idea why he wanted this time with her. Whatever his reason, she had to be careful. She couldn't stop herself from feeling attracted to him. But she could at least keep her distance emotionally.

"I don't know . . . it's like I sensed something earlier, when we were cleaning up. Like you didn't want to look at me." Marcus slowed his pace so he could see her. "Or was that just my imagination?"

Mary Catherine was glad for the cover of night. She uttered a single laugh. "Well, Marcus. I mean, you have Shelly. I wouldn't want to be too friendly."

He nodded slowly. "Okay. If that's all it was."

"Tell me about her. You and Shelly." Mary Catherine was proud of herself. This was a good way to turn the conversation.

"There's not much to say." He stayed quiet for a few minutes while they walked. Then he turned to her. "So what's your story, Mary Catherine? Tyler tells me you grew up in Nashville. Why'd you leave?"

"Good question." There had been times when she tried to tell herself Marcus was shallow. He was a pro ballplayer, after all. But that simply wasn't the case. His tone was kind and tender, and she sensed a depth in him that surprised her.

"Didn't you like the South?" Their pace was easy, relaxing.

"Actually, I loved it." She laughed lightly and looked up at the stars. "I guess I was too comfortable. Everything felt predictable and safe."

"Hmm." Marcus laughed, but barely hard enough to be heard. "Sounds like you. Sami says you like jumping out of planes and riding your bike down Santa Monica Boulevard."

"And swim with dolphins." She laughed. "That actually happened right here."

"Really?"

"Yes. It was amazing." She cast him a look. "I like feeling alive." She walked a few more steps and shrugged. "That's just me."

"Now we're getting somewhere." They turned a corner and kept walking. "Were you like the oldest of six kids or what? Locked in the house till you were eighteen?" He chuckled. "Why live life on the edge?"

"Actually, I was an only child. My parents did well for themselves. The right house in the right neighborhood, the best social clubs and affiliations." She smiled. "They loved me, but . . . they didn't stay together." This was the part of her story where her health came into play. Both of her parents worried about her, wanted her close to them, where she could be safe.

Mary Catherine wanted adventure.

She skipped that part. Marcus didn't need to know. There would be no reason.

"Okay. Why Los Angeles?" He seemed genuinely interested.

She grinned. "It was everything Nashville was not. Wild and loud and crowded and godless." She nodded once. "In LA, I don't go an hour without knowing how desperately I need the Lord. I like it that way."

"So did you break some poor guy's heart back in Nashville?"

"Hardly." She laughed out loud. "I dated

a few guys, but I never found *that* guy. You know . . . the one I could be real with." She thought for a moment. The last guy she dated was a good one. They loved to laugh together. But in the end, he wasn't the right one. Just as well, given the news about her heart. "I guess I'm picky."

"I could use a little more of that." He grinned at her.

He had to be talking about Shelly, but Mary Catherine didn't want to push the issue. She slowed her steps. "Another thing . . . have you noticed how selfish everyone is? We're all about our own social media, our own platform, our own interests. I still haven't found a guy who can be in the moment. You know, carry on a conversation without checking his phone halfway through."

Marcus stopped walking and looked down. He checked the ground in front of him and behind him, and then reached into the pockets of his jeans. When he found them empty, he patted his other pockets. Then he shrugged.

"You lost your phone?" Mary Catherine glanced at the sidewalk behind them.

"No." He slipped his hands in his pockets and looked straight into her eyes. "I didn't bring it. Figured I'd rather be in the moment."

Touché. Mary Catherine felt something strange and unfamiliar in her heart. He was right. Where so many guys were too distracted to pay attention, Marcus had asked for this time with her and he'd remained truly present. "Thank you." She felt her smile soften.

They started walking again. "For what?"

"For being in the moment. That's one of the greatest gifts people can give each other. It's like a lost art. Listening. Caring enough to look into someone's eyes." She couldn't fall for him. Absolutely not. But she would be wrong not to express her gratitude. "Just . . . thanks."

"You're welcome." He looked happy with himself. "Maybe next time we have a conversation among friends you'll look *me* in the eyes. The way you didn't do today."

"I told you . . ." She giggled, not really frustrated.

"I know . . . you didn't want to seem too friendly. I'm dating Shelly. I get it." He gave her a knowing look. "Let's just say today at the center no one would've thought you even knew me."

"Good." She kept a straight face. Much as she wanted to laugh, she needed him to know how serious she was. "I didn't want to overstep my bounds."

"Obviously." The quiet between them for the next few steps felt comfortable. Marcus looked at her a long time before his next question. "So is it a faith thing, your living dangerously? Jumping out of planes and swimming with sharks?"

Her laughter felt wonderful. "Not sharks. Dolphins."

"Whatever." He chuckled. "Really, Mary Catherine. Why?"

The truth wasn't something she was willing to talk about. Her doctor had told her anything that released too much adrenaline was bound to be hard on her heart. A quiet life, they told her. Keep to the house, the daily tasks and chores. Learning and reading were fine. A desk job, maybe. Anything out of the box would knock days off the life of her heart.

Her mother had begged her to follow her doctor's orders.

Mary Catherine would rather have died young. She took a deep breath and imagined a way to explain all that without talking about her health. "There's a Bible verse in John, chapter ten, verse ten."

He shook his head. "Don't know it."

"Jesus is talking. He says, 'I came that they

may have life and have it abundantly.' " Her tone held a passion never far from the surface. "I figure if Jesus came to give me that sort of life, well, then . . . I might as well live it."

"Hmmm." Marcus nodded. "Fair enough."

"How about you, Marcus Dillinger? You ever jump out of a plane or swim with dolphins?" She loved this, walking with him at midnight. This far up in the hills, the stars shone bright overhead, the moon a sliver in the sky.

His laugh was quiet again. "Hardly." He sighed. "For me it was baseball, baseball, baseball. My dad was a blond, blue-eyed ballplayer for the Giants back in the day. Played a few years and then got cut. He moved to the Bahamas to try to figure out his life and met the most beautiful woman he'd ever seen." He smiled. "That's how he tells the story. My mom was just eighteen, six years younger than my dad. Born and raised in the Bahamas. They fell in love and got married six months later at a little white church in downtown Nassau. Right in the heart of the city."

Mary Catherine had figured one of Marcus's parents must've been white. His light skin and eyes told her that much. But she had never heard his parents' love story. "That's beautiful."

"It was. My dad got a job in San Diego in computer engineering. He and my mom had me and two girls. Dad and I played ball all the time. He was one of my coaches. Believe it or not, I had a choice about playing baseball. He wasn't one of those fathers." Marcus grinned. "I just loved the game."

"So no time for planes and dolphins?" She could feel her eyes sparkling as she looked at him.

"Exactly."

Their teasing made her feel like she'd known him all her life. *He has a girlfriend,* she told herself. *Don't let yourself fall.* "Hey, wait!"

"What?" He looked intently at her. He had definitely perfected the art of being present.

"I know that little white church. The one in Nassau. Is it on the main street, right past the pink government buildings?"

He looked surprised. "Yes. That's the one."

"I went there once on a mission trip." She laughed. "I know. Not the roughest place to do mission work. Anyway, on Sunday most of our group went to service there. It was super colorful. They passed out tambourines

109

and percussion instruments." She nodded. "I loved it."

"You and my mom should meet." His tone remained genuine. "She grew up in that church. She'd love to hear that story."

They had turned around and now they were nearly back to the Waynes' house. Mary Catherine wasn't going to bring up Shelly again, but this time Marcus did. "You asked about Shelly. She's interesting. A little aggressive." He raised his brow. "It's awkward, her being Coach's niece."

"Mmm." Mary Catherine didn't want to say too much. "You think Coach Ollie is in favor?"

"I'm not sure." His laugh sounded nervous. "Just feels awkward. I kind of fell into the whole thing before I knew what was happening."

Up until then, Mary Catherine wondered whether Marcus had a chink in his armor. She had assumed the guy was a typical pro ballplayer, but her assumptions had been wrong.

Until this.

She considered her words before she spoke. "So . . . are you pursuing her?" She was careful not to sound mean. Just curious. "Or the other way around?"

"I asked her out, if that's what you mean.

But more to kind of see if we were compatible." He was quiet for a long minute. "Actually, I guess she asked Coach if I was interested. I didn't really know about her until a month ago."

Mary Catherine didn't respond. Maybe it was better if Marcus was allowed to sit with his own thoughts for a bit.

"Yeah, maybe she's doing the pursuing." He looked troubled. "To answer your question. I guess I hadn't thought about it."

They were back at the house. Mary Catherine smiled. "The Waynes are great. I love the way their home feels." She was finished talking about Shelly. Marcus could figure that out later.

"They're my second family." He looked to the front door. "They seriously always have a light on." He chuckled. "Like that old motel commercial my dad used to like."

They both laughed and headed inside. Mary Catherine said goodbye and thanked Rhonda and Ollie for having her.

"Come anytime. Seriously." Rhonda hugged her. "We health foodies need to stick together."

"I'll be back." She grinned from Rhonda to Ollie. "I want to meet your daughter next time."

The only thrill greater than jumping out

of a plane or bungee jumping off a bridge was investing in people. Mary Catherine worked with the youth group every Sunday at church. She didn't lead it, but even as a volunteer, girls were always talking to her. Telling her their struggles.

It was another wonderful reason she loved being alive.

Marcus walked her out and opened her door first before he slid behind the wheel. The whole way back to the apartment, Mary Catherine couldn't stop from dreaming. Even just a little. And in the time it took them to reach the freeway, she allowed herself to imagine the greatest possible plans ahead. If she could, she would walk that way whatever the cost. However many steps the journey might hold.

For tonight, she could dream about the possibilities. As if for this one moment she might pretend Marcus was *her* boyfriend and the two of them were facing life together. Head on.

She looked out her side window. *Don't be ridiculous,* she chided herself. *There are a hundred reasons why it could never happen.*

Because Mary Catherine had no time for a relationship. If God was going to give her more than thirty years — the way she truly believed — then she would spend it living and serving and loving people.

Just not the sort of love her wayward heart had dreamed about tonight.

10

Mary Catherine hated seeing her time with Marcus come to an end. He parked in front of the apartment and walked her to the front door. She hoped he couldn't hear how hard her heart was beating. The rush she felt had nothing to do with her health. Something about being with him stirred feelings she'd avoided most of her life.

He stood closer than she liked. Or maybe she liked it more than she wanted to admit. Either way, he looked deep into her eyes before he spoke. Like he had all the time in the world. "I had fun tonight."

"Me, too." She folded her arms in front of her. "Thanks again . . . for not bringing your phone."

He chuckled lightly. The sound sent chills through Mary Catherine, and she could do nothing to stop them. "You, too. Looks like we're both good at being present."

"Yes, sir."

" 'Yes, sir'?" He angled his head. The look in his eyes took her breath. "You had that Southern thing in your voice just then."

She giggled. "Blame it on the upbringing. You can take the girl out of the South . . ."

He grinned at her, as if he wanted to stretch the moment as badly as she did. "But you can't take the South out of the girl."

"Exactly."

"I love it. And you still have an accent, by the way."

"Maybe." She was enjoying herself more than she wanted to admit.

"Anyway . . . I'll say this, Mary Catherine." He paused, searching her eyes. "Sami was right about you."

"About how wild I am?" She blinked a few times. Under his gaze, her walls didn't stand a chance.

"No . . . that you're one of a kind." He looked up at the sky and then back into her eyes. "I had to find out for myself."

"I'll take that as a compliment."

"As it was intended." She wondered if he was going to hug her. Instead, he did the slightest bow. Like a knight from a long-forgotten era. "It's been a pleasure, m'lady."

"Oh, now look." She laughed softly. "Southern gentleman, are you?" The sound faded and she looked deeper into his eyes, all the way to his soul. "Marcus Dillinger . . . you're not who I expected."

"Now, now . . ." A twinkle lit up his eyes and he waved his pointer finger at her. "You thought us ballplayers were all the same."

"I did. I confess." No matter what she'd told herself up to this point, she didn't want the moment to end. She could've stayed out here beneath the stars with Marcus Dillinger, being far too friendly, until daybreak.

"Well" — he took a step back — "happy to prove you wrong." His teasing lifted like morning fog and for several seconds he stood there, just watching her. Again she had the sense he didn't want to leave any more than she wanted him to go. "See you later, Mary Catherine."

"See ya." She put one hand on the door, but she didn't turn around until he did, until he jogged to his Hummer, climbed inside, and pulled away.

Inside, she was grateful Sami was already asleep. She didn't want to answer questions about the night or her walk with Marcus or what she might be feeling. She stood at the window and peered through the crack in the curtains. Her heart was giddy with love and life and every wonderful thing. Springtime reigned in her soul and sunshine followed her into the apartment despite the dark of night outside.

Had the last few hours really happened? Had Marcus really just driven off at one thirty in the morning after spending the most wonderful time with her? And what was she thinking, allowing herself to feel this way?

Mary Catherine had no answers for herself.

For once she didn't care about her sensibilities, about her determination to keep herself unattached, to never fall in love. She always thought she could find a grander purpose outside of love. Learning to fly, or feeding children in Africa, or sneaking Bibles into North Korea. She had believed her wild side was enough to soak all the life she could out of the time God gave her.

But she would never have this night again and right now she would've given up every adventure ahead for the chance to be loved by Marcus Dillinger. Something that would never happen. She drew a shaky breath.

Right now she didn't feel wild. She felt scared and unsure and lonely. Just for tonight, she wished for the freedom to fall in love if she wanted to. She wished she wasn't sick and that tonight wasn't only a dream. And something else.

She wished she had a hundred years.

It was a half hour back to his house in Silver Lake, and Marcus was pretty sure he'd need every minute to sort through his feelings. The ones that had made it hard to feel the ground beneath his feet a minute ago.

Mary Catherine had filled his senses for the past two hours like no girl ever had. Yet, he was pretty sure she wasn't available. She didn't have a boyfriend — at least he didn't think she did. But she gave off no real proof of being interested, either.

Marcus gripped the steering wheel and gritted his teeth. What was he thinking? Of course she wasn't interested. Hadn't she said that at the beginning? Sure, she'd opened up to him tonight. But in front of their friends she'd been just short of rude. Too concerned with offending his girlfriend. Which was another problem.

He had never intended to have Shelly be his girlfriend.

The thing with Shelly just sort of happened. She was relentless when they were together, and when they weren't, well, she texted him constantly. Always her texts were forward and laced with innuendo. He came to a stoplight and checked his phone.

Another two texts had come in from Shelly while he was saying goodbye to Mary Catherine. The light was still red, so he glanced at them. The first was short. *Miss you.* The second was longer. *All I can think about are those long legs of yours and . . . well, you know. See you soon.* Each text was punctuated by half a dozen emojis.

Of course he hadn't brought his phone on the walk with Mary Catherine. Her texts came in like clockwork.

He tossed the phone on the passenger seat as the light turned green. How had things gotten this way so fast? The two of them hadn't been alone except for their goodbyes — which was a good thing. Even when he took her home, she was all over him, kissing him and asking him to park further down the street. "Let's take our time," she always told him.

Mary Catherine had asked the most profound question of the night. Who was pursuing whom when it came to Shelly? Marcus sighed, and the sound rattled around in the empty Hummer. He knew so little about being a Christian. Sure, his dad had been a good man. He'd met Marcus's mom in church, after all. But as far back as Marcus could remember there had only been baseball.

A good life, a nice family, and baseball.

He thought about how easily Mary Catherine had rattled off the Bible verse. What was it? John something. Marcus had never even read the Bible, at least not as far as he could remember. It wasn't something he and Tyler had talked about, either.

Mary Catherine's face came to his mind, consuming his senses. She was the sort of girl a guy could pursue. No question. But if they'd had another hour, if their walk had gone on longer, eventually the questions would've turned to him and his past.

He had basically told her everything there was to know — at least from his high school days. He had played ball. Period.

But his time in college and the pros? Those years, there was much more to his story. A sick feeling came over him. There didn't seem to be enough air in the SUV, so he rolled down his window. Pitching for the Oregon State Beavers came with certain expectations. Different girls every weekend. Others on the road and still more midweek on campus. It was all part of the game.

Marcus liked to think he was better than some of his teammates. He didn't drink, didn't party. But he couldn't remember the names of all the girls he'd been with.

Shame burned through him, so that even

the skin on his hands felt hot. He could never tell Mary Catherine about his past. She wouldn't want another conversation with him. He squinted at the freeway ahead of him. *Dear God, what sort of pathetic, wretched man am I? How many girls do I owe an apology to?*

He rarely thought about this. Especially in the last few years, when he'd cleaned up his act and stayed away from women. But if he was honest with himself, things only grew worse after the draft.

Los Angeles was a place without values or morals. Everyone was out for themselves, on the hunt for money, fame, sex. The thrill of the one-night stand worked both ways in LA. The girls Marcus hooked up with hadn't wanted a commitment any more than he had.

People using people. Until recently, that was Los Angeles for Marcus.

He tried to imagine what Mary Catherine would think about that. If she were telling him the whole story, the girl hadn't had a serious boyfriend. Maybe not ever — though he found that hard to believe. One thing was for sure — Mary Catherine wasn't going to settle. Not in life, and not in love.

The weight of his past pressed in around his shoulders. Sure, he'd made a deal with

God, and God had come through. But where did that leave him? The question that had plagued him after Baldy's death suffocated him again. Here in his Hummer. If he didn't make it home, if a drunk driver drove the wrong way onto the freeway and he never saw it coming, where would he be at night's end?

Heaven or hell?

Yeah, he needed to talk to Ollie Wayne. The family opened their home week after week. They hosted church every Sunday, but Marcus had never talked about his past, about what to do with it.

Let me just say this, Lord . . . I'm sorry. If I could do things over again, I'd avoid every bit of it. The girls . . . they were nothing to me. But . . . it was something to You. I'm sorry.

The breeze through the open window brushed against his face and the pressure on his shoulders eased. He didn't hear any response, the way he had earlier on the way to the youth center. But he felt something. Hope, maybe. Yeah, that was it. Hope.

He would talk to Ollie and Rhonda and he'd start reading the Bible. He'd start with Mary Catherine's verse in John.

Her name brought him back to the moment.

Tonight was a dream. He could've talked

to the beautiful redhead all night. She carried with her a childlike joy, the kind that could warm an entire room. Her very presence was intoxicating. But he didn't dare dream about her.

God might forgive him for his ugly, sordid past. But Mary Catherine would never even have the chance because he could never tell her. If he ever did, the magic of tonight would be gone as soon as he said the words. The simple truth was this:

A girl like Mary Catherine deserved better.

11

Lexy felt a hundred years old as she walked into her grandma's house. It was only nine thirty, but already the woman was asleep. Her grandma didn't belong in this generation or this neighborhood. She was a God-fearing woman who had nowhere else to turn.

Lexy crossed her arms and stared out the window. A kid had died tonight. One of EastTown's youngest. Dwayne had no choice — that's what he said. The rules had changed. Now if he wanted to be leader of the WestKnights he needed two murders. A kid from EastTown and Marcus Dillinger.

He was halfway there.

Vomit rose in Lexy's throat. Sure, she'd been around a lot of killing. Still, tonight was different. Dwayne hadn't been able to find one of the EastTown Boyz. They were headed home and he was cussing at her. Like it was her fault.

Dwayne didn't have to treat her like that. Lexy was his, heart and soul. He could at least be a little nice. That's what she was telling him when all of a sudden he slowed the car down.

"There." Dwayne had cussed under his breath. "Two-bit punks. Say goodbye to life." He had rolled down his window.

Lexy had heard him cock the gun, but she didn't want to look. For all her time on the streets she'd never actually seen someone shot and killed. Not close like this. But at the last second she looked. She turned and everything happened in slow motion.

The two EastTown Boyz had been sitting on trashcans, their backs to the street, red bandanas proudly wrapped around their heads. And Dwayne had started cussing again, saying something about getting the younger one. Then before Lexy could take another breath, Dwayne fired at the smaller of the two guys.

And both boys had turned and looked right at them and Lexy had gasped. Because they were young. Too young. Twelve, maybe thirteen. Both of them. And she watched the kid's eyes grow wide, watched the fear as Dwayne's bullet ripped through his head.

And the blur continued as the other kid screamed and the one who'd been hit fell to the ground, and the screaming . . . the screaming echoed in Lexy's heart and mind and soul and Dwayne had sped away and that was it.

Her boyfriend had met the challenge.

But Lexy hadn't been able to speak or breathe. All she could see were the boy's eyes as he fell to the ground. And terror shook her body, her knees, her hands. And Dwayne had said, "Don't get soft on me now, baby."

She had turned and looked at him. Dwayne still had the gun in his hand. She said nothing, but she had one thought. The thought she still had now sitting here in her grandma's house.

Maybe she didn't want to be Dwayne's girl.

Anyway, the police would be looking for them by now. The other kid would say it was one of the WestKnights. The chase would be on. It was only a matter of time. Dwayne must've figured that out because right after the shooting he drove her back here. "Don't need no other witness hanging around." He nodded for her to get out. "If you hear a tap on your window later tonight, be ready. I still need to celebrate."

Lexy's breath was still shaky. She turned away from the window and sat in her grandmother's rocking chair. The darkness felt heavy around her. She could already feel the prison bars. There was no way out of this life, not if she wanted one. And where would she go if she did want out? She might as well run in front of a moving train.

The gang would destroy her — one way or another. Behind bars or on the streets.

Being part of the WestKnights was all she knew.

And Dwayne was about to be leader of the gang. The rocking chair creaked in the dead of night. Something moved a few feet from her. Lexy turned but nothing was there. Her heart beat harder. One time she and her friends had watched a movie about demons. Lexy walked away believing they were real. You could feel them even if you couldn't see them. A skin-crawling feeling of horror and evil.

Which was what she was feeling now.

Lexy folded her arms tight around her chest. She could text Dwayne and tell him how scared she was. She was his. She tried to remember that. But all she could see were the kid's eyes as his body fell off the trash-can. As he took his last breath.

She needed a light on. Even if it woke up her grandma.

Another sound over her other shoulder.

Lexy put her hands to her face. She didn't want to stand, didn't want to move. But she needed light. Needed it in the most desperate way. Finally she stood and braced for an attack of some kind. From whatever was here with her, whatever was hunting her.

Somehow she made it to the light switch and flipped it on. There. Her breathing resumed, fast and shallow. There was nothing there, no one with her in the room. The sounds must've been her imagination. Demons weren't real. She was just freaked out by the shooting.

Lexy waited until her breathing relaxed a little. The house was small, two rooms and a kitchen. Nothing more. But it was always clean. Her grandma saw to that. The heaviness in the air remained — even with the lights on. Lexy walked to the kitchen and there on the broken table against the wall sat her grandma's Bible. It was open, like maybe her grandmother had been reading it before she went to bed. Lexy came closer and looked. A section was highlighted, but Lexy couldn't read half the words. Her grandma had tried to teach her, but Lexy had long ago stopped learning. School meant nothing to her.

She sat down, weary and sick from the killing. The Bible was ancient looking, the letters so small her grandmother used a magnifying glass to read it. The letters at the top spelled R-O-M-A-N-S. Lexy had no idea what that meant. She pulled the Bible closer and looked at the yellow part. She could read a few of the words.

Hate what is evil . . . cling to what is good.

A strange feeling came over Lexy, like someone was watching her from the shadows. Hate what is evil? Did the Bible really say that? She looked at it again and read it more slowly this time. Yes, that's exactly what it said. Cling to what is good. Lexy wasn't sure what *cling* meant. Dwayne always told her not to be clingy in front of the guys. Not too much hand-holding and hanging onto him.

She let the idea sink in. So then . . . according to the Bible people were supposed to hate bad things and hold on to good. Lexy dropped slowly to the hard wooden chair and stared at the wall, at nothing, really.

Demons or not, her whole life was built around evil. She didn't think about it that way most of the time, but tonight? Watching the kid from the EastTown gang die right in front of her? That was evil. No one could say different.

But what about the good? Lexy felt ice in

her veins. Anger came around her and made the muscles in her face tight. Who was she kidding? There was no good, none at all. Her grandma was good, but no one else. Lexy stared at the Bible and then, in a rush of frustration, she slammed the cover shut. What good could come from an old book, anyway? People had to believe it; they had to read it for it to make a difference.

She stood and thought about going to bed, but she couldn't. She couldn't stop looking at the Bible and thinking about the words her grandma had colored in yellow. Hate evil. Cling to good.

And suddenly she remembered.

There was someone good out on the streets, someone trying to make things better. Someone who cared about the broken kids and homes without mamas and dads. There was someone willing to put his own money into giving all of them a better way.

His name was Marcus Dillinger.

And tomorrow night at this time Dwayne would be leader of the WestKnights and Marcus would just be another victim. Another guy in a body bag. Tears stung her eyes. She could stop it. Never mind the evil around her, Lexy could cling to good — even if only for tonight.

She dug around in her purse and found a

small bag of change. Quarters mostly. Money she'd stolen from her grandma's nightstand. Then she clutched her bag to her side and headed back out the front door. Two blocks down there was a bar with a pay phone outside. From what she'd heard, a caller couldn't be traced on pay phones. If Dwayne found out about this, he'd kill her. Lexy had no doubt.

Four different cars drifted slowly past her as she walked. The drivers looked ready to kill someone, ready to fight. The guys in each of the cars called out to her as they went by. Rude things. Words that reminded her how many times she'd been forced to do stuff she didn't want to do.

Tears trickled down Lexy's cheeks. She wasn't upset, not really. She was just mad at Dwayne. He should've said he'd kill off more of the EastTown Boyz. Not Marcus Dillinger.

Lexy wiped at her tears, her pace hard and fast. The pay phone was just ahead. She reached it and looked over one shoulder, then the other. No one watching, no West-Knights to rat on her. She picked up the phone and dialed 911.

A woman's voice answered. "Nine-one-one, what's your emergency?"

What was her emergency? Lexy's entire

body shook, her mouth so dry she wasn't sure she could talk. She could feel the evil, feel it gaining ground. *Cling to what is good . . . cling to what is good.* She swallowed a few times. "It's . . . it's not an emergency today."

"Ma'am, I need you to be specific." The woman sounded frustrated, like she couldn't be bothered. "What's the emergency?"

"It's . . . Marcus Dillinger." Her heart was pounding so loud she could barely hear herself. Two guys left the bar a few feet from where she was standing.

She hesitated. "Marcus Dillinger, the baseball player?"

"Yes." Lexy looked over her shoulder. What if someone recognized her and told Dwayne? She clutched the phone. *Be brave, Lexy . . . come on.* She squeezed her eyes shut and found her voice. "Someone from the WestKnights is gonna kill Marcus Dillinger tomorrow night at the new youth center."

"Someone's going to kill Marcus Dillinger?"

"Yes." Fear grabbed at Lexy, hissing at her from all sides. She was crazy to do this. They would kill her for it. "Please help him." She slammed the receiver back down and stared at the phone. She could feel it. That scary feeling again. Demons, maybe. Or people behind her, coming up to her. She spun around and there they were. Three East-Town Boyz, red bandanas, eyes blazing with hate.

Coming for her.

Lexy pressed her back against the cold metal phone. She was going to die here. It was only a matter of minutes.

"You dead, WestKnight girl." The older one narrowed his eyes at her. "But we gonna have some fun with you first."

Before Lexy could scream, before she could tell them she wasn't afraid, that they could do what they wanted because she was not a coward, because for once in her life she was clinging to the good, before she could even think about what to do next, a huge police officer stepped out of the shadows. He had big shoulders and longish blond hair.

"Go home, boys." His voice was loud. So loud it rattled through Lexy's soul.

The EastTown Boyz turned toward him and one of them drew a gun. But the cop kept coming, walking right at them. His eyes looked bright, like something weird from a movie. He never blinked. Just kept walking up to them, slow and serious. "I said . . . go home. You don't want to do this."

"Stop, man. I'll shoot!"

The officer looked more like a mountain as he got closer. "Go ahead." He stepped in front of Lexy. He was so big she couldn't see the guys around him. Then the cop pulled a club from the leg of his uniform. "Don't give me a reason."

"Look, man, you're not from around here." One of the EastTown Boyz laughed. "You're the one needs to go."

"In the name of Jesus." His voice was quieter now, calm and different. Like nothing Lexy had ever heard. The man raised his club. "Leave."

A gun versus a club? Lexy figured the EastTown kid would go ahead and shoot. Instead, she could hear their shoes shuffling. Lexy peeked around the cop and saw the three of them backing up fast, their eyes scared. Then they turned around and started to run, and when they did, the kid with the gun stopped, turned, and shot at the cop.

Fired right at him.

But at the same time the officer didn't flinch, and . . .

Lexy gasped. "What . . . Where's the bullet?" *What happened?* Lexy felt a strange sense of something she'd never felt before. Peace, maybe. Or comfort. Who was this guy? What had he said? Speaking in the name of Jesus? Cops didn't talk like that. She moved out from behind him and looked up at him.

The officer wasn't listening. He was still staring at the EastTown Boyz, watching as the reality hit them. The bullet seemed to have gone right through the officer and then ricocheted off the wall. Just a few feet from her.

They began to run as fast as they could down the street until they were out of sight.

Only then did the officer turn to her and put his hand on her shoulder. "You're okay. You need to get home."

The man's eyes had a hundred colors. Green and blue and even a white kind of light. "Who . . . are you?"

"Officer Jag."

She caught the name on his uniform. J-A-G. "How . . . did you know I needed help?"

"Lexy." The cop was calm. "God sees your heart. He has a plan for you." Officer Jag looked down the street and then at the bar a few feet away. When he looked at Lexy again, his eyes were sad. "God's plan for you . . . is so much bigger than this."

Lexy gulped. She didn't know what to say. "How did you know my name?"

"Come on." He looked fierce as he started walking in the direction of her grandma's house. "Stay with me. You need to get home."

Sure enough, the officer didn't leave her side as they walked the few blocks home. Lexy didn't understand anything that had just happened. "I'm serious. How did you know my name?"

"The bigger question is this." He looked down at her, his eyes kind like they had been at first. "Why are you with Dwayne Davis?"

Lexy felt the toughness rise up in her. "Dwayne's my man."

"No." Officer Jag shook his head. "Dwayne's working for the enemy. You stay with him, he'll destroy you."

In all her life, no one had ever spoken to her that way, like there was a plan for her life or like God knew who she was. They reached her grandma's house and the cop walked her to the door. "Think about what I said, Lexy." He looked right through her. "And stay inside."

"Okay."

"Your grandma's Bible is true. Hate evil. Cling to good. Like making that call for Marcus Dillinger." The cop took a few steps back down the stairs. "How you live, it's your choice."

Lexy felt chills on her arms and legs. "How did you . . ." She couldn't finish her sentence. Everything was just too weird. Like maybe she was having a dream. She watched the man turn and walk slowly back down the street. Then in a rush she hurried inside, shut the door, and locked it.

Only then did she realize several things all at once. The officer had no car, not that she had seen. And he had been working alone. Which cops never did in this neighborhood. And the biggest question. How had a bullet gone straight through his gut without hurting him?

A thought came to Lexy and she felt her mouth hang open for a few seconds. What if Officer Jag was an angel? Come to tell her to hate evil and cling to good? Like her grandma's Bible had told her half an hour ago? She thought about that. An angel named Jag who wore a police uniform and was bulletproof? Not possible. Just like the demons she'd imagined earlier. The whole thing was all in her imagination. Probably because of watching that kid get shot earlier. Like seeing that had made her a little crazy. Yeah, that was it. She was just a little crazy. Maybe she would open her eyes and she'd be in bed.

Lexy blinked a few times and looked around. But she wasn't in bed.

She sat down at the kitchen table and reached again for her grandma's Bible. Slowly she ran her thumb over the soft, crinkly page. The Bible was too old to matter today. Lexy felt the reality of her situation more than ever before. She had done her good deed. She had called and told the police about Marcus Dillinger.

Officer Jag had told her doing good was her choice.

But he was wrong. What was she supposed to do? Find a new family? She was a West-Knights girl. There was no way out, even if she wanted it. She brushed her teeth and fell into bed, but she couldn't sleep.

The man's face, his eyes, stayed with her. Like an Instagram picture in her mind. What kind of regular person could not be hurt by a bullet? Or guess her name? And how had he known exactly what she had read in her grandma's Bible? Maybe he was some kind of magician. And she was about to be on some reality show. There had to be an explanation.

Because angels and demons weren't real and neither was God.

The streets were proof of that.

12

Marcus had a heavy heart as he arrived at Chairos Youth Center at just after four o'clock and found the paint buckets in the back closet. A twelve-year-old boy had been killed the previous night, one of the East-Town kids. Police had ruled it a gang killing, probably for points. Gang members ranked themselves by the points they accumulated.

The murder made Marcus sick to his stomach.

He carried the paint to a worktable in the room that needed the most help. As he did he smiled at volunteers working throughout the building. More volunteers than before. The community was behind his efforts. They had opened the place at two that afternoon, and now tutors at several tables were helping kids with homework.

The dream was coming true. Just not fast enough.

Before he could brainstorm ways to keep kids like the twelve-year-old murder victim off the streets, Marcus had to finish the work at hand. In the conversion of the old warehouse to a youth center, several rooms still needed painting to cover up a decade of graffiti and desperation. Tyler, Sami, and Mary Catherine planned to show up around five to help, and by seven o'clock kids would start arriving for pickup basketball and pizza.

Given the gang situation, police and a few volunteer high school basketball coaches would be on hand — to keep the teams fair. The pizza was set to arrive around seven thirty and the activities would wrap up a few hours later. Marcus had been looking forward to this Tuesday for weeks.

Yes, it was a school night. But on the streets kids stayed out till far later regardless of school in the morning. This was one way to give them an alternative. A way to say no to the gangs that were ever willing to accept them.

Marcus made a few trips from the closet to the table getting the cans of paint and brushes and buckets set out. All the while Marcus thought about the murdered boy. What if the center had opened sooner? The kid might've found his way through the doors and never looked back.

He might be alive today.

Marcus was organizing the paint according to room when he heard the sounds of his friends. Mostly Mary Catherine, her voice, her laugh. She hadn't been far from his mind since Saturday night. And while he'd fielded dozens of texts from Shelly in that time, he hadn't heard from Mary Catherine at all.

Another reason why she was special.

They entered the room, dressed in old T-shirts and sweatpants. "A-One Painting Crew at your service!" Tyler had his arm around Sami's shoulders. "Fastest painters in Los Angeles." He grinned at Sami and Mary Catherine.

"That's right. Don't blink." Sami laughed. "The whole place'll be painted."

Mary Catherine looked happy, relaxed. And when her eyes met his, Marcus could feel the same pull, the same attraction from the other night. The chemistry between them made him dizzy. He gave Tyler and Sami a hug as the three approached but when it came to Mary Catherine, he hesitated, slightly awkward.

She sidestepped him. "I get first dibs on the brushes." She grinned. "It's all about the brushes."

"I've heard." He stepped back. Why hadn't he hugged her? Not the other night and not now? He tried not to feel frustrated. Of course he hadn't hugged her. He had a girlfriend and she wasn't interested. Or she wouldn't be if she knew his past.

They got busy, filling trays with paint and dividing the work. Before they started covering the walls, Marcus told them about the boy killed last night.

The news hit them hard. Tyler gritted his teeth. "That's why we gotta get this thing up and running. Kids killing kids. It has to stop."

"They need another way of living." Sami took Tyler's hand. "It's just so sad. Such a waste."

Mary Catherine stayed quiet. She looked at her paint, stirring it slowly. Whatever she was thinking, she didn't say it. Marcus hoped he would have time to ask her later. She cared so much about making a difference. Did the recent violence make her want to do more? Or find somewhere else to serve?

Marcus had a feeling it was the latter.

They started painting, and gradually the mood lightened. Tyler and Sami were amazed by home church at the Waynes' house a few days ago. "I never thought about the family of Jesus like that." Tyler seemed like he was really thinking about the teaching that day. "The cost of being connected to Jesus had to be so great. So emotional. I guess it makes the Bible feel a lot more real."

Marcus agreed. The Sunday service at the Waynes' house had been tremendous. He only wished Mary Catherine had come. But her work with kids at her church was important. She wasn't going to miss that. She cared too much for those kids. And these kids.

Which was the real reason she was here. No matter what attraction Marcus felt between them.

Sometime before seven, Shamika and her little boy, Jalen, showed up to help paint. Jalen wanted to play basketball, but his mom explained that tonight was for the big kids.

"You know what, though, buddy?" Marcus cleaned his hands on a rag and stooped down to the boy's level. "I bet I can find that other hoop for you. We have room right here for a little pickup game."

"Really?" Jalen's eyes lit up. "Can I, Mama?" He turned his bright brown eyes up to Shamika.

She laughed lightly and shook her head.

"Marcus, you don't have to do that. We're here to help paint. He knows that."

"Yeah, but a guy has to play hoops." Marcus winked at Jalen. "Right, buddy?"

"Right!" The boy fist-bumped Marcus.

Hope infused Marcus's troubled heart. Playing ball with Jalen later would be fun. He found the junior hoop and set it up in the middle of the room so Jalen could play while his mom painted. Marcus was handing a small basketball to Jalen when he felt someone watching him. He glanced over his shoulder and saw Mary Catherine looking right at him.

Their eyes met and she smiled. Then without a word she returned to her painting. No, the two of them would never date. But Mary Catherine was becoming his friend. And despite the way his heart skipped when she walked into the room, he welcomed her friendship. At least that.

The teens started arriving before seven, hanging around the gym and talking about the teams. A few minutes later the coaches showed up. Without supervision, a pickup basketball game could easily become a reason to fight.

A reason to kill.

But with it . . . well, Marcus could only hope that this might be a place the kids could get their aggression out, a way they could move and compete and connect without bringing the gangs and guns into it.

As Marcus expected, the kids who showed up that night were young. He looked at the teams as the first game started. He'd have been surprised if any of them were older than fifteen.

"Good turnout." Marcus was standing next to Tyler, watching the coaches working with the players. "Thirty-three kids."

Tyler smiled. "Thirty-three boys who won't be hanging with a gang tonight."

A dozen or so girls gathered along the sidelines. Two more played with the guys on the floor. By the time the games were under way, it was almost seven thirty. The pizza would be there any minute.

Marcus watched, and deep satisfaction welled within him. *God, if you would please bless this youth center.* He studied the kids, willing a change for them. *Give these kids a reason to believe in life, in people. A reason to believe in You. And help me know how we can really change things here in the —*

"Marcus!"

His prayer cut short, Marcus turned around. Officer Charlie Kent looked in a hurry as he walked up. His partner hung back, talking to Tyler, Sami, and Mary Catherine.

Marcus felt his heart sink. "More trouble?" He wiped his brow with the back of his hand. There was no relief around here.

"Always." The officer folded his arms and looked squarely at Marcus. His voice was as angry as it was defeated. He was careful to let no one else hear him. "We got a tip yesterday. The WestKnights have a contract on you. They're planning to take you out tonight."

"Me?" A partial laugh came from Marcus, but only out of disbelief. "Why would they wanna kill me?"

"Who knows. The WestKnights lost their leader this past week in a drive-by. Gangs do deadly things when a position is at stake. Sounds like that's what this is."

"The shooting yesterday, the twelve-year-old kid? Was that a part of this?"

"Probably." The officer shook his head. "We're close to making an arrest. A kid named Dwayne Davis. Has a list of robberies and attempted murder charges. We think he's the shooter from last night."

"So . . ." Marcus didn't understand. "Can't you arrest him?"

"It's not that easy. These guys don't have a residence. They're always moving, living on someone's floor. Every door we knock on has a bunch of armed kids."

Marcus nodded. The danger was worse than anything he ever imagined. It made him wonder — just for a moment — if he'd picked the wrong city to build the youth center. He could've built this in the suburbs and at least there wouldn't be bullets flying out front.

Maybe this was a mistake. If someone wanted to kill him for trying to help, then —

No, he told himself. Don't think like that.

God had given him this idea. The Lord had provided the broken down warehouse, the funds to renovate it, and the volunteers to help staff it. There was a reason he was supposed to be here. He looked out at the action on the basketball court, even as the officer kept talking, warning him about the dynamics between the rival gangs in the area.

But all Marcus could think about were the kids on the court. That's why he was here. Threats of violence wouldn't make him give up. He'd simply have to be careful. He turned to the officer. "What should I do?"

"The front of the building will be the most dangerous. We have officers patrolling, looking for Davis. But we think maybe you should call it an early night."

Marcus hesitated. He hated breaking up the basketball game. Hated letting the gangs win — even for a night. Any minute the pizza would be here. He clenched his jaw, frustrated. He couldn't put the kids and volunteers at risk. He stared at the officer. "Whatever we need to do."

The officer studied the teens on the court. "Let's dismiss them after this game."

"What about the pizza? It'll be here any minute."

"Maybe they can grab a piece on the way out. Then we can shut down." He pulled his radio from his belt. "I'll call for additional backup until everyone's cleared out."

Marcus studied the kids again. They had no idea their fun tonight was about to come to an abrupt end. Marcus looked across the room at the faces of his friends. The other officer was talking to them and by the look on their faces, they knew about the threat.

A thought occurred to him. Now he wouldn't get to play with little Jalen, either. Everyone would have to go home. He looked over at the junior hoop, but Shamika and Jalen were nowhere to be seen. Marcus had a strange feeling about the mother and son. He hadn't seen them in several minutes. "Hold on." He nodded to the officer.

148

"I have to find someone."

He turned to jog toward the back room where the water bottles were set up, but then something caught his eye. He turned and watched Shamika and Jalen walk toward the entrance of the center. Shamika saw him and waved. "The pizza's here! Me and Jalen are gonna help bring it inside."

"No!" Marcus shouted, but it was too late. Shamika and Jalen were already through the front door.

Marcus ran for the door and tore outside into the night. The pizza guy was out of the car, a stack of boxes in his hands. Cars seemed to be everywhere, cruising down the street, parked across from the center. Marcus could feel the danger, he could sense it to the core of his being.

But where was it coming from?

Suddenly out of the shadows, a woman lunged at him. "Get down!"

Everything happened so fast, the action around Marcus became a blur. He heard gunfire and the sound of squealing tires and felt something burning in his leg. Before he could register any of it, he heard Shamika scream.

"Jalen! No, not my boy! God, please!"

Marcus scrambled to his knees and the pain sliced through his leg. He looked down and saw blood coming from his thigh. *Flesh wound,* he told himself. But Jalen . . . What had happened to the child?

Volunteers were shouting and sirens sounded in the distance. But what about Jalen? Marcus pulled himself to his feet and pushed through the crowd. "Jalen!"

Shamika was still screaming. "Someone help us! No, God, not my boy! Please not my boy!"

Marcus could see him. There was blood everywhere as he knelt next to Shamika. Jalen wasn't moving and now Marcus could see where the blood was coming from. The boy had been hit in the back of his head. He had probably turned when he heard Marcus yell and now . . .

Dear God, no . . . not this child, please! "Has someone called nine-one-one?" he shouted, desperate.

"They're on their way," one of the parent volunteers answered.

Across from him working on the child was the woman who had knocked him to the ground. It was Aspyn. One of the volunteers. She had her hands on Jalen's chest, giving him CPR. Then, as if she could sense Marcus looking at her — despite the screaming and crying happening all around — she looked straight at him. "Pray." She continued her efforts to save Jalen's life. "Pray for the boy. Pray in Jesus' name."

Marcus stared at the boy. Someone had to stop the bleeding. He took off his shirt and put it against the child's head. He didn't know CPR, but Aspyn seemed capable.

Pressing the shirt against the boy's skull, Marcus tuned out the wailing and shouting and took hold of Shamika's hand. "Let's pray."

"I can't lose him!" Her words were a panicked scream. "He's all I have. Please . . . God, please!"

Marcus had never been in a situation like this. He wanted to rewind the clock and have this moment over again. If only he could've stopped Shamika before she walked outside. The bullet intended for him had hit Jalen instead. It was more than he could bear.

But even with all of that, even desperate for Jalen to survive, Marcus knew Aspyn was right. They had to pray. The blood was spreading. He couldn't watch. Marcus closed his eyes and raised his voice, raised it above the crying and shouting and sounds of the approaching sirens. "We need a miracle, Lord. Please, don't let him die. Please . . . save his life. Please, help us! God, I beg you!"

Shamika was sobbing now, but she managed to say, "Amen. Jesus, please, amen."

The ambulance pulled up and paramedics rushed through the crowd. Marcus sat back on the grass and watched as Jalen was whisked onto a stretcher. Shamika stayed with him, running alongside the men as they took her baby to the ambulance.

He should've taken that bullet. Not Jalen.

Behind him he heard Tyler's voice. But at the same time another set of paramedics rushed up and surrounded him. "Marcus, you've been hit. You need to get to the hospital."

His leg? He wanted to tell them he'd be fine. "Go find the shooter. Someone find him!" That's all that mattered now.

Tyler was at his side. "Man, it's a nasty wound. You gotta get in."

"The boy . . ." Marcus stared at the place where the ambulance carrying Jalen had disappeared. "Pray for the boy."

"We will." Tyler squeezed his shoulder. "I'll bring Sami and Mary Catherine. We'll meet you at the hospital."

The paramedics lifted him onto the stretcher. Marcus looked back as they carried him toward a second ambulance and a sudden thought hit him. What about Aspyn? How had the woman known Marcus was about to be hit? She had shoved him to the ground and then just as quickly she was at Jalen's side doing CPR. As if she'd known all this was about to happen. Was she someone connected to the gang? Did she have inside information?

Marcus would tell the police to talk to her. Just in case she knew something. In case she could lead them to the shooter. He scanned the crowd looking for her. Aspyn had volunteered at the center Saturday night. She was a pretty woman, thin with long, straightened hair and green eyes. She must've gone back inside the building.

Because she was nowhere in sight.

The paramedics loaded Marcus into the waiting ambulance and he closed his eyes. How could this have happened? It was supposed to be a fun night for the kids. This was supposed to help the gang problem here on the streets of LA. Everything they'd done, the time and money and prayers for this place. It was supposed to make a difference.

Instead, little Jalen was fighting for his life.

13

Jag was furious.

He knew Angels Walking were required to stay in control emotionally, but he was seriously struggling. He exhaled and replayed the truth in his mind. Angels on earth could feel human emotions. Anger. Fear. Sorrow — all were possible, especially when angels took on human form. By the power of God, an angel walking on earth had to control himself.

That had never been a problem before. Jag had been on many missions over time. The successful mission he and Aspyn had done during World War II, for instance. They had rescued a pilot shot down over Germany. Destruction, hate, violence.

None of it had moved Jag the way this had.

The futility of kids shooting kids. The same gang violence that had killed Terrance Williams.

Jag steadied his breathing. He waited with

Aspyn across the street from the youth center. How could this have happened again? The entire mission was in jeopardy. They had known the shooting was possible. He and Aspyn were both on site, ready to intervene, and Jag had done what he could to delay Dwayne. He had disabled the kid's vehicle. But apparently not well enough. Because the shooting had still happened.

Just like ten years ago.

Either way, right now they didn't have time to wonder about what went wrong. Jag had a job to do.

He wanted Dwayne Davis behind bars. Where he belonged, according to man's law. Where he could do no further harm to mankind.

"Aspyn." He looked straight at her. "You did the right thing. You saved Marcus. I'm the one who failed."

"No." Aspyn's eyes were damp with tears. "You did what you could. Police mean nothing to Dwayne."

Anger stirred in Jag's heart again. "If it were up to me . . ."

"Don't." She touched his shoulder. "We need to stay focused." A tear slid down her cheek and she caught it with the back of her hand. "This feeling . . . the sadness. It's the hardest part of being on mission. So much heartache here on earth."

"Exactly." Jag willed the strength of God to settle his being.

Across the street the teens were still milling about; Officer Kent seemed to have things under control. He was dispersing the young people, telling them to go home.

Jag turned back to Aspyn. "We will ask the Father for a miracle where the child is concerned."

Aspyn nodded. "I didn't see this coming. I thought the boy was out of the way. I thought —"

"It's okay. We don't know all things." This was the hardest part of being an angel. Having more knowledge than humans, more power. But not nearly the knowledge or power of the Father. God alone knew when someone would be called home, when a person's time on earth ran out.

But why allow angels to intervene if people were going to die anyway? Again Jag forced himself to relax. *Stay controlled, Jag,* he told himself. *Keep the mission in mind.* One day the answers would be clear, even to angels. For now they were to do their jobs, carry out their assignments.

"I want to be at the hospital." Aspyn straightened.

"You should go." Jag studied her. She

looked stronger than before. She would come back and she would work as hard as possible to see the mission accomplished. Jag had no doubt.

Aspyn looked at him, her eyes still filled with sorrow. "The most important thing is prayer. Always."

"You go. I have another matter to tend to."

"Jag." Her voice held the familiar warning. "Be careful. Work in God's strength. Don't let human emotions guide you."

Her words hit their mark. He clenched his fists and relaxed them again. "I won't." He exhaled. "The mission is God's. Not ours."

"Exactly." She nodded to him. "See you soon. Stay low."

With that they were both gone. Jag felt the sense of purpose deep inside him. He needed to stay hidden better. Aspyn was right about that, too. Angels Walking had to stay invisible as much as possible. Sure, they had to materialize. That was part of the mission. And when they took on human form, sons and daughters of Adam might wonder. Christians familiar with God's word knew that sometimes they would entertain angels unaware. But too many displays — like not being harmed by flying bullets — and people wouldn't wonder. They would know.

God sent His angels to clandestinely work as messengers and protectors among His people. So that He would get the glory. Otherwise humans might worship angels and miss the One who created them.

Almost as soon as he left the spot in front of the youth center, Jag arrived two blocks away, invisible, just down the street from Dwayne and Lexy, who were standing on the sidewalk outside his car. Angels had keen hearing — so Jag could clearly hear Dwayne cursing Lexy, threatening her.

Anger filled Jag again. He wouldn't let the young man hurt the girl. She was important to the mission. He moved closer to Dwayne. Why so much hatred? How could one created in the very image of God be so full of evil? Jag heard a rush of movement in the air around him. A cold wind came with the sound and in a blur the street was filled with demons. Hissing. Laughing. Taunting him and pushing their way closer to Dwayne.

Then suddenly — as if Dwayne could sense the dark support around him — he raised the gun and pointed it straight at Lexy's head.

Jag had to act quickly. He instantly moved to the pay phone near the bar a block away. He slipped into a tight spot between two houses and materialized as the towering blond officer.

Jag stepped up to the pay phone and dialed 911.

The operator answered on the first ring. "What's your emergency?"

"I'm an officer. I know who tried to kill Marcus Dillinger."

"Identify yourself."

"I'll give you the address. I'm in a hurry." He quickly rattled off the information. "Send several squad cars. You don't have long." He hung up and stepped into the shadows, and instantly he was back on the street with Dwayne and Lexy, invisible. The entire phone call had taken mere seconds.

The demons were closing in on Dwayne and Lexy. A team so murderous and dark. Treacherous and evil. The smell of death hung in the air. One of the demons dug its invisible claws into Dwayne's back.

Jag breathed deep. *I need you, Jesus . . .*

Instantly he was in the midst of the demons. "Go!" He held both hands toward the evil spirits. "Go now!"

One of them hissed and his spiky wings brushed up against Jag. "Fight us, mighty warrior. Our time is short. These two belong to us."

Again Jag felt the rush of anger. This

159

wasn't right. Nothing should stop an angel, not unless . . . What was he thinking? How could he forget?

The name of Jesus.

"In the name of Jesus, be gone!" The humans couldn't hear him, but his voice boomed through another dimension. "Now!"

At the sound of the name of Jesus, the demons withered in size, shrinking back, repulsed, wounded. And instantly the evil band disappeared. They would find someone else to torment tonight.

He stepped out of hiding directly behind Dwayne and Lexy, this time as the police officer again. "Stop." His voice pierced the night air. "Both of you! Police!"

"What the —" Dwayne spun around and pulled his gun.

Jag covered the ground between them in fractions of a second and grabbed the gun from Dwayne.

Jag looked at the pistol in his hand and felt a surge of power. *So this is what it's like?* he thought. He ran his thumb over the handle. He pointed the gun at the teenager. He could kill Dwayne now, but there would be eternal consequences.

It wouldn't take much. The slightest pull on the trigger and Dwayne would no longer be a threat. Jag was breathing harder. He ran his finger along the smooth metal at the center of the gun. *One pull . . . just one.*

Suddenly Lexy cried out, "Jesus, help us!" *Jesus.*

At the sound of His name, Jag instantly came to his senses. He felt a heavenly calm wash over him and he moved his finger from the trigger. He would not shoot. Not now. Not ever. The sound of sirens in the distance told him it wouldn't be long. Help was on the way.

"The punishment you're about to receive, you have earned." Jag kept the gun trained on the kid. "But it is nothing to what will come after this life." Jag was within his bounds now. Eternal truths, life-altering messages — these were the job of angels.

Dwayne glared at him. He grabbed Lexy by her hair and held her close.

Before Jag could speak again, three police cars pulled up from different directions and skidded to a stop, their bright lights on Dwayne's car. Six of them jumped out, guns drawn.

Jag was invisible by then, the gun on the ground where he had been standing. He moved, unnoticed, to a place where the shadows were dark and the lights of the police cars could not reach. And like that

161

he was gone.

Immediately he was at the hospital, in the room where surgeons frantically worked on little Jalen. Aspyn stood nearby, praying. Constantly praying. Jag took his place beside her.

He closed his eyes.

That was close back there. He could still feel the gun in his hand, feel the strange and powerful desire to kill. His anger had nearly consumed him. *I'm sorry, Father. I was wrong.* He would need to be more careful. Another moment like that could jeopardize the entire mission.

Jag closed his eyes. Prayer. That's what he needed. More time in prayer. He could not work successfully as an Angel Walking unless he stayed connected to God. His breathing slowed down and a deep peace came over him. He blinked his eyes open and stared at the injured child lying on the operating table. Yes, he would pray. For the child fighting for his life a few feet away and for himself.

That human rage would never consume him again.

14

On the way to Cedars-Sinai Medical Center, Mary Catherine sat in the back and prayed. Tyler was behind the wheel, Sami in the passenger seat beside him. The car stayed quiet except for the occasional sound of a whispered prayer. Mary Catherine stared out the window. How could this have happened?

Of course the youth center was in a dangerous part of town. But none of them ever really thought the gangs would shoot at them. Why would they? Marcus was only trying to help.

They turned into the parking lot and found a spot near the emergency room entrance. The ambulances were still there, parked close to the doors. Mary Catherine squeezed her eyes shut. *Dear God, be with that child. Please.*

Tyler hurried out of the car and around to Sami's door and then Mary Catherine's.

"Is the bullet still in Marcus's leg?" Mary Catherine hadn't wanted to ask until now. She had seen the blood on his jeans before the paramedics took him.

"I couldn't tell." Tyler looked pale, worried. "I hope not."

Inside they checked in at the front desk and explained they were there for Marcus.

"Come on back. He already has visitors, but we're slow tonight." The nurse opened a set of double doors and met them on the other side. "Can't believe those gangs. Trying to kill Marcus Dillinger? Guy only wanted to do something good for the city."

Mary Catherine trailed after the group. Where was the little boy? Where was Jalen? Was he in one of the rooms with the curtains drawn?

Her heart ached at the thought. Precious little child. He had only wanted to help bring in the pizza. She fought back tears as they walked. They reached Marcus's room and stepped in.

The Wayne family was already there, including Shelly. She was sitting next to Marcus's bed, running her hand along his arm.

"Hey." He seemed to shake off Shelly's touch. He looked at Tyler and Sami and then held Mary Catherine's gaze. The fear in his eyes was tangible. "Any word on Jalen?"

"We came here first." Tyler reached out and clasped Marcus's hand.

"I'm fine." His mouth sounded dry. "I need to know about that boy. The nurse won't tell me."

Shelly slid her chair closer to his bed and ran her hand over his hair. "I'm sure he's okay."

"He's not okay." Marcus shot her a harsh look.

Shelly's sad smile didn't waver. She moved her hand to his shoulder. Meanwhile Coach Wayne and his wife were talking quietly, whispering a few feet away.

Mary Catherine felt out of place. The cold, shrinking feeling deep inside her could only be jealousy. Which she hated. She focused her attention on Marcus's injured leg.

He lay stretched out on the bed, one leg of his jeans cut off. The bandage was halfway up his thigh and, if the wrap was any indication, the wound was serious. He had an IV in his arm, and he looked tired.

Sami looked at Marcus's leg. "Did they get the bullet out?"

"It didn't go in. Just grazed me."

"Poor baby." Shelly was on her feet, hanging over the side of the bed like she wanted to crawl up next to Marcus.

Mary Catherine had seen enough. "I'm going to go find Jalen's mother. I'll let you know what I find out."

She didn't wait for a response. Out in the hall she found the nurses' station and asked how to get to the pediatric ICU. "Take the elevator to the fourth floor." The woman hesitated. "Other than parents, patients are only allowed one visitor at a time."

"Thank you." Mary Catherine was already on her way to the elevator. At the fourth floor she walked quietly to the nurses' station, but before she could ask, she saw Jalen's mother in the hallway outside one of the rooms. She was sitting on a chair, her head in her hands.

Mary Catherine approached and took the seat beside her. "Shamika. It's Mary Catherine. From the youth center." She put her arm around Shamika's shoulders. "How is he?"

The woman lifted her head. Her eyes, which had shone with hope earlier today, were swollen from crying and dark with fear and defeat. "How did this happen?"

She wasn't looking for answers, so Mary Catherine let the moment pass. "Is he in surgery?"

"Yes." She sniffed and brushed the backs of her hands beneath her eyes. "They have to remove part of his skull. Because his brain was swelling." She shook her head, bewildered. "They have to get the bullet out. It went from his head into his neck."

Mary Catherine didn't want to ask any more questions. Especially when Shamika probably didn't have answers. Like whether the boy would walk again or how much damage had been done to his brain or his spine . . . or if the doctors even expected him to live.

All of it was one minute at a time. Mary Catherine took her arm from Shamika's shoulders and reached for the woman's hands. "Can I pray with you?"

"Would it matter?" She probably wasn't trying to be rude or difficult. Her question didn't sound cynical. "I mean it. God could've protected my boy from that bullet. Why pray now?"

Mary Catherine had spent a great deal of time on this issue. She had done a summer of Bible study on the power of prayer and the reasons bad things happen in the first place. She kept her tone even. "I'm not sure anyone knows exactly why certain things happen, but I know this. Evil doesn't come from God."

Shamika thought about that for several seconds. Gradually she nodded her head. "I suppose." She stared at her hands. "But really . . . why did this happen?" Fresh tears began to fall down her cheeks. "He was just being good."

For a long moment Mary Catherine said nothing.

"I'm serious." Shamika's voice was sharper this time. "If you can tell me, then tell me."

Mary Catherine hadn't planned on saying anything. She had no real answers. She took a deep breath. "The Bible says this place, this earth . . . it's broken and fallen. God gives us a way out through Jesus. Even still, every one of us will die someday." She paused. "This isn't our home, Shamika."

She ran her right thumb over her empty left ring finger. "Jalen's daddy left me when I was six weeks pregnant. I figured if he couldn't love me, no one could. Not even God."

Mary Catherine put her hand alongside Shamika's face. "That's not true. God loves you so much. He has a plan for you and Jalen and whatever that plan is, it's good. Even now."

Confusion lined Shamika's face. "There's nothing good about this."

"No." Mary Catherine felt frustrated with

herself. She wasn't helping at all. "Of course not."

"So what does it mean?" Shamika's eyes filled with tears again. "God loves us. He has plans for us. But here we are, sitting in this hospital while Jalen fights for every breath."

There were no simple answers. "I only know that God is great. If we choose Him, then one day we'll have eternity together. No more tears, no sorrow, no pain. No shooting or gang violence. No lonely nights. Never again."

Her tears came harder. "I just want my baby back. I want him to live and laugh and be . . . like he was three hours ago."

Mary Catherine took hold of Shamika's hands once more. "Then let's pray. Let's ask God for that."

"Okay." Shamika looked like a little girl, desperate and lost. She took tight hold of Mary Catherine's fingers. "Please . . . go ahead."

Mary Catherine nodded. "Dear God . . ." Tears flooded her eyes and fell onto her lap. The little boy had been so happy, so trusting that all of life would stay the way it had been in that moment. Filled with love and joy and fun. She tried to find the words. "Lord, we don't understand evil or why things like this happen. But we need Your help to get through it." She struggled to keep her voice steady. "Father, we ask You for a miracle for Jalen. That he would live and laugh and that he would one day soon be just like he was a few hours ago. We ask this in Jesus' powerful name, amen."

When she finished praying she hugged Shamika. "Let me give you my number. So you can update me on how he's doing."

They exchanged information and Shamika was just starting to explain how Jalen's birthday was coming up in a few weeks when the doctor opened the door at the end of the hallway and walked toward them.

His face was taut, his expression deeply concerned. "We've done what we can. We removed the bullet. He's resting now."

Shamika stood. "Is he . . . breathing on his own?"

"No." The doctor looked troubled. "He's on life support." He paused. "I have to be honest, Mrs. Johnson, Jalen may not make it through the night. He's a fighter, but the damage . . . it's considerable."

Quiet sobs came over Shamika. Mary Catherine stood next to her and turned her eyes to the doctor. "Will you bring him back here?"

"Yes. In a few minutes." He put his hand

170

on Shamika's arm. "He's unconscious. Once he's back in his room, you can talk to him. He may be able to hear you."

Mary Catherine helped Shamika into the room and again her tears came. The woman covered her face with her hands, stifling her sobs. "Not my boy, God . . . please . . . bring him back to me. I can't do this."

Shamika didn't seem to be able to move at all. Not toward the room or toward Mary Catherine. Not at all. Mary Catherine prayed silently. *God, give her peace and strength. Help her be strong for her little boy. Show us You're here. Please.*

Gradually Mary Catherine felt the woman beside her start to relax. After a while the doctor brought Jalen back to the room. He looked so small, lost in the sheets and bandages, tubes and wires. Mary Catherine stayed by Shamika as she took up her place beside her son.

"I'm scared," Shamika whispered. She lowered her hands from her face. Jalen's head was fully wrapped and he had a breathing tube in his throat and mouth.

Shamika put her hand on Jalen's much smaller one. "Baby, it's Mama." She hung her head and grabbed a few quick breaths, clearly fighting for control. When she lifted her head, she studied her boy and then brushed her knuckles softly against his cheeks. "Mama's here. Jesus too, baby. It's gonna be okay." She wiped her tears with her free hand. "You keep fighting, Jalen. You're gonna be stronger for this." She looked back at Mary Catherine and the smallest flicker of hope flashed in her eyes. Then she turned back to Jalen. "We'll both be stronger."

The door to the room opened and an older nurse poked her head in. "Mary Catherine?"

"Yes?" She turned to the woman.

"Your friends are out here. They want to talk to you."

Mary Catherine hugged Shamika again. "Want me to stay? I will. I can call in to work tomorrow."

"That's okay. I wanna be alone with my baby."

"I understand." Mary Catherine searched Shamika's face. "Call me or text me if you need anything. We'll get everyone to pray for Jalen, all right?"

"Yes." She managed the slightest smile. "Thank you."

"You're not alone."

Shamika nodded and turned to Jalen again. "I'll be here. Until he opens his eyes and talks to me again."

That was all they could ask for. That Shamika might believe enough to expect the impossible. To look for a miracle.

Mary Catherine stepped out of the room. Tyler and Sami were waiting for her. Sami hugged her first. "How is he?"

"Fighting." She blinked back a wave of tears. "The doctor said it doesn't look good." She pulled a tissue from her purse and pressed it to her eyes. "We have to pray for a miracle. We need to believe."

"Poor little guy." Tyler put his arm around Sami.

Sami sighed. "We all prayed in Marcus's room."

Mary Catherine didn't want to think about Marcus. "Is he staying overnight?" Spending time with Shamika had been good for her. She hadn't once pictured Shelly sitting next to Marcus earlier, or the way the scene had jabbed at her heart.

"No." Tyler stepped up. "Shelly and the Waynes are gone. I guess the doctors are finishing up paperwork. We can take him home." Together the four of them had only Tyler's car. "We could come back and get you later."

"I'll be ready in a few minutes. I can meet you downstairs." She took Sami's hand. "Is that okay?"

"Of course." Sami looked beat, too. They all did. She and Tyler hugged Mary Catherine again. Longer this time. Then they left for the elevator.

Mary Catherine had spotted a small chapel just down the hall. She didn't want to interrupt Shamika's time with her son, and she hardly wanted to be with Marcus after seeing him with Shelly earlier. Not tonight. Not when she couldn't get a grip on her emotions.

She waited until Tyler and Sami were gone, then she headed toward the chapel. It was right across from the elevators. She went inside and found it empty.

The room was small and dimly lit. Just eight pews and a wooden cross at the front. Mary Catherine sat in one of the middle pews, dropped to her knees, and brought her hands to her face. She prayed for Jalen and for his mother and for the future of the youth center. She prayed the shooter would be caught and that progress would someday be made on the streets of inner-city Los Angeles.

Not until she had talked to God about all that did she pray for the thing that was weighing most heavily on her heart. Her words came in quiet whispers. "I let myself start to fall for Marcus, Lord . . . and that

174

was a mistake. I'm sorry. That's not the life You want for me. You've made that clear. So protect my fragile heart, God. Please. When I see Marcus let me see him as a brother. Only that. In Jesus' name, amen."

She lifted her head and gasped.

Sitting across the narrow aisle from her was a police officer. Big and blond, his hat in his hands. He looked at her and nodded politely. "Sorry to startle you. I didn't want to interrupt."

"Is something . . . did Jalen . . . ?"

"No. The boy is still with us. Your prayers matter, Mary Catherine. Keep praying."

"I will." She sniffed and squinted at him, trying to make out the name on his badge. "Have I met you? At the center?"

"No." He put his hat back on his head. "I'm Officer Jag. I'm not from around here, but I was there when the shooting happened. I wanted to update you."

Mary Catherine felt her heart beat faster. "Did they catch him? The shooter?"

"They did. Dwayne Davis is behind bars, which is where he'll stay. But the girl . . . she's very young. She still has a chance."

"What girl?" Mary Catherine turned in the pew so she could see the man better. He had the most unusual eyes. Like a hundred colors in one. And a peace seemed

175

to emanate from him. Maybe because of his uniform. She wasn't sure.

"The girl is Lexy Jones. Dwayne's girlfriend. She's been heading down a dark path." The officer clearly had more to say. He glanced at the back door of the chapel as if he were in a hurry. "Anyway, Marcus asked about the Scared Straight program."

That was true. Mary Catherine knew about that. "He was told it didn't work that well."

"We have another program now. It's newer. More involved. It's called Last Time In. Kids get a tour of the jail, the inmates tell them the truth about being incarcerated. Then they get four weeks of counseling — three times a week. It's intense, but it can work."

Mary Catherine nodded. She liked the idea. "Did you tell Marcus?"

"I can't stay. I'm hoping you might tell him."

"Okay." Mary Catherine had just asked God for a break from Marcus. Now this. "Is the program available here?"

"It's in place, but they need a grant to continue. Ten thousand dollars." Officer Jag stood and moved out of the pew into the aisle. He held his hand out to Mary Cather-

ine. "If you could tell Marcus, I'd appreci-
ate it."

"I will." Mary Catherine stood and shook
the man's hand. As she did, the connection
worked its way instantly to her soul. Like
there was power in his touch. Their eyes met
and held and Mary Catherine had the
strangest feeling. Like she was on holy
ground.

"About your prayers. Just remember . . .
God knows better than we do. He always
does. Even when it doesn't make sense." He
looked to the door again. "Keep praying."

His bright eyes held hers and then he left.

Questions pelted Mary Catherine's soul.
How had the officer known she was here?
And how did he know she was a friend of
Marcus's? How did he know her name? She
had no answers. The nurse at the desk
must've seen her come this way and told
him. And maybe the nurses also knew who
she had come with and that they were here
with Marcus.

What other explanation was there?

Mainly the officer wanted her to tell Marcus about the Last Time In program. The
idea sounded amazing. Certainly kids like
Lexy Jones weren't going to stay away from
gangs and violence just because a youth
center opened in their neighborhood. They

needed something more.

If the program needed money, Mary Catherine could fund it. She had an account her parents had set up. Money they put aside for her every year as a birthday gift. She didn't need it, so she hadn't touched it. When the time came to use it, she could only justify using it to help someone else.

This would be a perfect reason.

Now she had to tell Marcus. She didn't want to talk to him today. In light of Jalen's life-threatening injuries and the terrifying shooting, the news could wait. At least until tomorrow.

But who was Marcus supposed to talk to about the program? Officer Jag said he wasn't from around here, so then who was the contact? Mary Catherine hurried out of the chapel and stared down the hallway. The man had been gone for less than a minute.

So where was he?

She walked as quickly as she could to the nurses' station. The woman sitting behind the desk was the same one who had been there before. "Hi . . . Officer Jag came into the chapel to talk to me. Can you tell me where he went?"

The woman blinked. "Officer Jag?"

"Yes. He's tall, blond hair. Light eyes." She could see the woman wasn't tracking with her. "He must've come by here."

"There hasn't been an officer on this floor. Not for an hour at least."

Frustration rattled Mary Catherine's nerves. "He was just here." She pointed down the hall toward the chapel. "He left from right there."

"I'm sorry, miss." The woman looked indignant. "I told you. I haven't seen an officer. Certainly no one by that description." She paused. "What did you say his name was?"

"Officer Jag." She realized that she hadn't gotten a full name. "He said he wasn't from around . . ." Mary Catherine felt her shoulders sink. "Never mind."

She jogged down the hallway toward the chapel and kept going to where it dead-ended. There was no way out. The only direction the officer could've left was right past the nurses' station. Mary Catherine headed that way. This time the woman at the nurses' station was buried in paperwork.

That had to be it. The nurse had been too busy to notice the man.

A sigh made its way through Mary Catherine and she walked to the elevator. Her friends would be ready to go. On her way to the emergency room, Mary Catherine remembered Officer Jag's words about prayer.

179

God knows better than we do. He always does. Even when it doesn't make sense.

That was what the man had said, right? Clearly, he had to have been talking about Jalen. The little boy needed everyone praying, everyone believing. Good that the officer was a man of faith.

The city needed more like him, wherever he was from.

She reached Marcus's room. He was sitting up now, getting instructions and paperwork from a nurse. Tyler and Sami were waiting near the door.

Marcus looked at her. "How is he?"

"Not good." She stayed by the door with her friends. "He needs a miracle."

The ride home was quiet. Marcus sat in the front with Tyler, and the two of them did most of the talking. "Police came in when you guys were gone." Marcus leaned his head against the seat. He looked exhausted. "They have the shooter in custody. His girlfriend, too."

"Good." Tyler didn't hesitate. "Makes me think they should arrest everyone in both gangs. Run their rap sheets. Figure out what new crimes they're linked to." He glanced at Marcus, his hand tight on the steering wheel. "Maybe then the younger guys wouldn't be so quick to join."

180

Mary Catherine stayed silent in the back-seat. She looked out the window and thought about Shamika, spending the night at her son's side. The conversation in the car faded and Mary Catherine lifted her eyes to the stars overhead.

God could do this, of course. He could give them a miracle for Jalen.

Now she could only pray that He would.

Jag stood next to Aspyn on the opposite side of the child's bed, invisible. Aspyn was ready to fight — just like Jag. She wanted to see the mission succeed and she wanted justice.

"Earth is so difficult . . . full of pain." She held her hand over the boy's head. "Jesus, heal him. Let him live."

Jag loved the heart of his teammate. She was a very great example to him, especially after tonight. "My anger . . . I nearly lost it."

She turned and stared at him. "Dwayne Davis?"

"Yes." Jag still felt ashamed. The feel of the trigger beneath his finger would stay with him always. "I could've killed that boy. I wanted to."

No matter what, they had to be honest with each other. Aspyn faced him. "Why didn't you?"

"I'm an angel. I want to do God's will. The name of Jesus reminded me."

Aspyn exhaled, relieved. "Who said it?"

"Lexy. The girl." He straightened himself, empowered, convinced that his perfect God was with him even in his imperfection. "God used her to get my attention. Just in time."

"She needs help." Aspyn's tone was heavy. She looked at Jalen again. "So many pieces of this mission. We can't miss a moment."

That had never been more true. "I spoke to Mary Catherine in the chapel."

"Do you think she has an idea? Who you are?"

"No." He felt another reason for regret. "I wasn't as careful with Dwayne. The guys on the streets think I'm some monster cop. I need to be careful." He looked deep into her eyes. "I'm sorry. I've talked to the Father about it."

"Then you are forgiven." Aspyn took hold of his hand for a moment. "Let this go." She moved closer to the bed and studied the child. "The hardest thing about earth is that love is not enough. It's never enough."

Jag let her words settle in his soul. He shook his head. "Love is always enough, Aspyn. But there are different kinds of love."

"True." She checked the monitors surrounding the boy. "The child is fading. We need to pray."

And so for the rest of the evening they begged God for a miracle, asking that He intervene in Jalen's body and that He give doctors wisdom beyond their abilities. Most of all they asked that Jalen be surrounded by love. Not the earthly sort of love that could so easily fail.

But heaven's love.

A love that would always be enough.

15

Marcus was in the middle of an upper body workout in his home gym the next morning when he received the text from Mary Catherine. He hadn't known what to say to her last night, how to bring up the fact that he hadn't asked Shelly Wayne to come to the hospital.

None of it mattered compared to the shooting. He'd gotten word from Officer Kent an hour earlier that Jalen had survived the night. He was still on life support. Still critical.

Now Marcus looked at his phone. The text said simply, *Can we meet this morning? If you're feeling up to it? I need to talk to you about something related to the shooting.*

Marcus had no idea what she wanted to talk about. He only knew that he wanted to see her. More than he wanted to do anything else today. He moved his fingers across his phone. *Definitely. I'd like that. How about eleven o'clock at the Silver Lake Whole Foods. They've got great coffee.*

Her response took a few minutes. *Great. See you then.*

The last thing he wanted was to finish his workout. He was out of danger, barring infection, but his leg throbbed. He couldn't run for a week, but otherwise he'd be fine. The bullet had only grazed him. Aspyn, the woman from the neighborhood, had saved his life.

Last night at the hospital Officer Kent had come by and Marcus had brought up the woman's name. "She pushed me out of the way before the guy fired. Almost like she knew what was going to happen."

"I saw the whole thing." The officer shook his head. "Like she had some sort of advance warning."

"Did you check her out? I mean . . . I guess I wondered if she knew something."

"She's not from the area. No record of her in any of the searches. But we don't think she was involved."

Marcus picked up a pair of fifty-pound dumbbells. Good that Aspyn wasn't working for a gang. But how had she known to push him out of the way? And how come she hadn't been hit? The whole night still didn't add up, but none of it mattered. Not compared with Jalen's struggle to live.

He pushed through his routine for another thirty minutes and then showered and shaved. If this were a different situation, he would've been thrilled at the chance to have coffee with Mary Catherine. But today would be different; he could feel it. Different from how things had been the other night when they walked around his neighborhood.

The incident with Shelly last night had changed things.

Mary Catherine's text had more of a businesslike feel. She was keeping her distance. Not that he blamed her. He really needed to call Shelly and let her know things weren't working out. The difficult part was Coach Wayne. His coach was also his friend, and the last thing Marcus wanted was to hurt the man's niece.

The whole situation was complicated.

He got ready faster than he expected and found a booth at Whole Foods a few minutes earlier than eleven. A baseball cap low on his brow would keep people from recognizing him — something that was rarely a problem. He was six-three and built like an athlete. But in a city like Los Angeles, Marcus didn't stand out unless he was in uniform.

Five minutes later he watched Mary Catherine arrive and he felt a little dizzy. The girl had captured his attention and maybe even his heart. No matter how poorly last night had gone, no matter how sad everyone was, he couldn't put into words how great it was to see Mary Catherine now.

She spotted him and as she approached she seemed to do her best to avoid a hug. They walked together to the coffee bar, poured their drinks, and then returned to the booth. "I heard from Shamika on the way in." Mary Catherine took the spot opposite him. "No change for Jalen."

"No." Marcus leaned his forearms on the table and waited. The fact that the child had taken the bullet intended for him was still more than he could bear. He stared at his drink and after a long moment he took a sip.

"Thanks for meeting." She seemed less comfortable than she'd been the other night. The shooting had deeply affected them all. "Last night, after I visited with Shamika, I went to the chapel."

"On the ICU floor?"

Mary Catherine nodded. "It's small. I was the only one there. At least at first." Her tone was intent, as if whatever was coming was very serious. "When I finished praying,

I opened my eyes and there was a police officer there. Sitting across the aisle from me."

"Charlie Kent?"

"No." She put her hands around her cup of coffee. "His name was Jag. Officer Jag, that's what he called himself." She shrugged one shoulder. "I didn't get his full name."

Marcus wished he'd worn a sweatshirt. The morning had been cold for Southern California. Not quite sixty degrees yet. They were inside, but a chill hung over the Whole Foods booth. "Jag. Sounds familiar."

"He said he wasn't from here." She looked out the window and then back at Marcus. "He told me about a new program. It's called Last Time In. He wanted me to tell you about it."

Strange, Marcus thought, *that he'd find Mary Catherine and ask her to bring the message.* "Why didn't he come tell me himself?"

"He was in a hurry."

"Oh." Marcus wasn't sure where this was going or why the officer wanted him to know. "Tell me about the program."

Mary Catherine pulled some paperwork from her purse. "I stopped by the police station on my way here." She spread the documents on the table in front of her.

"Charlie Kent gave me this. It looks amazing."

For the next ten minutes Mary Catherine went over the information. The program was created by a couple of police officers, looking for an alternative to the Scared Straight program. "Prison is always scary, of course." Mary Catherine sounded more relaxed than when she first arrived. "But this takes kids beyond the scared part."

The program involved a prison tour with volunteers acting as chaperones. Police guards would introduce a group of young offenders to actual prisoners. "So they get a realistic picture of prison?" Marcus liked that part. There had to be a sense of reality if the program was going to make a difference.

"Definitely." Mary Catherine turned to the last page of the paperwork. "What makes it different is the group meetings after the prison tour."

Apparently the meetings were run by the same people who volunteered as chaperones. "I'm assuming the volunteers have to be cleared by police?" Marcus looked up, straight into Mary Catherine's eyes. She was more beautiful every day. At least it seemed that way.

"Yes, and trained." Mary Catherine took

another drink of her coffee. "It's freezing in here."

"I know." He held his cup and let the steam warm his face. "I have an idea." He stood and nodded to the store. "I'll be right back."

Marcus jogged to the clothing section at the front of the store. His leg didn't hurt as bad as it had this morning. In no time he found two navy blue sweatshirts with white writing that said simply, "Live Life." *Perfect,* he told himself. He grabbed a small for her and a large for himself, paid for them, and hurried back to the booth.

"Here." He handed her the small one. "Maybe now we can actually think."

She laughed and the sound was music to his soul. There hadn't been a reason even to smile since last night. "Thank you." She took it from him, removed the tags, and slipped it over her head. "Mmmm. Much better." Her smile remained. "I love impulsive."

"I figured." He put his sweatshirt on and instantly felt better. "Okay. Where were we?" He had to be careful around her. She had a way of making him forget what he was doing, what he was saying.

"The program." She furrowed her brow, like she was trying to find the serious place

from a few minutes ago. "So, it's all voluntary. The kids have to sign up, and they have
to agree to the weekly meetings. Volunteers
can share their faith as long as they're clear
about it up front. It's up to the kids and
their guardians if that type of counseling
will work for them. The group meetings are
very loosely structured. More of a time for
kids to open up."

Marcus was starting to understand. "So
Bible study could be a part of the group
meetings?"

"Exactly. It's a private program. Police
involvement is voluntary and outside official
work hours." She looked at the paperwork
on the table and then at him again. "As long
as the kids agree to be led by that volunteer,
then the group can take whatever direction
of encouragement everyone agrees on."

"Wow. Amazing." Marcus hadn't heard of
anything like it. "So this officer, he wanted
me to know?"

"He did." Mary Catherine took a sip of
her drink and then sat back, pensive. "Last
Time In costs around ten grand. Without
that there's no program. Maybe Officer Jag
thought you could help."

"Of course." Marcus leaned forward, his
arms on the table. Mary Catherine looked
adorable in her sweatshirt. She could've

designed it herself. He forced himself to focus. "I can get the money to Officer Kent today. Is that how it works?"

"Actually" — she smiled — "it's taken care of. Don't worry about it."

Marcus was surprised. But the topic seemed off limits. Maybe one day he would be close enough to Mary Catherine to know where the money had come from and what other secrets she hadn't shared. He guessed there were many. "Great." He nodded. "So how do I help?"

"You chaperone." Mary Catherine looked straight at him. "Charlie Kent says most of the kids from the streets love you. Whatever you tell them to do, they'll do it."

"Not Dwayne Davis." He raised his brow.

"But his girlfriend, Lexy Jones. She's a different story." Mary Catherine began folding up the papers in front of her. "Police think she made the call, the one that tipped off the department about the fact that someone from the WestKnights wanted you dead."

"His girlfriend?" Marcus tried to imagine that life.

Over the next few minutes Mary Catherine explained more of the details. The police wanted to offer Lexy a chance at the Last Time In program. "It's either that or she serves five years. At least. She was in the passenger seat when Dwayne fired." Mary Catherine frowned. "Even if she tried to save your life by tipping off the police."

"Has anyone talked to Lexy about it?" Marcus liked the idea. If someone could reach the girl now, it might change her life. It might save it.

"No. She's in jail for now."

Marcus remembered something he hadn't asked Charlie Kent. "How old were these kids?"

"Dwayne's eighteen. They have evidence he committed at least two other murders. He can be tried as an adult, so he's probably looking at life." Mary Catherine sighed. "Lexy . . . she's just sixteen."

"Man." Marcus shook his head. He looked down at his empty cup. The problem was so much bigger than he ever imagined. *God, whatever You want me to do, I'll do it.* He met Mary Catherine's eyes again. "If you're asking if I'll volunteer, the answer is yes."

"Good." Her smile started in her eyes. "I told them I would, too. I'll talk to Sami and Tyler later. They'd be perfect. The whole program takes about four weeks. It's one Saturday and then eight weeknights."

"Perfect. I leave for spring training February eighth." Marcus felt his hope surge. He checked the calendar on his phone. "The timing couldn't be better."

"So . . . that's why we had to meet today." She looked hesitant. "Training starts tomorrow at noon and again Friday night. Saturday is the prison tour. Not a lot of warning." She paused. "I guess usually the volunteers are family or friends of the kids who go through the program. The police volunteers oversee it, but the others who help out usually have a personal reason why they're involved."

Marcus uttered a sad chuckle. "I guess after last night we're qualified."

"Yes." Mary Catherine slid the folded documents across the table. "Look these over." She checked the time on her phone. "I have to run. If you don't hear from me, I'll see you tomorrow night at the police station a few blocks from the youth center. The one on Fourth."

Apparently their time together was over. Marcus stood and waited while Mary Catherine stepped out of the booth. Again she seemed in too much of a hurry for a hug. She did smile, though. "Thanks for meeting. I think this will help. Really."

"I hope so." Marcus didn't have time to say anything else. She was already distancing herself from him. "Thanks for including me." He raised his hand. "See you tomor-row."

She waved and then turned and headed for the exit. Before he had time to think of what to do next she was gone. He picked up the papers from the table and slipped them into the back pocket of his jeans. There was still so much more he wanted to say. He would've wondered whether the last hour had happened at all if not for two things. His navy sweatshirt with the words "Live Life."

And the faint smell of her perfume.

She couldn't have stayed another moment. Mary Catherine rushed across the parking lot to her car and left in record time. Another minute with Marcus and she would've cracked. She would've asked him why Shelly had been there last night and what he was doing with a girl he didn't really care about.

Her eyes would've given her away and Marcus would've known for sure what she was feeling. How she had never felt more drawn to a guy in all her life. She had tried to talk herself out of everything she felt for him. Nothing about it made sense, and most certainly nothing would ever come from it.

But until she could figure herself out, she

couldn't allow Marcus to know any of this.

Not until she was home did she remember the sweatshirt. She looked down and thought again of the sweet, impulsive moment. Marcus running through the store getting them both warmer clothes. Once she was inside she looked at herself in the mirror.

Marcus had no idea how apropos the message was. "Live Life." Yes, that's exactly what she needed to do. And she needed to do so without thinking about Marcus Dillinger. Especially over the next few days. *Treat him like a brother,* she told herself. Yes, she had to learn to think about Marcus differently, stop herself from reacting every time she was with him.

No matter what her heart had to say about it.

16

Tyler was thrilled when he heard about the Last Time In program. It was the first time since the shooting that he and Sami felt there was something they could do. Something that might help the kids on the streets. The youth center alone wasn't enough. Tyler agreed with Marcus.

Mary Catherine had presented the idea, and now Sami was on board, too. Tonight, though, Tyler didn't want to think about the prison program or the little boy still fighting for his life at Cedars-Sinai. Even if only for a few hours.

Tonight was the double date with Marcus and Shelly.

Marcus had talked about canceling. He didn't seem as into Shelly as he'd been at the beginning. But Tyler had talked Marcus into sticking with the plan. Now Marcus and Shelly would meet Tyler and Sami at the restaurant in just a few minutes. Cherry

Lane, it was called. A beautiful place situated in the hills above Los Angeles. Tyler walked with Sami through the dining area to a table by the window.

A balcony just off the back gave people a place to admire the view, so after they had their lemon water, Tyler led her outside. He put his arm around her and they looked at the stars. "Reminds me of that night on your grandparents' roof. All those years ago."

"Feels like yesterday." Sami looked into his eyes. "I sort of wish we were having dinner alone. It's been so crazy."

"I know." He took gentle hold of her face and kissed her. "I think Marcus needs tonight."

"With Shelly?" Sami was clearly trying to be nice. But she couldn't hide the disdain in her tone. "I don't get it with them."

Tyler laughed. "No one does. That's why he needs tonight. I have a feeling being around us . . . you know, it'll help him see."

"See what?"

Certainty filled Tyler. "That she's not the right girl."

"I hope so." Sami looked out over the city. "He never looks at Shelly the way he looks at Mary Catherine."

"I wondered about that." Tyler put his arm around her again. "We haven't had time to

198

talk. Feels like weeks." He thought about the two of them, Marcus and Mary Catherine. "Does she like him?"

Sami hesitated. "Everything is complicated with Mary Catherine. She hasn't said, but I can feel it."

"Time will tell." Tyler put his hands on her shoulders and faced her. "You look beautiful. If I haven't told you lately."

"Not since we pulled into the parking lot." She grinned at him. "What if I hadn't found you?"

"What?" He pulled out his most surprised look. "You didn't find me, baby. I found you. Remember? On Facebook."

Sami laughed. "You have a point." She swayed in his arms. "So what if you hadn't written to me? Where would we be?"

Times like this Tyler could easily be overcome with the impossibility of all that had led them to this place. His blown out shoulder, his time being homeless, and then his job as a maintenance worker at Merrill Place. But nothing really turned around until Tyler met Virginia Hutcheson. The fact that her daughter knew Marcus Dillinger and would think to contact him on Tyler's behalf? No one could've seen that coming, or the fact that Sami would break up with her boyfriend after her few hours with Tyler in Florida.

A movie script with everything that had happened would have been tossed in the trash. Too impossible.

Yet God had done it all.

"Which reminds me." Tyler had asked Marcus to be a little late tonight. He had his reasons. "I know it hasn't been long, you and me. We only found each other a few months ago."

"That's not true." Sami linked her hands around the back of Tyler's neck. "We found each other when we were kids."

"True." Tyler loved her more every day. He let himself get lost in her eyes. "I mean, we've only been seeing each other a few months this time around." He caught her face in his hands. "But I want you to know something."

"What?" She grinned. The stars overhead had nothing on the sparkle in her eyes.

"I love you, Sami . . ." His words stacked up in his heart and he couldn't stop himself. "I know you want things between us to go slow. I understand. You and Arnie were serious and . . . well, I don't want to rush you. But . . . I love you. I do." Suddenly he stopped and at the same time he started laughing. "Maybe I could let you talk."

Sami's smile took up her whole face. "I

was wondering." She laughed and the sound mixed with the music to become the most beautiful thing Tyler had ever heard. "First . . . I love you, too." Her laughter faded, and her eyes held his. "I've always loved you."

Tyler looked down. Just to make sure he wasn't floating. He turned to her again. She loved him? "Really?"

"Always." She brought her lips to his and kissed him. "Every day I wake up and thank God for bringing you back into my life." She searched his eyes. "I don't want to think about what would've happened if you hadn't written to me."

"Me either." Tyler wanted to raise his fists in the air and shout for joy. But he controlled himself. "So . . . I know you said you needed time . . . you just got out of a relationship. But . . . I can't wait to ask you." He searched her eyes. "Would you be my girlfriend, Sami? I mean, I'd like to ask you to be more than that." He grinned at her. "But first things first."

She dipped her head for a moment, laughing again. When she looked up he saw nothing but absolute assurance in her eyes. "Yes, Tyler. I'd love to be your girlfriend." She hugged him and the two of them swayed some more. She whispered close to his face.

"I thought you'd never ask. With you I'm myself. I feel like I can breathe."

"You believed in me when no one else did."

"Always." She put her head on his shoulder. "Don't ever leave me."

"I won't." Just then one of their favorite songs came on. James Taylor's "You've Got a Friend." "Dance with me?"

"Forever." They waltzed around the deck, and Tyler could picture where this would go. The wonder of it all filled his heart. But then, wonder was part of the process. Choosing to see and believe, to hold on to faith even when nothing made sense. The way he'd felt a year ago. But all of that might as well have been a lifetime away. Someday soon he would ask her grandfather for her hand in marriage. And one day in the not too distant future they would dance like this at their wedding.

Tyler could hardly wait.

Marcus and Shelly were fifteen minutes late to dinner, just like Tyler had asked them to be. They reached the table just as Tyler and Sami were returning from the deck out back.

"Hey, guys!" Marcus hugged Tyler, then

Sami. Shelly did the same. "You two look happy."

"It's official!" Tyler held Sami's hand as they sat down. "We're in love."

Shelly looked confused. "I thought you two were already . . ."

"It's a long story." Tyler laughed. "But it's all good now."

Marcus looked from his friends to Shelly. He figured she might need more of an explanation, but she was checking her phone. No longer interested in Sami and Tyler. Marcus hated the way that made him feel about her.

Shelly looked at him. "Sweetie, order me a glass of chardonnay. Whatever the waiter recommends." She winked at him. "Restroom break." And with that she left the table and headed for the back of the restaurant.

Marcus watched her go. Was she serious? Shelly was only nineteen. He looked at Tyler and put his elbows on the table. "She's not twenty-one."

"I was thinking that." Tyler made a face to show he empathized with him. "Difficult."

Sami seemed to be checking the ice in her water. She smiled at Tyler and then Marcus. "How was your coffee with Mary Catherine?"

"Short." Marcus could feel his heart

soften at the mention of her name. "Hey, I'm happy for you two. I know Shelly doesn't get it. But the two of you, it means a lot. Another piece of the most unbelievable story ever."

"Thanks, man." Tyler smiled and slipped his arm around Sami's shoulders. "How are things with you and Shelly?"

Marcus furrowed his brow. "I'm trying to figure it out, but it's not really working. I mean . . . just being around you two, it's kind of obvious. She's very young."

The waitress came, and Marcus ordered a Perrier and lime for Shelly. She returned to the table as the drinks were being delivered. Marcus had no idea how she would react. She looked at the drink and then at him. "Tell me this is a Tanqueray and tonic."

"Perrier and lime." He smiled at her. "Come on, Shelly. You're not old enough. No one else is drinking."

"Are you serious?" Shelly rolled her eyes. She was clearly frustrated. "I've been drinking since I was seventeen. You know that."

This was getting awkward. It was as if Shelly didn't remember Tyler and Sami sitting right across from them. "Well. Drinking's not my thing. I think *you* know that."

"Fine." She raised one eyebrow at him. "Your loss. I'm a better date after a few glasses of wine."

"I'll have to settle for sober." Marcus wished he could dig a tunnel beneath the table, usher Shelly back to the car, and take her home. He smiled weakly at her and then at his friends. "Are we ready to order?"

The entire night continued that way, in fits and starts. Shelly never found the social rhythm that his dates usually found. He felt himself counting down the minutes, glad that it was only a dinner date and not an all-day hike. Something he couldn't have gotten out of.

Throughout dinner, Shelly hung on his elbow. She would pat his arm and lean up and kiss his cheek. Already people were looking at their table, the way they sometimes did if they recognized him as the pitcher for the Dodgers. But with Shelly acting this way, they drew even more attention. The kind of attention that didn't seem to have anything to do with his being a baseball player.

Before dinner ended, Shelly looked over her shoulder. "You think the paparazzi might be here? You know, waiting for us outside?" She fixed her hair. "I've always wanted to be in the tabloids!"

Marcus folded his napkin on his plate. That was all. He smiled at Tyler and Sami.

"Early morning for me tomorrow. Running stairs again."

"No!" Shelly gasped. Her voice was definitely louder than anyone else's around them. "Not with your injured leg!"

"My leg's fine." Marcus could feel the stares they were getting. "Anyway" — he slid four twenties to Tyler — "this is for the bill. I think we'll get going."

Tyler stood and so did Sami. Another round of hugs and Tyler seemed to try to ease the awkwardness. "I have to be in early, too. Fun dinner, though."

Shelly was still sitting down.

"We're not leaving! Please tell me we're not leaving!" Her voice was whiny and high-pitched. She wanted to be noticed. There could be no other explanation. So someone would realize who Marcus was and just maybe take their picture.

Marcus felt anger well up inside him. How could he have thought this would be a good time? He clenched his jaw and reached for Shelly's hand. "Come on. I really do have an early day tomorrow."

Thankfully, she stood and slinked up next to him like they were attached at the hip.

"Well, you two lovebirds." Shelly waved her fingers. "It's been real!" She nuzzled Marcus's neck. "Till next time!"

On the way out, Shelly whispered to him, "No one's home at my house. I planned it that way."

Marcus ignored her. Dating Shelly reminded him of every wrong girl he'd ever been with. He felt sick about it. What had he been thinking?

Once they were inside his Hummer, Marcus turned to her. "Shelly."

"Yes, love?" She leaned forward, so her low cut blouse left nothing to the imagination.

Marcus kept his eyes on hers. "Look. Tonight . . . it wasn't good."

She seemed to come to her senses. "What do you mean?"

"Everything." He took a jagged breath. "You seemed really pushy."

"It's a date." She sat back against the passenger door and crossed her arms. "How was I supposed to act?"

Like Mary Catherine, he wanted to say. Instead he found a dose of compassion. "It's fine. Let's just go."

They drove home in silence, and Marcus turned up the radio. Otherwise the silence would've been deafening. He kept his right hand on the wheel so she wouldn't think about trying to hold it. There was no point explaining how he felt. Maybe it wasn't all

Shelly's fault. Ever since his walk with Mary Catherine, since her question that night, he found himself wondering the same thing. Who was pursuing whom? And why couldn't he stop comparing Shelly to Mary Catherine?

Marcus walked her up to her front door, but before she could press up against him, he kissed her cheek. "Goodnight, Shelly."

"Are you breaking up with me?" She batted her eyes. She looked sad, but her eyes were dry.

"We aren't in an official relationship. We're just dating." He slipped his hands into his pockets and walked down the stairs. He didn't wait for Shelly's response as he climbed behind the wheel of his SUV and drove off. Only then did he actually feel like he could take a breath. What in the world was he thinking, dating Shelly Wayne? He needed to talk to Coach and explain that things weren't working with her. And not just because of Shelly's antics.

But because all night long the face that filled his heart and mind wasn't Shelly's.

It was Mary Catherine's.

17

Mary Catherine met Marcus in the parking lot of the police station around noon the next day. Despite all her determination to see Marcus in a different light, to remember the way he looked with Shelly fawning over him, she couldn't get her heart in line.

From the moment he walked up to her she felt the heat in her cheeks. Felt her heart beating faster than before. The faint smell of his cologne made her breathless. *Come on, Mary Catherine.* She swallowed, desperate for a grip. "I have no idea what to expect." Her voice sounded shaky. She looked up at him as they reached the door of the station. She needed to keep her mind on the matter at hand. Learning how to work with the girls during their prison visit.

"Can I say something? Before we go in." Marcus stopped and smiled at her. "You look beautiful. Just didn't think I should miss the chance to say so."

She held her breath for a few seconds. "Thank you." Her rebellious heart soared at his compliment. He looked great, too. Dark blue jeans and a white short-sleeve shirt. But Mary Catherine didn't dare say so.

Even being attracted to him was wrong. He had a girlfriend, and she had promised God she wasn't going to date. Not ever. But then why did she feel like this? And why was Marcus making things more difficult by being so kind?

"I heard about your date last night." Mary Catherine started walking again. She shot him a teasing look. "Sounds like a good time."

Sami had spilled all the details back at the apartment last night. About Shelly's request for wine and the way she clung to Marcus throughout the night. Sami had said Marcus couldn't get out of the restaurant fast enough.

Now Marcus rubbed the bridge of his nose and shook his head. "She's a lot of work, for sure."

"Well . . ." Mary Catherine grinned, enjoying the game. As long as she could joke with him, she wouldn't have to worry about why it sometimes seemed he felt attracted to her, too. She tilted her head, as if she were genuinely concerned about Shelly and him. "I'm sure you two will figure things out."

Marcus opened the door for her and they walked inside. At first he looked like he might disagree about figuring things out with Shelly, but before he could speak, Charlie Kent approached them. "Marcus. Mary Catherine." He held out his hand. "Great to see you both!"

"Thanks." Marcus took the lead. "Our friends will be here, too. Sami Dawson and Tyler Ames."

"Great. I'm expecting them." He checked a clipboard on the nearest table. He scanned the page. "It looks like we have six young ladies going through the program and a dozen volunteers. Those are the numbers we like."

"We won't meet the girls tonight, right?" Mary Catherine hadn't been sure about that.

"No." Officer Kent smiled. "They're back at home. Once they agreed to the program, we released them from jail." He frowned. "Jail and prison are very different. These girls haven't seen the inside of a prison. This will be an awakening for sure."

Sami and Tyler arrived and together with the other volunteers they were ushered into a classroom. Officer Kent led the training.

"These kids are hard and angry and defeated. The only reason they agreed to this program is it beats serving time. They won't change easily. That's important to know."

Mary Catherine pulled her notebook from her purse and scribbled down everything the officer said. Marcus sat next to her and every once in a while their arms brushed against each other. Mary Catherine discreetly moved her chair a few inches away.

His touch was more than she could take.

Charlie Kent continued, explaining another reality for these girls. "Girls around this age, thirteen, fourteen, fifteen . . . they've most likely been sexually abused; many have been raped. More than once for some of them." He leveled his gaze at them. "You feel good about yourself if you feed a teenager a healthy meal? Parents of these girls feel good if a teenager doesn't get raped under their roof." He paused. "They come from broken homes. There's no supervision much of the time."

He told a story where he was talking to the stepmother of a girl who had gone through the program a few years ago. "She told me she couldn't understand why her daughter didn't want to be at home. She said, 'She's been raped by her uncles and cousins. But never at my house. You'd think that would matter to a kid.' "

Mary Catherine couldn't decide if she felt angry or just nauseous.

Dear God, what difference can we make with these girls? What's the point? She thought about the faces on her refrigerator, the kids from Africa she sponsored each month. *I'd be better off going to their village. Building them a home and providing them food and love,* she thought. Things were too far gone here.

"You okay?" Marcus whispered to her. He studied her eyes. "This is tough."

"It is." She smiled. Why was he so kind to her? "I didn't know . . . it was so bad."

"Me either." He looked sad. "Glad I'm here."

She nodded.

Charlie Kent explained that another problem was the girls' dishonesty. "They lie about everything. Just to feel like they have power. They don't want to share the truth and you can't force them to. Truth makes them feel vulnerable. Remember that when you get to the group-share part of the program. They have to talk a long time before the walls fall enough for them to be honest."

Great. Mary Catherine wrote the word *liar* in her notebook. The girls had been raped and used and sucked into gang activity. They were hard and callused and they wouldn't tell the truth for a long time, if ever.

So what was the point?

The training went on for another hour. They talked about the EastTown Boyz and the WestKnights, how the gangs formed, what their purposes were, and how easily the younger kids got drawn into joining.

"It's all these kids know." Officer Kent folded his arms. "Mom was a WestKnight, Dad was a WestKnight, brother and sister were WestKnights. A kid turns twelve, there's no question about what his future holds. He'll be a WestKnight. Unless someone shoots him first."

Mary Catherine tried to table her discouragement. The training was important. They learned that the EastTown Boyz mainly dealt heroin. WestKnights dealt cocaine. Heroin wasn't as costly as cocaine but the customers were more desperate.

"For the most part kids in gangs don't do the heavy drugs, they deal them. They smoke pot and they drink. But the hard drugs are business to them. They get them from the Mexican cartels and entrepreneur street dealers. It's how gangs stay afloat financially."

When the training was over, the volunteers each collected a booklet of additional information from Officer Kent. "Read through this. Tomorrow we'll talk about prison life. You need to know what to expect. After a week or so we'll give you materials for your group sessions. How to transition these girls from gangs to getting an education and even a job. Practical ways they can find a life outside of what they've known."

Officer Kent also gave each pair of volunteers the name of the girl they'd be working with and her contact information. "We encourage you to reach out before the prison visit Saturday. You can call or text. Just some way so they know you're there for them. You care. Whether they believe that at first or not."

Back outside in the parking lot, Mary Catherine and Marcus met up with Tyler and Sami. All of them looked drained. "That was a lot." Sami linked arms with Tyler. "I didn't feel ready for this before. But I feel way worse now. How can I help a girl who's gone through all that?"

"Who'd you get?" Tyler looked from Mary Catherine to Marcus.

"Lexy Jones." Marcus looked at the information card on the girl. "I think Officer Jag arranged that."

Mention of the man's name reminded Mary Catherine she hadn't talked to Charlie Kent about Jag. Where exactly did he work, and how was he connected to the local department? She turned to Sami. "What about y'all?"

"I love when you say *y'all*." Tyler smiled at her. "Just for the record."

Mary Catherine returned the smile.

"We know, we know." Sami laughed. "It's that Southern thing."

"Exactly." She grinned. "I can't help it if y'all weren't raised right."

"About our girl." Tyler looked intently at the information card he and Sami had been given. "Her name is Alicia. She's fourteen. Arrested for grand theft auto and truancy."

"Looks like we've got the rougher of the two." Marcus made a face that said how serious things were for Lexy. "Our girl's connected to one of the most brutal killers on the street."

"Again . . . how are we supposed to help?" Sami looked lost, like she wasn't sure she could go through with it.

"I think this is where faith comes in." Tyler sighed. "I mean, none of us is prepared, but we're willing. I guess we ask God to make up the difference."

"He's right." Marcus put his hands in his pockets. "Maybe we could do that now?"

"I like it." Tyler gave Marcus a friendly slap on the arm. "You always have the best ideas, man."

The group huddled up, their arms around each other's shoulders. Mary Catherine was between Sami and Marcus, but all she could feel was the way Marcus's arms felt around her. Strong and warm and secure. She had her arm around his waist. Nothing in all her life had felt so natural and wonderful.

So real.

God, help me . . . I can't stop these feelings. Mary Catherine closed her eyes, tried everything possible not to think about Marcus beside her. *See, God? Nothing works. I can never have this except in random moments. Marcus will never be mine. So please . . . help me keep my distance. Help me keep my wayward heart in line.*

Tyler started the prayer and Mary Catherine did everything she could to focus. Tyler asked God to give them super-natural wisdom and protection, that their efforts might truly change the lives of the girls in the program. Mary Catherine listened and prayed along with Tyler, but she found herself wishing the prayer would go on forever.

When it was finished, and after Tyler and Sami headed for his car, Marcus gave her shoulders a light squeeze. His smile warmed her all the way through. Mary Catherine drew a long breath. "Well . . . I think I'll go visit Lexy. Take her to Elysian Park for a hike. She doesn't know me, so she might not want to go. But I want to try."

"Good idea." Marcus's eyes lit up at the idea. "I'll go with you. I was sort of thinking the same thing."

"Well . . ." Mary Catherine shook her head. "Maybe not this time." She willed him to understand. "Sometimes girls open up better to a girl. At least at first."

Marcus thought about that. "Okay. I guess." He seemed disappointed. "I really would like to meet her before we see her Saturday morning."

"Maybe tomorrow." Mary Catherine folded her arms in front of her. "Thanks for being so kind. And for doing this. It doesn't seem like it, but I have to believe it'll help."

"It has to." He put his hand on her shoulder, but she was already pulling away.

She waved. "I'll let you know how it goes."

He chuckled. "You're always in a hurry."

"I guess." Mary Catherine gave him her best smile. So he wouldn't know how she was really feeling. "I've always got somewhere to be." She turned for her car. "See you tomorrow!"

"See you."

Mary Catherine watched him in her rearview mirror. He stood there, watching her until she drove away. Only then did the tears sting at her eyes. She blinked them back. It was nothing to cry over. She would never have Marcus Dillinger. "Come on, MC." She wiped her cheeks. "Get over it. You're stronger than that."

She had no choice, really. Her heart would figure it out eventually.

A few blocks down the road, she pulled over and used the number on Lexy's information card to text her. *Hey. It's Mary Catherine. I'm the volunteer who'll be helping you this weekend. I wondered if I could come by and take you for a walk. Maybe get coffee.*

Lexy must've had her phone with her, because she was quick to respond. *No coffee.*

"Okay." Mary Catherine tried to think of what to say next. Her fingers worked their way over the small keyboard. *A milkshake, maybe?*

The response took a little longer this time. *Fine. I can't be out late.*

Lexy's answer made her smile. The girl was clearly guilty of far more than staying

219

out late. But like Officer Kent said, these kids would lie. They didn't trust anyone. Least of all some stranger. Still, Mary Catherine felt a glimmer of hope. Lexy was willing. Before she pulled away she texted Shamika. *How's Jalen? The two of you have been on my mind all day.*

Shamika texted back quickly. *The same. His doctors say the longer he's in a coma, the worse it is. Please pray.*

I am. I will. Just like that Mary Catherine had plans for both day and night. She tapped out another text. *I'll come up and visit after dinner.*

Thank you. Shamika included a praying hands emoji. *Sometimes I like to sit here alone with him, because that's most like usual for us. Just him and me. But other times I feel like I'll go crazy if I don't have someone to talk to. I'll see you tonight.*

Mary Catherine appreciated the joy that filled her heart and mind as she drove away. She didn't need Marcus to feel happy about what God was doing in her life. Didn't need his arm around her shoulders or his kind eyes looking into hers. Days like today it was enough to simply carry out the message on the sweatshirt he'd given her. *Live life.*

With God's help, that's exactly what she planned to do.

18

Mary Catherine wasn't surprised at the small house Lexy lived in or the fact that it appeared to be in one of the roughest projects, just a few blocks from the youth center. Even so, she didn't worry about her own safety. This was the sort of thing Mary Catherine lived for. She knocked on the door and waited.

A young teenage girl answered. She looked down the street one way and then the other. "Come in. Hurry."

Clearly the girl didn't want to be seen talking to her. "Are you Lexy?"

"Yeah." She cocked her head back. "My grandma wants to meet you."

An older woman shuffled into the room. "My name's Anna." She shook Mary Catherine's hand. "I don't understand . . . Why do you want to take my Lexy out?"

Mary Catherine was actually glad the woman cared enough to ask. She explained her role as a volunteer for the Last Time In program. "The goal is that this will be their last time behind bars."

"I have my own crimes. Years ago." The old woman nodded. She was still beautiful, and clearly Lexy favored her. But her hands shook and she looked frail, timid. "Too many men. I'm trying to make up for it now." Tears filled her eyes. "The guns and violence, kids killing kids. It gets worse every year. You aren't someone unless you're a WestKnight or an EastTown gang member. It's not good for anyone." Anna looked at her granddaughter. "It's not too late for Lexy. She needs a way out."

Lexy stared at the floor, like she was unwilling to look at her grandmother or acknowledge the truth in the woman's statement.

Mary Catherine was still standing. She took hold of the older woman's hand for a brief few seconds. "I want to help." She looked back at Lexy. "The police agree with you. They think she has a chance. That with help she could find her way out of this life." Mary Catherine paused. "If she wants to."

Anna nodded. "Very good." She looked deep into Mary Catherine's eyes. "Take care of her." She wiped at a tear. "She's all I have."

It was a common theme here in the projects. People were broken and battered, scared and alone. Most of them were lucky to have one person who cared for them or lived with them. For Anna, that was Lexy. Her granddaughter. The only family she had.

"We'll be gone a few hours, if that's okay." Mary Catherine had a plan in mind. But she wanted to clear it with this dear woman first.

"Yes. Please." She was trembling again. "Lexy won't talk to me. Maybe she'll open up with you."

There was so much Mary Catherine wanted to say. Questions she wanted to ask. But she needed to get to know Lexy first. "Yes, ma'am." She nodded to Anna. "I hope so."

They were in Mary Catherine's Hyundai and nearly out of the neighborhood before Lexy said anything. "Do all the volunteers do this? Take their kid out for ice cream?"

Mary Catherine thought for a minute. "Probably not." She glanced at Lexy. "I figured it'd be better if we knew each other at least a little before Saturday."

"You know what I did?" Lexy looked small and uncomfortable in the passenger seat. She stared at Mary Catherine with big eyes.

"Cops tell you?"

"Yes." Mary Catherine kept her eyes on the road. "You're Dwayne Davis's girl. You were with him when he robbed a Seven-Eleven and you were with him when he killed a boy from the EastTown gang." The light ahead turned red. Mary Catherine looked straight at Lexy. "You were also with him the other night when he shot that four-year-old."

Lexy exhaled and stared out the window. After several minutes she muttered, "Why you want anything to do with me?"

"Do you want to be in a gang?" Mary Catherine felt funny using the word. But it was all Lexy would understand. "Or is it just because of Dwayne?"

Maybe it was the first time Lexy had thought about it. She took her time answering, and for a long time she stared straight ahead. Finally she looked at Mary Catherine. "I like it. Every girl wanna be Dwayne's shorty." Defiance rang in her voice. "But he picked me."

Mary Catherine thought about correcting her English but then let it go. One step at a time. "We're here." She pointed to a Dairy Queen up ahead. "You want a milkshake or a sundae?"

Lexy seemed stumped by the question.

225

They pulled into the parking lot and the two of them walked inside. At the counter, Mary Catherine pointed to the menu. "Have whatever you want."

"Anything?" The word sounded almost angry, as if Lexy didn't believe this. Like there had to be a catch. "What about a burger?"

"Sure. Get a burger and ice cream, if you want." Mary Catherine wasn't hungry. Besides, there was nothing on the menu she could eat. She had to give her heart a fighting chance.

"Okay." Lexy looked up at the menu, then back at Mary Catherine. "What's the thing where they chop up candy and ice cream in a cup?"

"A Blizzard?"

"Yeah." It was the first time Lexy had smiled since Mary Catherine stepped into her house. "I'll have a cheeseburger and that."

The girl behind the counter looked impatient. "What kind of Blizzard?"

Lexy settled on vanilla ice cream with Oreo cookies and hot fudge sauce. "And whipped cream."

" 'Please,' " Mary Catherine reminded her.

The surprise on Lexy's face was as real as

the air they were breathing. She turned back to the cashier. "Please."

Good, Mary Catherine thought. *It's a start.*

"Where we goin'?" Lexy focused on her Blizzard. "You said we'd be out for a couple hours."

"I'm taking you to Elysian Park. It's near Dodger Stadium." Mary Catherine used her GPS to lead the way. The park was another fifteen miles from the Dairy Queen.

Lexy looked nervous. "You been there before?"

"No. They have trails. There'll be people all around." Mary Catherine smiled, her eyes on the road. "I thought we could walk for a while, get to know each other. We can leave whenever you want and then I'll take you home."

Lexy didn't say anything. Either she didn't have an opinion or she didn't care. Twenty minutes later they parked in the lot at Academy Road and Elysian Park Drive. Mary Catherine had read that the other side of the park could be shady. This part was supposed to have well-marked trails with beautiful views of the city and the stadium.

It was a park Tyler and Sami had told her about.

They started up the trail and Mary Catherine waited until they found their stride.

Lexy was still finishing her Blizzard. "What do you want to tell me, Lexy?"

She peered over the edge of her cup at Mary Catherine and shrugged. "Got nothing to say."

This wasn't going to be easy. But the time was worth it. She could feel the girl's guard dropping, even just a little. "Why do you want to be Dwayne Davis's girl?"

Lexy cocked her head back again, doing her best to look tough, no doubt. "Dwayne gonna be leader of the gang. That makes me famous, too."

Mary Catherine resisted the urge to roll her eyes. In Lexy's world, her reason mattered. Mary Catherine was careful to use a gentle tone: "Lexy . . . Dwayne's behind bars. He's not getting out. Not ever."

The cockiness in Lexy's expression faded. Suddenly she looked like a lost little girl. "That ain't true. Dwayne told me he was getting out."

"He's not." Mary Catherine looked at Lexy. They were walking, but their pace was slow. "They've got Dwayne on at least two counts of murder. Attempted murder. Dealing. Robbery. I talked to the police, Lexy. They don't believe Dwayne will ever get out."

The girl looked at her nearly empty ice

cream cup, and at the next trashcan she threw away what was left. Again they walked in silence for a while until Mary Catherine could think of the right next question.

"You'd be locked up, too. That's why you're doing this program. So you don't have to. Because you're so young." Mary Catherine wasn't sure how much the girl understood. "You know that, right?"

"I guess." She crossed her arms tightly in front of herself as they walked.

"What happens when your guy goes to prison? Are you still part of the gang?"

Lexy looked frightened again. "The guys, they take turns. They'll fight it out. Who gets me next."

Her answer wasn't entirely clear but Mary Catherine figured she'd heard enough to know. The guys would take turns with her? That could only mean one thing. Lexy was little more than a child, and yet she took it in stride. Like being treated that way was a rite of passage.

"You know something, Lexy?" Mary Catherine had to start speaking truth into the girl. "You don't have to let them do that. What's in it for you? Being in the gang and having guys do that?"

"They keep me safe." She jerked her head back again. "Once a WestKnight, always a

WestKnight. EastTown Boyz don't mess with you if your man's a WestKnight. You in, then."

"So the EastTown Boyz don't hurt you . . . but the WestKnight boys do. How is that a good thing?" Mary Catherine kept her words slow and even. She didn't want to make Lexy too upset. Officer Kent had warned that when pushed too hard most of these girls would shut down. Sometimes for good.

But Lexy wasn't shutting down. Her expression softened, like maybe she had never thought about that before. How staying in the WestKnights could be a good thing when she was going to be hurt either way.

Lexy looked up at her. "What other choice I got?"

"That's what we're going to try to figure out, me and you." Mary Catherine hesitated. "You know who your other volunteer is?"

The girl looked straight ahead, her steps slow. "I get two?"

"You all do." She smiled. "The other one is a guy. Marcus Dillinger."

Lexy stopped walking. She stared at Mary Catherine and her eyes grew wide. "From the Dodgers? The pitcher?"

"Yes." Mary Catherine let that sink in for a few seconds. "The one Dwayne tried to kill."

"No." She started to shake her head. "He can't come. He can't see me." She looked over her shoulder like she might run. "He'll know it's me."

"Lexy." Mary Catherine put her hand on the girl's back. "Honey, Marcus knows who you are. He wanted to do this *because* of that. He wanted to come today. We both believe you have a chance. A way out of this."

"I don't want to meet him." She looked away and began walking again, faster this time. As if she were in a hurry to finish the hike. "I just wanna go home."

Mary Catherine kept up with her. Lexy was shifty and hesitant and probably — like Officer Kent said — ready to shut down completely. Whatever the girl felt deep inside her heart, it would take much effort to find it.

If they could find it at all.

Lexy had never felt like this in all her life. She didn't want to say too much, didn't want to open up. But something about Mary Catherine made her do it. Like the white girl really cared.

231

"Tell me about your parents." Mary Catherine wouldn't give up. No matter how quiet and rude Lexy was, the girl kept trying.

"What's to tell?" Lexy stared at the ground as they walked. "My dad was killed when I was a baby. My mom's in prison. You met my grandma." She was about to tell Mary Catherine how she'd raised herself, but at that exact minute they rounded a corner and stopped. Two police officers were arresting a skinny white man with a long beard. Right here on the trail.

Lexy stopped and next to her Mary Catherine did the same thing. The guy looked creepy.

"Come on." Mary Catherine put her arm around Lexy's shoulder and eased her past the scene.

One of the officers turned to her. "You girls okay?"

"Yes, sir." Mary Catherine answered first. "Is it safe?"

"This park?" The officer glanced at the guy in handcuffs. "It's never completely safe up here. But yes. You can get back to the parking lot okay. Call nine-one-one if you see anything out of the ordinary."

"We will, sir. Thank you." When they got past the men, Mary Catherine gently released her hold on Lexy and picked up her pace. "Let's get back."

"Yeah. Maybe the park wasn't such a great idea."

They didn't talk much on the way back to the parking lot, but Lexy couldn't let go of the feeling that she wanted to trust Mary Catherine. The older girl seemed really interested in her answers. In her as a person. The reality made her feel a lot of things. Hope, maybe. Happiness — if this was what happiness felt like. But something else, too.

Fear.

Lexy had learned a long time ago that the worst thing on the streets wasn't the thugs or the bullets or the way a brother threw a girl on a bed and had his way with her. It wasn't a break-in or a drug bust or getting arrested.

The worst thing was caring.

Jag and Aspyn hovered over the house where Lexy lived. They watched the two girls pull up in Mary Catherine's car and walk inside.

"Thank You, God." Jag was exhausted. He and Aspyn had more strategizing ahead. No mission had ever been more taxing. Despite that, Jag was overcome with relief. "The things that man on the path planned to do to Mary Catherine and Lexy . . ."

Aspyn closed her eyes. "Unspeakable. You stepped in at just the right time. Pulling him out of the bushes onto the path was the right thing to do. Instead of running, he was forced into the light."

The bearded man had been waiting in the bushes, ready to attack Mary Catherine and Lexy. Jag had appeared from the shadows and ordered the guy to step onto the path.

When the man pushed further back into the brush, Jag grabbed his arm and pulled him out. In one swift move, Jag had the guy pinned to the ground, his arm bent behind his back. That's when Jag had seen the gun in the man's sock. He grabbed it and the guy's cell phone and called 911. Two officers were already at the park. Just before they turned the bend on the trail and drew their guns, Jag dropped the gun, stepped into the brush, and disappeared.

Jag was grateful for the control he'd learned the last time. He had no desire to kill the man in the bushes. Protecting Mary Catherine and Lexy was all that mattered. Orlon had been right. The mission was very dangerous. Evil lurked around every corner and this much was certain.

The stakes had never been higher.

19

Marcus met Tyler at the hospital that afternoon to give blood. Whether Jalen could use it or not didn't matter. Someone could. They were in the lobby waiting their turn when Charlie Kent came in.

"Brought in another two gunshot victims today. They'll both live but they're in bad shape." The officer looked weary. "I haven't seen this much violence in years."

He took the seat opposite Marcus and Tyler. "We made an arrest an hour ago near Dodger Stadium. Story could've wound up very differently."

Marcus couldn't imagine being a police officer in Los Angeles. "What happened?"

"An officer from another precinct was walking the trail. He found a man in the bushes and recognized him from the wanted list. Called for backup and a couple of our guys made the arrest." Officer Kent shook his head. "The guy's on our most-wanted list, multiple homicides, rape, attacks on kids. Escaped prison in Northern California a year ago."

A sense of satisfaction came over Marcus. "Glad you caught him."

"What was he doing in the bushes?" Tyler also seemed gripped by the story.

"That's the scary part. A couple of girls were walking the trail. A few minutes more and they would've walked right past the guy. We think he was planning an attack. Waiting for the young women to walk by."

The pieces came together, and Marcus felt like he was falling, like he couldn't feel his feet beneath him. "What . . . what park did you say it was?"

"Elysian Park. Near Dodger Stadium." Officer Kent stood. "You two here to see the little boy?"

"Yeah." Marcus stood and shook the officer's hand. Were the girls at the park Mary Catherine and Lexy? He tried to focus. "We're giving blood, too. It's something we can do."

The officer shook Tyler's hand next. "That's how we all feel. Trying to make a difference best we can." He tipped his hat. "See you tomorrow night for training."

"Looking forward to it." Marcus slowly sat back in his seat. His heart pounded so loud he thought it would break through his chest.

Tyler stared at him. "You okay?"

"Elysian Park." Marcus couldn't slow his heartbeat. "That's where Mary Catherine took Lexy."

Tyler let the pieces connect for a moment. "You think maybe the two girls were . . ."

"It's possible." He put his face in his hands for a few seconds and then looked up. "I should've gone with them. Forget that girl-bonding thing. The city isn't safe."

"Text Mary Catherine and ask her."

Marcus didn't want to wait that long. He pulled his phone from his pocket and tapped Mary Catherine's number. She answered after two rings.

"Hello?"

"Where are you?" His words sounded too loud, too intense. He forced himself to calm down. Wherever she was, at least she was okay.

"Leaving Lexy's house." Mary Catherine was clearly taken aback by his tone. "What's wrong?"

Marcus put his head in his free hand and exhaled. *Slow down,* he told himself. "Did you take her to Elysian Park? Like you said?"

"I did. It wasn't perfect, but it was a start.

She's tough." Hesitancy still rang in Mary Catherine's words. "You sound upset. What happened?"

"Did you see police there?"

"Actually, yes." Mary Catherine paused. "Two officers arrested a man on the path just ahead of us. Kind of creepy."

Marcus stood and paced the length of the waiting room and back. "He was a very dangerous guy. I just talked to Officer Kent and he said . . . the man might've been lying in wait."

"For us?" It was the first time Mary Catherine sounded fearful.

"Possibly." Marcus couldn't believe it. Mary Catherine and Lexy had been in danger and if something had happened . . . He couldn't finish the thought. "God was with you. Looking out for you."

"The officers didn't tell us." Mary Catherine's voice held a fear Marcus hadn't heard from her before. "If Lexy had been hurt, I never could've forgiven myself. We had no idea."

"It's behind you now. Just . . . please, Mary Catherine, be careful. You should've let me come with you." He sat down and leaned back hard. It felt so good to hear her voice, to know she was okay. His tone lightened some. "Remember that next time."

"You're right." A warmth filled her voice. "Sorry. I was kind of quick to turn you down."

"We're in this together, this volunteer thing." He leaned his elbows on his knees. "Let me help, okay?"

"Okay." For the first time since she answered the phone he could hear her smile across the phone line. "Where are you?"

"At the hospital." He wasn't a fan of needles, but this was important. "Tyler and I are giving blood."

"Nice." Again her tone was softer. "How's Jalen?"

"About the same." Marcus felt the heaviness of the child's situation. "We're going to see him and Shamika next."

"I'll be there in a few hours." She sounded like herself again. The fear from earlier gone. "I'll probably miss you."

"See, there you go again. Trying to avoid me." He chuckled. "Just kidding." He paused. "Be safe, Mary Catherine. Please."

"I will."

The call ended as Marcus and Tyler were called back. They took cots next to each other and in no time they were hooked up and watching bags fill with their blood.

"I hate needles." Marcus looked away from the one in his arm. "I have to believe this is for kids like Jalen."

"Really, though?" Tyler moved his arm and winced. "It'll probably help the two gang guys just brought in."

Marcus hadn't thought about that. The possibility didn't sit well with him. Give blood for guys caught up in gang violence for what? So they could get back out on the streets and shoot each other again? He gritted his teeth and tried not to think about it.

"You and Sami doing anything this weekend?" He put one arm behind his head so he could see Tyler better. "Besides the prison tour, obviously."

Tyler laughed in a way that was more concerned than humorous. "That'll probably leave us pretty worn out."

"True." Between donating blood and the prison tour, Tyler was right.

"Hey, I almost forgot." Tyler faced him. "Tomorrow morning Sami and Mary Catherine are going to the beach. Supposed to be another warm day like last week."

"Sounds fun." He uttered a brief laugh. "Mary Catherine didn't tell me about it."

"Well, Sami did. She asked us both to come."

"Really?" Marcus smiled. "Did she check

with Mary Catherine?"

"Come on, Dillinger." Tyler laughed. "You don't really think MC's trying to avoid you. I mean, she agreed to work with you on the prison program, right?"

"She didn't really have a choice." Marcus gave Tyler a wary look. "Remember? A police officer asked her to talk to me about it."

"Well . . . don't forget she could be a little leery, what with Shelly Wayne and all."

Marcus sighed. "Yeah. About Shelly." He looked out the window and thought about the situation. "I need to talk to Coach."

"Why?" Tyler made a face. "He won't be upset if things don't work out with you and Shelly."

"She's his niece." Marcus felt trapped. "I never should've agreed to call her."

Tyler waited, a knowing look on his face. "Whatever you do, you need to figure it out. The other night was awful."

They finished giving blood and Marcus gulped down the orange juice and crackers. He stayed close to the wall until he felt less light-headed. Tyler took it all in stride. "You live with your arm hanging halfway to your knee for a few months and giving blood'll feel like a day at Disneyland."

The two friends laughed as they left the

unit. But as they reached the elevator and rode it up to the intensive care unit, they grew quiet. "I keep praying." Tyler drew a tired breath as they walked down the hall toward the nurses' station. "I just wish God would wake the boy up."

Tyler had agreed to wait while Marcus visited the boy. Marcus felt the familiar ache in his heart as he reached the child's room. The door was partly open and Shamika was inside, sitting close to her son, holding his hand and talking softly. She looked up as Marcus stood at the doorway.

"Please. Come in." Shamika stood and hugged him. "Thank you for coming."

"How is he?" Marcus walked up to the bed and put his hand over the boy's much smaller one. He looked up at the machines, whirring and buzzing and clicking like before.

"He's still in a coma." Shamika's face looked tearstained. "I'm begging God he might wake up today." She paused and her voice fell. "Doctor says it needs to be soon. For Jalen's brain to work right."

The weight of the situation pressed in on Marcus's shoulders and sucked the air from the room. Jalen had been so trusting, so willing to help that night.

"Is there anything I can do? Do you need help?"

"Ask people to pray. Please." Her eyes grew watery. "I want God to know I'm not giving up."

Marcus nodded. "I can do that. I'll tell everyone." He needed to do more of that. Of course he and his friends had been praying. But who else had he asked? More than half a million people followed him on Twitter and he hadn't said a word. He pursed his lips. "I promise you, Shamika. I'll get people to pray for your boy."

As they left the hospital, Marcus and Tyler were quiet. They didn't talk until they were outside in the parking lot. The whole time Marcus thought about Twitter. All of Los Angeles knew he'd been shot at. The *Times* had run the news on the front page. So everyone who followed him on Twitter would've already heard that he'd been a victim of gang violence in his attempt to make the youth center a success.

Why hadn't he asked anyone to pray for Jalen?

"I have an idea." Marcus pulled out his phone. "You still on Twitter?"

"Yeah." Tyler hadn't started the car yet. He found his phone in his front pocket and looked at it. "I haven't used social media since I came here."

"Maybe now's the time to start." He opened his Twitter app. "You got a hundred forty characters to ask everyone listening to pray for Jalen. Let's do this."

Marcus's tweet was simple.

There's a little boy fighting for his life in an LA hospital. He took the bullet intended for me. Ask God for a miracle. #prayforJalen

Marcus reread his words and then looked out the window. *Lord, forgive me for not thinking of asking them sooner. I'm new at this. And please . . . help Jalen. He needs You more than ever, God.*

He sent the tweet and looked at Tyler. "Done."

"Me, too." Tyler slipped his phone back in his pocket. "Let's see what happens."

They went to In-N-Out across the street for burgers and talked a little more about Jalen and Shamika and the youth center. And whether they were in over their heads.

Marcus thought maybe they were.

Halfway through the meal Marcus checked his Twitter. "This is crazy!" He couldn't believe it. "Almost a hundred thousand people have retweeted it. And it's only been twenty minutes."

Tyler checked his and found a similarly high number of retweets. Marcus stared at his phone and blinked back tears. The gesture meant more than any of his followers could've known. Reading their comments, Marcus could see some of them were doing more than simply retweeting. They promised to pray. At a time when violence seemed the norm and kids didn't seem to care about each other, clearly there were some who actually did.

It was a surge of hope Marcus needed — especially since he needed to go by the youth center later and see how things were going. He'd hired a full-time director a week ago, and today the guy had reported that things were calm.

Marcus wanted more than calm, of course. But in light of the events this week calm was an improvement.

As they walked to their separate vehicles, Tyler gave him a light punch in the arm. "You're going with me tomorrow morning. To the beach." He slid his phone back in his pocket. "No excuses."

He still lived with Tyler, so it'd be easy to go. But Marcus wasn't sure. "Someone should ask Mary Catherine."

"Sami said she'd be fine." Tyler held up his hands. "Really, man? You're letting the girl intimidate you."

"We'll see." Marcus tossed his keys in his hands. "I'll think about it."

"We're all friends." He pointed at Marcus. "See you at nine tomorrow."

The discussion was over.

Marcus drove to the youth center, and the whole way he debated whether he should go. He thought about Mary Catherine all the time and found himself counting down the hours till the next time they would see each other. But going with Tyler to the beach felt a little intrusive. Mary Catherine hadn't invited him, no matter what she told Sami.

He tried to put the thought from his mind. At the center he checked in with the new director. The report was mostly good. Kids were still coming for help with their homework, still showing up to play basketball every night around seven. Lots of them had asked if there would be pizza again this Tuesday.

"You'd think the shooting would keep them away." Marcus still didn't understand life on the streets.

"It has no effect at all." The director used to be a football coach at an area high school. He was perfect to manage the youth center. "These kids think nothing of a shooting.

Very different from the way you and I might see it."

The futility stayed with Marcus as he left. He planned on going home and getting in another workout before turning in for the night. But there were too many thoughts battling for his attention.

Instead he drove to Dodger Stadium.

Spring training was coming fast. A couple of months at Camelback Ranch in Arizona, and then they'd be in full swing for the season. He was on the roster as their top pitcher again, so his time with Mary Catherine would be infrequent at best.

The stadium was empty, the way he expected for a Thursday night in early January. Marcus used his key to get into the back of the facility and then found a spot near the top of the bleachers. The sun was setting, spreading pink and blue across the sky.

Something about being here always helped him think. Helped him get his priorities right. He'd been reading his Bible now — ever since the walk with Mary Catherine. He'd bought the e-reader version of the Voice Bible — a new translation designed for people like him. People who had no real experience with Scripture. He could read it any time he wanted right on his phone.

This morning he'd read the book of James.

Don't just be hearers of the Word of God. Be doers. The message stayed with him still.

The first chapter was the reason he'd asked Tyler to go with him to give blood today. It wasn't enough to wish people well and offer a quick prayer. God's people needed to act. Matthew West had a song about it. "Do Something."

He rested his forearms on his thighs and stared out at the stadium. His surface wound from the bullet was healing. One day soon the place would be packed, people cheering on his team, screaming his name. But what did they know of Marcus Dillinger? Sure, he was clean-cut. He stayed away from drugs and drinking and he'd given a bunch of money to open a youth center for kids in the inner city.

But what about his faith?

The question had plagued Marcus many nights, even since he'd known for sure that God was working in his life, that God had answered his challenge back in October. Okay, so he believed. So he did a few good things for the community — if they actually were good.

Did that mean he was a Christian?

Marcus breathed in sharply through his nose and sat up straighter. *God, I'm here . . . What do You want from me?*

No answer whispered across his heart. But another Bible verse came to mind. The one he'd read yesterday in Romans, chapter ten. He pulled out his phone and read it again. *Romans 10:9 — So if you believe deep in your heart that God raised Jesus from the pit of death and if you voice your allegiance by confessing the truth that "Jesus is Lord," then you will be saved!*

He had heard people pray for salvation before, but sitting here, the winter breeze cool against his face, Marcus wasn't sure he'd ever actually done that. He'd attended house church at the Waynes' week after week. But even though he appreciated the stories and the teaching, he'd never made the message personal.

Never made that sort of a deal with Jesus.

Marcus lifted his eyes to the sky and like a parade, he could see all the girls. All the careless nights. The reason he could never stand before Mary Catherine as anything but her friend. *Lord, I know I already apologized for those times. For who I was back then. But where do I go from here? What happens now?* He thought about his anger toward the shooter, the futility and impatience that had consumed him most hours since Jalen had been shot. *I guess sin can be more than sleeping around. I'm sorry for my attitude, too.*

Suddenly, there in the quiet of the empty stadium, he could feel the presence of God. Marcus did the most natural thing he could do. He lifted his hands toward heaven and prayed.

The verse from Romans played again in his mind. This time he spoke out loud. "Father, would You get rid of the filth in my heart, please? I believe in You."

The cool breeze picked up speed, sending a low whistling sound through the stadium.

Marcus wasn't finished. "From the depth of my heart, Jesus, I believe You are God and that You died on the cross and were raised to life for me." His words were quiet but powerful. "I want You to be with me. I want to be saved. I am nothing without You. I mean it." Marcus felt tears on his cheeks. "Even if I were the only person on earth You would've died anyway. So here's my confession, Father. Jesus is Lord. Now and forever."

He lowered his hands and dragged them across his cheeks. There was no describing the feeling inside him. He felt whole and clean and full of light. Of course he would mess up again. He could never be perfect. But at least now he had assurance. If the bullet hit him next time, he'd go from life on earth to life in heaven.

Because the Bible said so.

But there was something else. He'd learned last week at the Waynes' that the Book of Acts talked about times when people got baptized. He spent the next half hour searching for the word *baptism* in his Voice Bible app. Every time, it seemed like people made the decision to get baptized after they decided to believe in Jesus for salvation.

Believe *and* be baptized. That's what the Bible said.

He remembered the beach trip in the morning. Could he be baptized then? Would that even be possible? Without hesitating he called Coach Wayne. "Coach. It's Marcus."

"Hey!" The man sounded happy, the way he usually sounded. "I've been meaning to call you. How's the little boy doing?"

"Still hanging in there. No change." Marcus felt a ripple of discouragement. "His mother's asking everyone to pray."

"I saw that on Twitter. Almost a hundred and fifty thousand people have retweeted it. That's incredible."

That many? Gratitude filled his heart. Who knew where the request would go from here? But he'd done what Shamika had asked and now — with so little effort —

people were praying. Marcus drew a breath and tried to focus. "I'm calling you for a couple of reasons."

"Go ahead." There was the sound of a closing door. "I just stepped outside. What's on your mind?"

"First . . ." Marcus wasn't even sure how to explain what had just happened. "I'm here at the stadium by myself. I just gave my life to Jesus. Like for the first time. For real."

"Marcus! That's amazing!" Deep emotion came across in Coach Wayne's voice. "Rhonda and I have been praying for that. Actually, I was going to pull you aside this Sunday after church and ask you where you were at in your faith journey."

"Now you know." Marcus laughed. "I've been reading the Voice Bible. I love it. Everything's so clear. Like God's speaking straight to me."

"Incredible, right?"

They talked a few more minutes about Scripture and how it was God's Word. God-breathed. But there was more Marcus needed to talk to the man about. He tried to find the right words. "Coach . . . something else. About Shelly."

"Yes." His voice grew more pensive. "I was going to talk to you about her, too."

Marcus stood and paced down the empty row and back. How was he supposed to say this? "I'm planning to talk to her later tonight. It's just not . . . it's not working out with the two of us." He paused. "I'm sorry, Coach, I really didn't mean to get this involved and now . . . I'm just so sorry."

For a moment there was only silence on the line. Marcus felt a pit in his stomach. Was his coach angry with him? If so, what could he do to make things right? He was about to offer another apology when he heard a light laugh coming from the man.

"I think you read me all wrong." Coach Wayne sounded almost relieved. "I was going to warn you about her. She's always been a little wild. Having her around more lately hasn't been good for our own daughter." He laughed again. "I was going to ask if you and Shelly would do your visiting outside of our home. Seriously."

Relief washed over him. He'd worried about this for nothing. "She looks for trouble, that's for sure."

"She's my niece, and I pray for her. One of these days something will get her attention and she'll need more than her good looks to get by." This time there was no denying the approval in Coach's voice. "Good decision, Marcus. You don't need that sort of distraction."

"Definitely not." Marcus realized he'd been holding his breath. He exhaled and sat back down. "So I guess that's two good choices tonight."

"Yes." His voice became more serious. "I know it won't be easy, talking to Shelly. But she'll understand. She's had lots of boyfriends."

"Thanks, Coach. There's one more thing." Marcus smiled. "If you're not busy tomorrow around nine thirty, could you meet us at Zuma Beach? Me and Tyler and Sami and Mary Catherine?"

"Sounds fun." There was a smile in Coach Wayne's voice. "Just because?"

"Because I want to get baptized. I wondered if you'd do the honors."

Again there was silence for several seconds. Marcus could practically see the man's face when he finally spoke. "It would be one of the greatest honors of my life, Marcus. Rhonda and I will be there. The kids, too."

The call ended and Marcus stared at the sky, soaking in the love and joy and peace that surrounded him. Mary Catherine would want to be there for his baptism. So would the others. There would be no fanfare, no media, no fear of bullets flying.

Just him and his closest friends and the greatest decision Marcus had ever made.

The decision to follow Jesus.

20

The sun was bright in the early Friday morning sky by the time Aspyn took her place at the short block wall that separated Zuma Beach from the parking lot. She watched Mary Catherine drive her Hyundai up and park near the wall.

Help me, Father. The timing has to be perfect.

She could picture her angel team in heaven, watching, all of them praying. Aspyn could feel their support.

Mary Catherine and Sami climbed out of the car and grabbed boogie boards, towels, and a few bags. Invisible and silent, Aspyn stayed with them as they headed down the sand toward the water. Her job was very specific. It would be nearly impossible to pull it off without being noticed.

The girls set up ten yards from the water, spreading their towels out on the sand. Aspyn watched closely, never taking her eyes off Mary Catherine. Finally it happened. Mary Catherine took her cell phone from her pocket and checked it.

Aspyn knew why. She was expecting two very important phone calls. One from her mother — who had called Mary Catherine the night before to tell her the news that her father's health was failing. Even though they were divorced, her parents cared about each other. Today the man was in a hospital in Nashville, where doctors were deciding whether he'd need lifesaving surgery.

The second call set to come in sometime this morning would be from Mary Catherine's own doctor. He had studied the tests she'd had done over a week ago and now he had the results. Aspyn watched Mary Catherine turn the ringer on her phone all the way up. Then she set it near the bottom of her towel.

"What time will the others be here?" Mary Catherine checked the time on her phone. "It's already nine."

"About half an hour." Sami was slipping her wetsuit on.

Good, Aspyn thought. She needed both girls to take to the water before the Wayne family and Marcus and Tyler arrived. Otherwise what she was about to do would be impossible.

Father, get them in the water. Please draw them in . . . I don't have much time. Suddenly in the nearby waves, a pod of dolphins appeared, splashing and chattering among each other. Aspyn looked up to heaven and smiled. God was beyond creative. *Thank You, Lord.*

Mary Catherine noticed the dolphins. "Look!" She tossed her phone on the towel and grabbed her wetsuit from her bag. "Hurry! Maybe we can ride with them again."

The girls hurried to finish getting dressed, grabbed their boards, and jogged to the surf. They jumped over the white water and made it out to the flat sea just before the breakers. The place where the dolphins were still tossing their heads and jumping through the waves.

Perfect. Aspyn slipped behind the closest lifeguard station and became a jogger. Simple navy shorts and a white tank top. The most discreet jogging outfit she could think to wear. She pulled her hair back with a rubber band from her pocket and studied the scene. The sand felt wonderful on her feet — something angels only experienced on missions. Sand in heaven was different. Softer.

Aspyn scanned the beach. No one else was

out here this early. The girls would have to stay distracted if she were going to pull this off. She took a deep breath and began jogging. She eased her way to the shore and started to close the forty-yard gap between her and the place where Mary Catherine's beach towel was set up.

Aspyn loved this feeling and hated it at the same time. The way her heart pounded was something intrinsically human. But the reason was terrifying. So much was at stake in the next few minutes.

Stay distracted. Please.

The dolphins weren't going anywhere. A few more seemed to join in, jumping and splashing not ten feet from where the girls were riding out on their boogie boards. *Hurry,* she told herself. *Get it done!*

Aspyn was closer now. She kept jogging, her face straight ahead as if she were any normal runner, enjoying any other day. As she neared Mary Catherine's towel she kept her eyes on the girls. They were still distracted by the dolphins, still too caught up in the moment to notice a jogger on the beach.

The plan could work. Aspyn reached the towel, stopped, and grabbed Mary Catherine's cell phone. In a quick move, she turned it off.

She had to hold the button a few seconds to see that the device was completely powered down. Then she dropped it back on the towel and resumed her jogging. Mary Catherine and Sami were facing the beach now, riding a wave into the shore, laughing and looking back at the dolphins.

They never once looked her way.

Aspyn kept jogging and a ways down the beach she met up with another jogger. Blond and tall. "That was textbook." Jag smiled at her. "And what about this sand?"

"I was just thinking that. So different than the sand in heaven." Aspyn could breathe again. "Rougher."

"Like all of earth." He lifted his face toward the sun as they jogged. "No time to waste, you know."

"Theme of this mission." She looked back. The girls were out near the waves again. Her action had gone completely undetected.

They jogged up the beach to the next lifeguard station, slipped behind it, and disappeared.

Jag was right. They couldn't waste a minute. They had a Nashville hospital to visit.

21

The water felt wonderful, cool and fresh and smooth against Mary Catherine's skin — the part not covered by her wetsuit. All that and a ride with the dolphins. Mary Catherine couldn't stop silently thanking God.

Sometime today she expected two difficult phone calls. One about her father's health. One about her own. But whatever news she received later, at least they'd had this time out here in the ocean. So far the morning couldn't have been more perfect.

And it was about to get better.

She and Sami had found out late last night that the guys were joining them along with the Wayne family for a very special reason. Marcus Dillinger was getting baptized. It was hard to believe that she had ever assumed Marcus to be shallow and predictable.

Nothing could've been further from the truth.

Marcus had a genuine love for people and a new faith vibrant and central to his life.

They rode another wave in and as Mary Catherine stood she saw the Wayne family and Marcus and Tyler walking in from the parking lot. She turned to Sami. "They're here!"

"This will be something." Sami stood and wiped the water from her face. "I'm so proud of Marcus. For wanting to do this."

"Me, too." They each held their boards under their arms and jogged back to their things. They pulled extra towels from their bags and dried off. They planned to go back in the water later, so they peeled their wetsuits only half off.

Mary Catherine had brought her Whole Foods "Live Life" sweatshirt for the occasion. Certainly baptism was a great time to think about living life. She slipped it on and worked her fingers through her hair. She hoped the calls didn't come in during Marcus's moment.

But if they did, she'd have to take them. If her father was sicker, she was ready to get on a plane in a few hours and fly to Nashville. Even if it meant missing the Last Time In program. Marcus could handle it by himself if he had to.

The others walked up and Tyler slung his arm around Marcus's shoulders. "Could there be a better day for a beach baptism?"

Sami led the way to meet them. She hugged Marcus and then Tyler, and stayed there, her arm around his waist. "We're so happy for you, Marcus."

"I don't know what took me so long." He smiled and then turned to Mary Catherine. "God's been talking to me about a lot of things."

The Wayne family joined them — Ollie and Rhonda and their three kids. Shane and Sam wore bathing suits and sweatshirts. Sierra looked distant in jeans and a light-weight jacket.

Coach Wayne spoke first. "Thanks for inviting us. We couldn't miss this." He and Rhonda gave hugs to the others. Ollie patted Marcus on the back. "I remember when our kids were baptized. It's a big day."

Conversations started between Rhonda and Sami and Tyler, and at the same time Ollie stepped back to say a few words to his kids. In the fraction of a moment when no one else was talking to either of them, Marcus walked up to Mary Catherine. He wore a bathing suit and a T-shirt, and he stood so close their arms were touching.

Never mind the sweatshirt she was wearing. Mary Catherine could feel every inch of contact with him.

"Hey." He smiled at her. "Thanks for being here." His eyes held the familiar teasing. "I sort of intruded on your beach morning."

"Not at all." She felt her defenses falling. Every time she was near Marcus Dillinger the attraction was stronger. "I'm glad to be here. Really."

The others were talking and for that moment it was just Marcus and Mary Catherine. He glanced at her. "I ended things with Shelly last night."

Mary Catherine felt suddenly light-headed. Marcus had cut things off with Shelly? Had he really just said that? She shaded her eyes. "You broke up with her?"

"Technically we were never in a relationship." His voice was little more than a whisper. He allowed a sad chuckle. "But she thought we were."

He was trusting her with his heart. Whatever that meant, Mary Catherine loved the feeling. She kept her voice quiet. "How did she handle it?"

"Not well at first." The breeze off the ocean wrapped itself around their private conversation. "I think she understood eventually. I told her she was too young and . . . well, truthfully I didn't see her the same way she saw me."

Mary Catherine winced. "Yeah, that would've been tough."

"She didn't hang around. Her friends were waiting for her back at her house." His smile melted her. "She'll be fine."

The feel of the ocean air, the sun on her shoulders, Marcus standing so close his words felt like velvet against her skin. All of it made Mary Catherine feel a little dizzy. She wasn't sure what to say.

"Anyway, I wanted you to know. That whole scene at the hospital the other night. The way she was at dinner with Sami and Tyler. I didn't want any of it. I needed to act on how I was feeling."

Mary Catherine reminded herself to breathe. "You seem happier."

"I am." He nodded toward the water. "And I'm about to make another great decision."

"Definitely." Mary Catherine wanted the moment to keep going. Even when standing here with him could never lead to anything. Feeling good wouldn't buy her a long life. "Thanks for telling me."

"I should've done it sooner." The sunlight caught his eyes. "Shelly wasn't real." He

265

didn't blink, didn't take his eyes off hers. "Next time I won't settle for anything less."

Real. That was her word. Mary Catherine didn't want their alone time to end but the others were done visiting. They circled around, looking to Marcus. Ollie Wayne wore a bathing suit and a T-shirt. "Let's do this!"

"I'm ready!" Marcus whipped off his T-shirt and threw it on Mary Catherine's towel. The group walked close to the water, Mary Catherine near the back.

Her head was spinning. She must've told Sami a hundred times before she got the news about her heart, about her years being cut short. Real was all she wanted in a guy. Back when she thought she had forever.

He would have to be real in his beliefs, real in his character. Real in the way he treated her and everyone else.

And now Marcus wanted *that* in a girl. She wanted to pull Sami aside and ask if she had somehow told Marcus. How else could he have known how that one word would speak straight to her soul? But that was impossible. Sami didn't have heart-to-heart conversations with Marcus.

She felt her feet sink into the wet sand a few inches, but she didn't care. The feeling was a reminder that she was really here, this was really happening. That Marcus had just stood next to her and told her he was done with Shelly because he wanted someone real.

The wind settled down — as if all of heaven wanted to hear clearly what was about to happen. Mary Catherine stood with Sami and Tyler. Rhonda Wayne and her kids stood nearby in another cluster, as all of them directed their attention to Ollie and Marcus. The two men walked out until they were waist deep.

Mary Catherine looked around, amazed. Not only was the beach quiet, it was empty. This divine moment was for them alone. She turned her eyes back to Marcus.

Ollie put his hand on Marcus's shoulder. "I've talked to Marcus Dillinger about Jesus for a long time." He hesitated, and after a few seconds it became obvious that the coach was struggling. Fighting to get the words past his emotions. Finally he coughed a little. "Anyway. This is a big day."

Marcus nodded. His smile was so big Mary Catherine could feel it all the way to the place where she stood.

"So you all know how this works." He looked at the rest of them on the beach. "Marcus asked Jesus to be his Savior. Now he wants to give a public demonstration of that faith. The symbol of dying to self and being raised to new life in Christ." Ollie looked at Marcus again. "You ready, man?"

"So ready!"

"What he means is, it's freezing out here without a wetsuit." Coach Ollie laughed. Then he turned his attention fully to the matter at hand. "Marcus, because you've placed your faith in Christ, and because you want to publicly declare your allegiance to Him, I now baptize you in the name of the Father, the Son, and the Holy Spirit."

Marcus put his hand over his face, plugging his nose, and Ollie dipped him beneath the surface of the water.

As Marcus went under, Ollie continued. "Buried with Him in baptism." Ollie helped Marcus back to his feet. "Raised with Him to new life in the power of the Holy Spirit." He pulled Marcus into a big hug. "Congratulations, my friend."

Mary Catherine led the applause on the beach, and the others quickly joined in. The moment was perfect. Flawless. Only as the two men headed back to the shore did Mary Catherine realize she was crying. She wiped the tears from her cheeks. Marcus Dillinger was exactly the sort of guy she had always dreamed about.

But she could never let him know, never

give him any sign that she was interested. In fact, she would be better off leaving Los Angeles altogether. Depending on what the doctor said, she might take a year and go to Africa. The way she'd always dreamed.

Anything would be better than feeling this way about a guy she could never have. The Wayne family rushed up to Marcus, congratulating him and hugging him. Mary Catherine and Sami and Tyler waited until he made his way to them.

"Man, that was beautiful." Tyler gave him a hearty hug. "I remember when I was baptized. Had a lot of years without God, but now look at us! Ready to change the world!"

"You got it!" Marcus looked exhilarated. The water beaded on his light chocolate skin and his green eyes flashed with joy. He hugged Sami next and then stepped up to Mary Catherine.

Every other time they'd been together, she had avoided hugging him, avoided being in his arms. Especially when it would only make it that much harder to admit the truth. That they could never be more than friends.

But this was not a moment to resist.

She put her arms around his cold, wet, bare waist and he pulled her into a gentle embrace that took her breath. Once, Mary Catherine had read about feeling born for a certain moment. If that was true, then this was that moment. Not jumping from a plane or swimming with the dolphins. But this.

The way she felt in Marcus Dillinger's arms.

He held on to her longer than the others and when he drew back he put his hand alongside her face. "Thank you. For being here."

There seemed to be so much more going on between them than their words could begin to acknowledge. Mary Catherine couldn't look away from him, couldn't remember that there was anyone else on the beach. She hesitated long enough to hold on to the feeling. "Congratulations. I'm so happy for you."

Marcus released her and turned to the others. The group talked for a few minutes, relishing the happy occasion. Sami shared about the dolphins, though now there wasn't one in sight.

"You girls and your imaginations." Tyler pulled Sami close, grinning at her. "What's next? You climbed on the back of a dolphin and took a ride up the shore?"

"Hey!" Sami gave him a playful shove.

"It's true." She looked to Mary Catherine. "Right? Tell him!"

"I believe you." Marcus was toweling off, shivering from the cold water. He winked at Mary Catherine. "I'll bet it was amazing."

"It really was." She laughed in Marcus's direction and then looked at the others. "There had to be a dozen of them. For like twenty minutes."

The conversation turned to the volunteer program and their training that night. "Let us know how it goes." Ollie Wayne looked at his daughter. "One of Sierra's friends is going through the program."

Coach Wayne didn't elaborate, but clearly the matter made Sierra uncomfortable. Mary Catherine remembered that Rhonda Wayne had said the family was struggling with their only daughter. She would have to ask Rhonda about it later.

After the Wayne family headed back to the parking lot, Tyler pulled a wetsuit out of his bag. "I promised my girl I'd ride boogie boards with her."

"Finally." Sami laughed and pulled hers back over her shoulders.

"You can use my board." Mary Catherine was still warming up from her time in the water earlier. Besides, she would rather stay on the beach with Marcus than get back in the ocean. She peeled off her sweatshirt and stretched out her legs. "I'll get some sun."

"Is that possible?" Marcus grinned at her. "You don't look much like the tanning type."

"I know." She rolled her eyes. "I have British skin. I can actually spend an hour on the beach and look more pale."

Marcus laughed. "I'll stay here with you. The water's freezing."

He sat next to her. Again their arms touched and Marcus smiled at her. "You're warm."

"The sun feels great." She lifted her face to the sky and closed her eyes. Could he tell how hard her heart was beating? Mary Catherine tried to still her nerves. What was she doing? And what was the point? This — whatever this was — couldn't go anywhere. Sitting this close to Marcus was like a form of torture.

But it felt too wonderful to even think about stopping.

For a while they sat that way, their arms touching, watching Tyler and Sami riding the waves. Tyler wasn't very good on the boogie board. No matter how hard he tried he kept falling off. The scene made for great entertainment, and after a few minutes Mary Catherine and Marcus were both laughing.

"That's my buddy! Mr. Surfer." Marcus laughed again. Then he leaned his head close to hers. "Good thing I don't have a wetsuit. Honestly, I'd be worse than him."

"I'd like to see you try. Someday."

"We'll see." Marcus sighed. "I should probably stick to pitching."

"Yeah, maybe." She shot him a teasing look. "If Tyler's any indication, pitchers might not be that great at riding waves."

Marcus drew one knee up to his chest and chuckled. He turned so he could see her better, but the move broke the physical connection between them. "So . . . what do you know about pitchers?"

"Hmm." She laughed. "Well, for starters they might be better on dry land." Her smile came easily. "Oh . . . and the fact that you're the best."

He tilted his head, searching her face, clearly trying to read her. "Have you ever seen me pitch?"

"Yes." Mary Catherine remembered it well. She had watched on TV as Marcus pitched the winning game of the last World Series. "You're very good." She felt the teasing in her eyes. "I'm actually a baseball fan."

"You are?"

"Yeah. But . . . not really the Dodgers. I

grew up loving the Braves."

"The Braves?" He stood and walked a few steps toward the water before returning. "Are you serious? That lousy team?"

"Yes!" She laughed out loud. "Definitely the Braves. We used to drive down to Atlanta for a couple of games each year." She loved this, the easy way they had together. It was more fun every time they talked. "Nashville has the minor league Sounds. But if you wanted the real thing, Atlanta was the place to be."

"Okay, then." He grinned. "I guess I can sit by you. Since you grew up not knowing better." He settled back on the towel and this time they sat closer than before.

"Very kind of you." The feel of his arm against hers was intoxicating. Mary Catherine had to work to feel the sand beneath her. Otherwise she would've thought she was floating.

"You know. Southern gentleman and all."

"Yes, sir." She milked her accent for all it was worth. "Kind gentleman like you doesn't come around every day."

He tipped his head back and laughed. "I love that! I should've been born in the South." He gave her a mock stern look. "That part about not coming around every day, don't forget it, young lady."

"Deal." She thought about finding her sunglasses in her bag, but the sun was still at their backs. Their faces still had enough shade to talk without the glare of the sun being a problem.

He stretched out his legs again. They were several inches from hers, but with every movement, his arm brushed against hers again. They fell quiet, watching Tyler and Sami. Finally she felt Marcus inhale. He looked at her. "I keep thinking about the other day, you at Elysian Park with Lexy." He shook his head and stared at the ocean for a beat before looking back at her. "I don't know what I would've done if . . . if something had happened to you."

"I'm glad the police were there." She was touched by his concern.

"The world can never lose a girl like you, Mary Catherine. You're the rarest kind of real."

Her head was spinning again, her heart leaping like the dolphins in the waves earlier. "Thank you." She had the strongest desire to rest her head on his shoulder. But she couldn't. This was all pretend. She wasn't being fair to him or to herself. If they were going to get close like this, she would need to tell him the truth about her heart.

Truth she was going to learn more about

any minute, when her phone rang.

"Tell me . . ." His voice was softer now. He looked at her eyes, straight to her aching heart. "Why do you run? When I'm around?"

"I don't run." She broke eye contact and turned to look at Tyler and Sami again. "I'm busy, that's all."

"No." His fingertips touched the side of her face. He waited until she looked at him. "You're not that busy. Only around me."

She wanted to beg him to stop this part of the conversation, stop it before she had no choice but to be honest. She shrugged and smiled. "Of course, you had Shelly, remember?"

"She wasn't the problem. You know that." He wasn't giving up. "I just want to know. Like . . . is there someone else? I know you said you hadn't found *that* guy, but maybe there's someone. Someone you didn't tell me about?"

A single sad laugh came from her. "No. That's not it." She wasn't sure how much longer she could look at him without giving in to her feelings, without forgetting every true thing about her health and her future and letting her heart win.

Just this once.

"So what is it?" He lowered his hand and

allowed the slightest space between them. "You don't like ballplayers?"

"You're the first one I've been friends with." She let her smile ease up some, enough that she hoped he could see she was being honest. "Relationships . . . they just aren't for me. It's complicated." She didn't wait for him to protest. "Maybe I'll explain it someday." She stood and stretched out her hand to him. "For now let's not think about it. Life's too short to worry."

He reached out his arm and their fingers touched and held. The feeling was as familiar as it was consuming. Like they'd held hands a thousand times before. He hesitated and then stood, still holding her hand. He looked down into her eyes and she could only allow the feeling between them. A heady wonderful feeling she was sure they were both experiencing.

When he spoke, his words were barely louder than the sound of the surf. "It feels right . . . being with you."

His words hit their mark. She hesitated and then grinned. "Come on!" She gently pulled him toward the shore.

"Don't tell me you're taking me back out into that water." His easy expression said he wasn't going to push the issue, wasn't going to insist on understanding everything about her right now.

But he also wasn't going to give up.

"Yes!" She led the way to the surf. "It'll be warmer now." They ran to the water. If she had wondered how he felt about her, now she knew. The pull she felt toward him, the way he could look straight through her, Mary Catherine could feel it long after they were waist deep in the water. She knew it because of one thing.

Marcus still had hold of her hand.

22

Marcus waited until he and Tyler were halfway home before he laughed out loud. "Okay, so what's with that girl? Just when I think I have her figured out, she throws me off again."

"I thought you might be thinking about her." Tyler laughed, too. He leaned against the passenger door and looked at Marcus. "Man, you got it bad for her. The whole beach could see."

"Just a couple of friends celebrating a great day at Zuma." He shook his head and kept his eyes on the road. "That's how she sees it."

"What about that holding hands thing?" Tyler was definitely enjoying the banter. "She didn't seem to fight that very much."

"True." He felt baffled. "She said she's not into relationships. Something like that."

"Well . . . maybe you'll actually have to chase her." Tyler grinned. "She might be the only single girl in the world who wouldn't jump at the chance to date you."

"She's definitely on the list." He replayed the moments with her again in his mind. "I know this. There's no other girl like her. It's like nothing could take her down. Like she'll be celebrating life until she's a hundred years old."

Tyler laughed again. "I just hope it doesn't take you that long to get her to change her mind."

Marcus rolled down the window and let the warm January air drift through his SUV. "I might just wait that long." He leaned back and smiled. "If she doesn't drive me crazy first."

Not until after Marcus and Tyler left did Mary Catherine realize she hadn't heard from either her mom or the doctor. *Strange,* she thought. She dug around on her towel and found her phone.

It was turned off.

That's weird, she thought. *Maybe the battery died.* She held the button at the top of the phone and the screen came to life. After a few seconds she could see for herself. The battery was still full.

So when had she turned it off?

Before she could figure out an answer she

watched several messages come through. Two of them were voice mails, one from her mother, one from her cardiologist. Sami was gathering her things, but Mary Catherine needed to check the messages first.

She noted the time of the calls. Her mother's came in right as Marcus was being baptized. The doctor's happened fifteen minutes later, when Marcus had just taken the spot beside her on the towel. She would've missed all of that if her phone had been on.

She had no time to worry about it. She played the message from her mom first. Her mother's voice came on the line and Mary Catherine put her hand over her other ear. She needed to focus, needed to hear every word.

"Honey, call me. Good news." That was it. All her mother said. The message was the last thing Mary Catherine had expected. She dialed her mother's number and waited.

"Hello, honey!" Her mom sounded happier than she had in months. "Your father's doing so much better!"

"What happened?" Mary Catherine felt the sting of tears. Her father wasn't healthy. She would need to get out to Nashville again soon. Before she could think about a trip to Africa. But for now he was at least out of danger. *Thank You, God . . . thank You.*

Her mom was explaining what had happened, how they'd gotten much closer since his illness. And how she'd been spending more time at the hospital with him. "He looked like he'd need heart surgery, and you know your father. With his weight . . . he's just not a candidate right now."

"I know." Mary Catherine felt the burden of her father's health again. "One day, maybe."

"Anyway." Her mother paused only long enough to catch a quick breath. "This new doctor visited us today. A pretty woman. She found a better medication for the IV. It only took an hour and his numbers were so much better." She sounded deeply relieved. "Makes me wonder if the woman was an angel. Anyway, just wanted you to know he's good for now. Your dad asked me to tell you that he misses you. We both do."

"Miss you, too. Tell Daddy I love him."

"I will. Love you, too."

The conversation ended and Mary Catherine stared out at the water, to the place where Marcus had been baptized little more than an hour ago. God was with them. No matter how terribly the week had gone or what evil existed in the world, the Lord was still at work.

He had allowed her divorced parents to find friendship again. And He had sent a doctor to heal her father.

Which meant now she could still do the Last Time In program with Marcus. Mary Catherine stared at her phone. The other message was from her cardiologist. But suddenly she didn't want to hear it. The news could wait. She only wanted to live in the moment and remember every amazing thing about the morning and her time with Marcus.

She stood and walked to the edge of the water, her eyes trained on the horizon. The time with Marcus today had been a dream. Better than a dream. He was funny and sensitive and he wanted to take their friendship deeper. To a place where there were no secrets.

Mary Catherine thought about the message waiting for her, the one from the doctor. Her failing health was her greatest secret, the one thing she never wanted to share with Marcus. She didn't want him feeling sorry for her or trying to convince her she was wrong about her decision to stay single.

Sami came up alongside her. "How's your dad?"

"He's great." She turned and smiled. "Some new doctor came on the scene today and gave him a different medicine." She still couldn't believe the news. "He won't need surgery after all."

"So you can stay with the prison program."

"Yes." She grew quiet, looking back at the ocean again. "Was it obvious?"

"You and Marcus?" Sami laughed quietly. "Very." She faced Mary Catherine. "Did you tell him? About your heart?"

"No." Mary Catherine wanted to run down the beach, far from the reality of her health. "I can't tell him. I shouldn't have told you."

"Why?" Sami sounded hurt. "Don't say that. I won't tell anyone. Not even Tyler." She didn't say anything for a few seconds. "It's just . . . with Marcus . . . you told me you didn't want to date. You might only have ten years. Remember?"

"I still feel that way." She exhaled and felt the weight of the entire beach on her shoulders. "I tried to tell him."

"What'd you say?" Sami wasn't pushing. She was only being a friend.

"I told him relationships weren't for me. I said it was complicated."

Sami looked surprised. "He didn't ask for

more of an explanation?"

"He would've." She ignored the hurt inside. "I made him go to the water with me instead."

"The hand-holding?" A sparkle started in Sami's eyes and turned into a smile. "It's okay, Mary Catherine. Why do you have to be so hard on yourself? You don't know what's going to happen. You might end up in a rocking chair next to me when you're eighty." She hesitated. "Only God knows the number of your days."

"True." She longed for the scenario Sami described, longed for a reason to believe it was possible. "But my heart condition . . . it's a real thing, Sami. I can't put that on someone else."

"Maybe you don't have to. Just wait it out. Have fun." She breathed in deep and did a little spin on the sand. Then she angled her face, empathy marking her expression. "Isn't that what you taught me?"

"Yes." Mary Catherine smiled. If only it were that easy. "In everything but love."

"Maybe especially in love." Sami wasn't giving up. There was a pleading in her voice. Like she was desperate for Mary Catherine to relax her way of thinking. "You told me to visit my old boyfriend when I was in Florida. And look at Tyler and me now."

"Sami." Mary Catherine needed her friend to understand. "I can't do that to Marcus. Don't you see? He deserves the sort of love that can live on and on." She felt tears choking her, making it impossible to speak. She turned to the ocean again and waited.

Sami came up beside her again. "I'm sorry. I didn't mean to make you sad. But you're just friends. You can at least give that much a chance."

"It's just . . ." She sniffed, still struggling. "I feel more. And I can't."

"Maybe you can." Sami hesitated. "No one knows the number of their days. I could fall over right here on the sand." Her words were gentle this time. "I would never regret loving Tyler. Even if we only had today."

Mary Catherine nodded. She understood what Sami meant. She really did. It just wasn't fair to either of them — her or Marcus — to let him think there was a chance. A chance at love and a normal life together. Why let something begin when the ending was already written?

They'd spent enough time talking about it. Mary Catherine smiled at her friend. "Come on. Let's get back." She walked slowly to her things and packed them into her bag. "Besides, I'm not sure he even likes me."

"MC, that's the most ridiculous thing I ever —"

"Okay, okay." Mary Catherine laughed and it felt wonderful for the moment to be light again. "Maybe he likes me just a little."

Sami made an exasperated sound. "You'll make plans to get your pilot's license, but you won't let yourself fall in love." Sami gathered her board and her bags. "Maybe just think awhile on your priorities. Okay?"

"I have." She grinned. "Conversation closed. But speaking of priorities, is it your turn to vacuum? Because I think it is."

They both started giggling and then walked in comfortable silence back to the car. Mary Catherine was grateful for Sami, for a friend who cared and could laugh with her.

The ride home didn't include a single mention of Marcus. Mary Catherine was relieved. There really was nothing to say, nowhere the topic could go.

Not until they were back at the apartment and Mary Catherine was in her room did she close the door and listen to the message from her cardiologist. The man's secretary had simply advised her to return the call. Her test results were in. Mary Catherine waited, her hands trembling. If only she could put off the news, put it aside and forget about it. *Father, I need You . . . I can't do this without You.* She closed her eyes and waited. After a minute or so a feeling of peace came over her. Peace enough to make the call.

She opened her eyes and tapped the call button.

A receptionist answered. "Dr. Cohen's office."

"This is Mary Catherine Clark." She couldn't shake the feeling that the news would be bad. "I missed a call from your office earlier."

"Yes, hold on." The woman sounded efficient. There was no reading her tone. "The doctor would like to speak to you."

"That's fine." Mary Catherine dropped on the edge of her bed and waited. The seconds felt like days.

"Hello? Mary Catherine?" It was Dr. Cohen. He was in his forties. One of the top cardiologists in Los Angeles.

"Hi. I missed your call earlier." She paused. "Is it about my test results?"

"Yes." He sighed. Not a quick sigh. But the kind that doctors tended to do when the information ahead might be difficult.

She closed her eyes again. *Whatever it is, God, You're in charge. You know the number of my days. I believe that.*

288

"Mary Catherine, I'm afraid the results were worse than we expected. Your valve has deteriorated greatly. But more than that, your heart is further enlarged." He paused. "I shared your results with a few respected cardiologist friends of mine. One in New York. One in Boston."

Mary Catherine slid off the edge of her bed to the floor. She brought her legs to her chest and let her forehead rest on her knees. "Okay. Yes?"

"We all came to the same conclusion. Mary Catherine, I'm afraid we'd like to put you on the heart transplant list. The sooner the better."

A black hole seemed to open up in the spot where she was sitting. Darker and darker, blacker and blacker. She could feel herself falling into it and the whole time she was certain of one awful reality. There was no bottom. She would keep falling for the rest of her days.

Because this was the worst possible news he could've told her.

"Mary Catherine? Do you understand, dear?"

"Yes, sir." Her voice was soft and shaky. "So . . . what's next? What should I do?"

"We have to have you into the office in the next week or so for a complete checkup.

You'll need more tests and blood work. Then there'll be a screening exam and some paperwork. All of that before we can get you on the donor list."

In the black hole where she was falling, Mary Catherine couldn't catch her breath, couldn't exhale fully. Like she was drowning in her own bedroom. "You mean . . . you want the surgery soon?"

"It's never that easy." He sounded discouraged by the fact. "Your heart and valve can go on for probably another nine months or a year. Even after your appointment it could be months before we get you on the transplant list. It's a process. Many people never get a donor, Mary Catherine. I need to be honest."

She still couldn't believe what he was saying. The transplant she'd expected in the years to come was supposed to be a valve replacement. Not a heart transplant. What about Africa? What about helping with the youth center? How was she supposed to get her pilot's license if she was waiting for a heart transplant?

"Did you hear me?" The doctor's words were kind. "I'm so sorry, Mary Catherine. I know this must be a shock to you. Frankly, it was a shock to me. That's why I sought the other opinions." He waited a beat. "I'm very, very sorry."

"It's okay." She was still falling, still trying to get a full breath. What about mornings on the beach and swimming with the dolphins?

"I'll transfer you back to the receptionist. I'd like you to book the appointment as soon as possible."

"Yes, sir." Mary Catherine couldn't lift her head, couldn't do anything but feel herself falling. What about her brand-new job as a graphic designer at Front Line Studios in Santa Monica? She was supposed to be there next year when their first movie hit theaters.

A heart transplant?

Sometime before the end of the year?

Falling . . . falling. Mary Catherine stood and steadied herself on the edge of her bed. Then with her remaining energy she walked to the window and looked at the blue sky. The beautiful Southern California sky. How could this happen?

She thought about her friends. Now she would have to tell Marcus. Not right away, but sometime soon. She'd have to tell all of them. If only she could stop falling, stop the blackness of the dark hole she'd stepped into. Before the call she'd thought she had till she was thirty. Another seven years at least.

Suddenly thirty felt like an impossible number. Like a gift.

Maybe there was some mistake. She felt fine, right? She wasn't short of breath or struggling with chest pains. People waiting for a heart transplant were very sick. Too weak to get out of bed. Mary Catherine clung to the window frame and thought about her morning, about the feel of Marcus's arm against hers. *What about moments like that, God?* There would be no time to make a difference, no time for learning the guitar or taking voice lessons.

She wouldn't live long enough for any of it. Mary Catherine closed her eyes, but the tears came anyway. The blackness was swallowing up the moment, and still she was falling. Everything was different now. Everything would change. And of course there was something else she would have to give up. The thing she only joked about every now and then and once in a while prayed about. The thing that would absolutely never be possible now.

Her hundred years.

23

Lexy couldn't stop shaking.

It was the morning of her prison tour. Mary Catherine and Marcus were going to pick her up and take her to the prison, an hour away. She stared at her full cereal bowl. She was too scared to eat. Too unsure about what was ahead.

Why had she agreed to the program? They wouldn't have given her very long at Eastlake juvie, right? Less than a year, then she'd have been back on the streets. But going to prison? Even a day there would be terrible.

Prison was the sort of place that took a person in and swallowed them up and never let them see the light of day again. The way prison had done to her mother. Lexy looked at the photo on the wall across from her. She and her mama before the arrest. Lexy stood and walked to the picture. She touched it, running her thumb over their faces. In the photo her mama's arm was around her shoulders and their smiles were the same. Their eyes, too. The arrest came the next day, an afternoon Lexy thought about all the time. The day her mama was locked up and sent away.

The last day the two of them had seen each other.

Lexy might've been maybe six in the picture. Her mama, maybe twenty-two. Her mom was beautiful and intelligent. She could remember sitting with her mom on the couch that week and watching TV. *America's Funniest Home Videos,* Lexy could still remember. Her mom was laughing and so Lexy had laughed, too.

When she was little . . . Lexy could remember laughing a lot with her mama. Why had her mom gotten into drugs? She could've done something different with her life. So why didn't she? Lexy stared at the photo and blinked. The reason was obvious. No matter how long she looked at the photograph, no matter how the two of them seemed there on the wall.

Her mother didn't love her.

Lexy was alone after her mama went away. Her grandma tried, but she never knew what was going on in the house. The summer Lexy turned eight was the first time she remembered the neighbor boy locking her in his bedroom and taking advantage of her. He was fourteen. At least she thought so. It had happened too many times since then. The bad all blended together. And none of it would have happened if her mama had been around.

Mamas are supposed to keep their babies safe.

Supposed to keep their babies in school and out of gangs.

Lexy felt her anger rising, taking over her heart and soul. If she had a soul. One day when she had babies, she wasn't going to leave them. She would move out of the slums to some nice place like Reseda. Lexy's grandma was from Reseda. Nice town in the San Fernando Valley.

Gradually a resolve built in her.

She had prayed to God for help and he'd given her the chance at this program. It was a little late to start wishing she'd served time instead. If she was going to make a change for her own kids one day, then this was the only way.

The Last Time In program. Whatever happened today, she could deal with it.

Her grandma's Bible was open again on the other side of the table. The way it was always open. *Hate evil . . . cling to good.* That's what the blond police officer had told her. And then he'd showed up again, right when Dwayne was going to kill her.

A sick feeling slammed into Lexy's stomach. Yes, Dwayne was definitely going to kill her. He had wanted to hide out at her grandma's house that day, but all of a sudden he looked at her like he was the devil himself and he ordered her back outside to the car.

"I can't have witnesses, baby. You gotta understand." That's what he told her. He said it again and again until they were almost to the car and then out of nowhere there was the blond police officer. Again. Towering and looking like he could take down a whole gang by himself.

Then the craziest thing Lexy had ever seen in all her life. The cop had appeared out of nowhere and grabbed the gun. That wasn't even possible. Anyone knew people couldn't just appear out of thin air.

But that's what the officer did.

Even that didn't scare Dwayne. Lexy thought the cop would shoot her boyfriend right there on the street. That's when she had shouted out for help from Jesus.

Lexy didn't understand it, even still. Didn't know why she had called out the name Jesus, but something about that moment seemed to change things for the cop.

Like he blinked a few times and he took his finger off the trigger. After that Lexy knew he wasn't going to shoot.

He was too good for that.

Hate evil . . . cling to good.

She was reminding herself when a text came through on her phone. It was from one of the WestKnights. *You in or not, baby? You're mine tonight. Dwayne's gone. I got next dibs.*

She stared at the text. Just stared at it as the words cut their way through her. Then she texted back without thinking. *I'm in.*

She looked at it and her heart felt hard and dead again.

He sent one last text. *Be ready.*

Tears slid down her cheeks. Who was she kidding? She would never have kids if she could help it. But if she did, she'd be just like her mama. How could she not? She was too far into the WestKnights to back out now.

There would be no babies, no family, no little house in Reseda. No life different from the one her mama gave her. No way to hate evil when it was a part of the air she breathed.

The time in prison today would not be her last time in.

It would be a preview.

24

Mary Catherine could've won an Oscar for how she pulled herself together and pretended to be fine. The acting had begun Friday night at the last training session and continued on to this morning when Marcus picked her up for the prison tour.

She was still in the dark hole, still falling. But she could see the light of day. If she didn't have a year left, she was going to live her days like never before. Starting today with the Last Time In program. This day wasn't about her.

It was about Lexy.

In the driver's seat beside her, Marcus seemed somehow aware that she was different. "You sure you're okay?" He'd asked her twice already. "Sorry. It's just . . . something in your eyes."

A smile lifted the corners of her lips. "I'm fine. Just tired. I was up late reading."

"Your pilot's manual?" He grinned at her.

"No, a novel." She told him the name. "My favorite author just had a book come out. I can't put it down." At least that much was true.

"I didn't know you were into reading." It sounded forced. Like he was trying to believe her. "Me, too. I love fiction."

"You do not." She laughed and she could feel the doubt in her eyes.

He raised his brow and pointed to himself. "Are you saying athletes don't read?"

"Not many of them." Even in light of her news, something about being with him made her forget everything but the moment.

"I take exception to that statement." He tipped his baseball cap to her. "This Southern gentleman loves to read. For real." His eyes stayed on the road. "When you finish this book that kept you up so late, I wanna read it." He glanced at her. "Deal?"

She was still laughing. "Deal."

The mood stayed light as they drove to Lexy's, but after they picked her up it changed. Lexy seemed completely shut down. More than she'd been the other day. Mary Catherine sat in the front seat next to Marcus and tried. "How were the last few days?"

Silence.

"Lexy." She kept her tone kind. "I know

this isn't easy. But please answer me."

Silence.

"Okay, then tell me about your grandma. How does she feel about you going for the prison tour today?"

Again nothing.

Marcus reached over and gently touched Mary Catherine's leg. Then he shook his head briefly, as if to say it wasn't worth it. He mouthed the word *later*. Then he turned the radio to the local Christian station. Francesca Battistelli came on. The song was a new one Mary Catherine loved called "If We're Honest." She hoped Lexy was listening to the words.

Mary Catherine sang along. " 'Truth is harder than a lie, the dark seems safer than the light . . .' " As the song played out a thought occurred to her.

The words applied to her own life as much as they applied to Lexy's.

Mary Catherine leaned back and let the lyrics wash over her. She loved every song by Francesca. This one and the one that had first given her hope that God might have more time for her than the doctors believed. The song was called "Hundred More Years." Mary Catherine looked out the window while the song played. Despite her best efforts at ignoring her own situation and trying to make today about Lexy, she felt the tears.

Life wasn't fair for her or for Lexy. Neither of them would likely ever have the lives they'd dreamed about. Mary Catherine's teardrops spilled down her cheeks before she could do anything to stop them. She wiped them with the back of her hand, careful not to catch Marcus's attention.

But he must've seen, because he reached out and took hold of her hand. He let the song play on, right to the last line . . . *If we're honest.*

Mary Catherine loved how her hand felt in Marcus's, loved that he would reach out and comfort her when he saw her tears. She smiled at him, no longer embarrassed by her watery eyes. Life was not all laughter and mornings at the beach.

It was okay to cry.

The music switched and it was Matthew West's "Strong Enough." Mary Catherine sniffed and settled into her seat. Crying might have been allowed, but it wasn't possible during Matthew's song. She sang along, quietly at first. " 'You must, you must think I'm strong, to give me what I'm going through.' "

Then, to her surprise, Marcus began to sing, too. Louder and more off-key than her.

"We'd make quite a duo for *America's Got Talent*." He was still holding her hand and now he winked at her.

It was impossible to stay sad around him. Plus the words to the song were too powerful. Okay, so she needed a heart transplant. And sure, not everyone on the list received one. Maybe she did only have a year left.

But she absolutely refused to use her days trying to stop falling, trying to see past the blackness. There would be time to cry, yes. But she had to believe in the message of the song. Especially with Marcus singing it at the top of his lungs beside her. That God was strong enough for her. Strong enough for Lexy.

After a minute, he released her hand and pretended to sing into a microphone. "I'm ready for *Fifteen Minutes*."

From the backseat Lexy said her first words of the morning. "Maybe not yet."

"Hey now." He looked at her in the rearview mirror. "You barely know me."

"Still." Lexy sounded disgusted. But it was a start. A way to connect. A bridge they could maybe cross again later today.

The rest of the drive was upbeat, and Mary Catherine didn't have to pretend to be okay. She actually felt it. Not until they reached the prison and started across the parking lot did Lexy hesitate. "I feel sick. Maybe we should turn back."

Mary Catherine stopped with her and so did Marcus. The prison loomed in the near distance, a monolithic structure made of block walls and razor wire. Everything about it looked intimidating.

No wonder Lexy felt sick. She was probably terrified, something they'd gone over in training. Mary Catherine put her hand softly on Lexy's shoulder. "Lexy, we'll be with you." The girl didn't jerk away. Mary Catherine smiled. "You'll be fine. I promise."

"Yeah." Marcus's voice was light and easy. Another tool they'd picked up in training. "Besides, I can't sing in there." Marcus had removed his baseball cap and left it in his Hummer. He peered at Lexy, clearly trying to see past her walls. "It's just a tour."

Lexy gave him a rude look. "I know." Whatever spurred her forward, she started walking again. "Come on." She looked back at Mary Catherine. "We can't be late. That's one of the rules."

They made their way past four security checkpoints, and then they were ushered into a large cement room with no windows and just one door. Tyler and Sami and the girl they were helping were already there.

Sami had tried to meet the girl before today, but she hadn't been willing to meet.

Which was too bad because, as it turned out, Sami and Tyler had Sierra Wayne's friend. Alicia Grange. The girl was tiny with pale blond hair. She looked barely old enough to be in middle school, let alone fourteen. Grand theft and truancy? Mary Catherine hoped the program worked for the girl.

For all the girls.

Over the next ten minutes the room filled up until all six girls were present along with their chaperone volunteers. At exactly ten o'clock the door opened and six prison guards pushed their way in. All of them seemed angry and put out, upset they had to be there.

This was part of the plan. Mary Catherine knew it. So did all the volunteers. But it was another thing to see the angry guards coming at them. Mary Catherine had to remind herself that these were volunteers. That no matter how it looked in this moment, these men and women cared very much for the girls in the program.

As for the volunteers, they would be advocates for the teens, people the teens could turn to when the reality of the prison visit became too much. That was one of the differences between Last Time In and Scared Straight. The point was to build connections between the teens and the volunteers. That way the volunteers would have a better chance of helping the teens stay off the streets in the days and weeks, even years, to come. At least that was the hope.

Mary Catherine tried not to think about the years she might not have to influence Lexy.

The guards moved toward them. They had their clubs out, and two of them were slapping them against their hands. *Here we go*, Mary Catherine thought. She stood close to Marcus, with Lexy standing in front of them. Already she was shaking.

"Got a buncha girls wanna spend their lives in here, that right?" The biggest prison guard lunged forward so his face was inches from the first girl. "You wanna be here? You gonna be a career criminal, missy?"

"No."

"That's 'No, sir'!" he screamed at her face. "Say it."

"No, sir!" The girl's voice could barely be heard.

"Louder!" He couldn't have been more than an inch from her. "Say it louder!"

"No, sir! I don't wanna be a career criminal, sir!"

The guard stepped back, his face an angry twist of knots. "That's better."

Mary Catherine had to remember to breathe. She could feel Lexy backing up, getting closer to her. Even in the first few minutes, Mary Catherine felt like the program was starting to work. Lexy was feeling a trust connection with her.

And the tour hadn't even started.

The other prison guards stepped into the action. Each of them went to a different girl. A muscled guard moved up to Lexy.

"Your guy's leader of the gang, right?"

Lexy didn't answer. She cocked her head back, the way she'd done when Mary Catherine first met her.

"We got a smart one here, do we!" He moved closer to her. "You dating the leader of the gang? Talk to me, gang girl. You've got no rights in here."

"He ain't the leader yet." Her words were soft, her eyes directed at the blank wall at the other end of the room.

" 'He's *not* the leader yet. Sir'!" He enunciated each word for her.

Lexy put her hands over her ears. "He's not the leader yet, sir." She still didn't sound very loud.

The officer towered over her, his physical presence intimidating to everyone in the room. "Next time you forget you'll do push-ups."

For a brief moment, Lexy looked back at Mary Catherine. Terror flashed in her eyes. Mary Catherine nodded. Lexy had to obey. That was part of the program.

"Don't look at your volunteer, gang girl." He twisted his head so his face was almost up against hers. "I changed my mind. Next time is now."

Lexy moved reluctantly to her hands and knees.

"You're going to do pushups, gang girl. Hurry up!"

Mary Catherine knew this would be the hardest part. Watching the guards treat the kids like they were prisoners. It was part of the program. After all, if they kept on the way they were headed, they would wind up here. And this would be a part of their everyday life. Having a prison guard in their faces, ordering them to obey.

This treatment was important. But it was almost impossible to watch.

Lexy began doing pushups. She was stronger than she looked. Mary Catherine would've guessed the girl wasn't quite ninety pounds. But her arms were strong.

Meanwhile, down the line the other guards questioned the teens. Some were being forced to do jumping jacks. Others looked terrified. One girl had to march to the opposite wall and back. Four of the six were crying by the time the guards stepped back and folded their arms. Lexy was one of those.

"Time for your fellow inmates. You make it back here, and these women will become your family. Your best friends." It was the first guard. He was still bellowing, still lunging toward the girls with every other word. "You don't wanna know everything they'll become to you." He looked at his fellow guards. "Right?"

"You don't want to know." One of the guards shook her head.

"We'll let *them* tell you." The shortest officer walked to the door. "Follow me."

Marcus put his hand on the small of Mary Catherine's back as they walked with Lexy into the hallway and down a corridor. On the way they passed a row of cells and every one they passed was teeming with angry women.

The inmates pressed up against the bars, shouting obscenities and gesturing to the girls. Mary Catherine wanted to turn back. She could only imagine how Lexy and the other girls must feel. *Please, God . . . let this work. It's so hard. Please speak to Lexy at the depths of her soul.*

At the end of the corridor there was another room — this one much larger. At least it appeared that way through the window. The short guard turned and faced the group. "This is where you meet your new friends." She unlocked the door.

All around the room, the guards unlocked the doors of the smaller cells and the inmates joined the group in the open space. The area had four cement tables, built into the floor, each of them with attached cement benches.

Otherwise the room was empty.

Sixteen prisoners came out and started walking toward them. The collective anger from them was like a physical force. Something Mary Catherine had never experienced before. She was tempted to put her hand on Lexy's shoulder but that wasn't allowed. The volunteers were supposed to be a presence of shelter, safety. Hope, even.

But they weren't supposed to interfere.

Suddenly Lexy crumpled to the ground. "No!" She turned around and glared at Mary Catherine. "You didn't tell me!" she shouted at the closest guard. "How come no one told me?"

Marcus took Mary Catherine's hand again. "Pray," he whispered to her.

"I am." She had no idea what was happening. But the meltdown seemed to be caused by an inmate walking straight for Lexy.

A woman who looked almost exactly like her.

"No, Mama, no! You can't do this!" Lexy started to turn around and run for the door.

But the guard caught her by the arm and turned her back around. "What's the matter, gang girl? Didn't you think you'd see your mama here? You wanna be just like her, right?"

Mary Catherine felt the blood leave her face. Lexy had said that her mother was in prison. But Mary Catherine had no idea the woman was in this prison. Mary Catherine felt sick. This was turning out to be the worst idea ever.

"No!" Lexy was still trying to run.

This time the prison guard lowered his voice, as threatening as he could sound. "You keep throwing a fit and I'll lock your mama back up. Then you won't see her at all."

Lexy grew calmer. Tears streamed down her face as her mother approached. For a brief few seconds, Mary Catherine wondered if the woman was going to start crying, too. She looked upset. But then, just like the other inmates, she came to Lexy and started yelling.

"Don't cry, little girl. This ain't a place for tears," Lexy's mother snarled at her. "Last time I saw you, you was all sweet and pretty." She jabbed a finger close to Lexy's face. "Now look at ya! You a gang girl now, Lexy. That it? All cool, hanging with the boys." The woman couldn't have been very old. She looked like Lexy's older sister.

"Stop it, Mama." Lexy turned her head, her body convulsing with sobs. "I hate you! Leave me alone!"

Mary Catherine felt tears in her own eyes. The scene was too disturbing. Lexy clearly didn't know she'd see her mother here. Let alone have her mama turn on her this way.

"No, little girl!" Her mom shouted louder. "I will not leave you alone!" Her mom moved so she could get her face up close to her daughter's. "You wanna be here with me, I'll show you what it's like."

Her mom rattled off a list: the danger of showers, the way young inmates could get owned by older inmates. The way inmates could sell the young ones to other inmates for a pack of cigarettes.

"You hear that, daughter!" Lexy's mother yelled. "A pack of cigarettes!" She practically spat in Lexy's face. "You want this.

311

Don't forget it!"

Lexy looked ready to faint. She was sobbing and only every so often did she manage to say anything. "Please, Mama. Stop it!"

Mary Catherine could feel her heart breaking. There was a reason for all this. But watching Lexy's mom shout at her, yelling at her mercilessly, was more than Mary Catherine had planned for. Only one thing could be worse than this sort of prison tour.

Coming here forever.

Aspyn and Jag had hovered over the prison tour from the beginning. It was the ugliest hour they'd spent on earth.

"I'm going to see the girl's mother." Aspyn nodded at Jag. "She's back in her cell already. You all right by yourself?"

"Go ahead." Jag looked like he understood. His job was to keep Marcus and Mary Catherine safe.

Instantly, Aspyn was an orderly ready to clean up after the prisoners. Her uniform was light blue and she had a mop bucket. She walked out of a janitor's closet and past a few cells to the one where Lexy's mother was. The woman was alone, her back to the others.

She was crying.

Aspyn slipped into the cell and shut the door behind her. "What's wrong, Camila?"

The woman spun around. Everything angry and hateful about the way she'd looked earlier was gone. She took a step back. "Who are you?"

"I'm new." Aspyn had one hand on her mop. "Gotta clean up. But I heard you crying."

It took a minute for Camila Hernandez to believe she wasn't in danger, that Aspyn didn't want anything from her. Aspyn started moving the mop slowly over the floor. So she wouldn't raise Camila's suspicions. This moment was for Camila alone.

"You didn't answer me." Aspyn moved her mop slowly in a circle between them. "What's wrong? Why are you crying?"

Camila melted against the back wall of her cell. "My girl . . . she was in there. I haven't . . . seen her in so many years."

Aspyn slowed the mop. "You wanted to be with her, right?"

"I did." She covered her face with her hands. "I love her so much. I never stopped loving her. This is the last place I wanna see her."

Aspyn and Jag had figured this was going to happen. They knew Lexy's mother was an inmate here. And now Aspyn felt herself

313

hurting for Camila. "You're doing the right thing. Don't give up." Aspyn set the mop aside and went to Camila. She took hold of the woman's hands. "Write your daughter a letter. Do it now. Do you have paper and a pen?"

The woman sniffed. "I do." She pulled a small plastic box from beneath her bunk. "In here."

"You write it. I'll make sure she gets it." Aspyn took a step back. "Your daughter will know you love her."

"I miss her so much." Camila allowed another wave of tears. "I wanted to run up and hug her. I missed . . . everything. All her growing up years. I'm the worst mama ever."

"No." Aspyn wanted Camila to hear her. "You're doing everything you can to keep her out of this place. That makes you a loving mother."

Camila shook her head. "She'll hate me forever."

"Write the letter." Aspyn needed to go. Lunch would be over soon and she couldn't be caught.

For a long time Camila only stared at the paper and pen. Then she sniffed and nodded. "I will." She lifted hesitant eyes to Aspyn. "Can you help me?" She looked embarrassed. "I'm not . . . that good a writer."

Aspyn felt her heart melt. "Yes." She took the paper and pen from Camila. "Tell me what you want to say."

"Okay. I'll try." The woman struggled to find the right words, but in the end the message was all hers. Camila seemed calmer. "You'll make sure she gets it?"

"I promise." Aspyn hesitated. "You ever pray, Camila?"

"I want to learn."

"There's a Bible study once a week in your cell block. Did you know that? Monday nights."

"I never go."

"Start." Aspyn smiled at her. "God has plans for you, Camila. Even now. Even here."

The woman looked dazed. Like the news was hard to believe. Aspyn couldn't wait another minute. She nodded. "I'll get the letter to Lexy."

With that Aspyn stepped out of the cell and back into the closet, and disappeared.

25

Mary Catherine wanted nothing more than to take Lexy in her arms and comfort her. The poor girl. The day was dragging on, but Lexy never recovered from seeing her mother as one of the inmates. After lunch it was more of the same, and by the time the prison tour was finished, Lexy looked like she might pass out.

Tyler and Sami's girl also spent most of the day crying. If Mary Catherine had to guess, she doubted the girl would ever steal again. School probably looked like a dream vacation compared with this.

Marcus stayed by Mary Catherine's side as they ushered Lexy through the main space and into the corridor. They were halfway to the holding room where they'd started when a woman mopping the floors stopped Mary Catherine. "I got something for you."

"What?" She stopped. The woman looked

familiar, but she couldn't place her.

"Here." The orderly kept her eyes averted. She handed Mary Catherine a folded piece of notepaper. "This is for Lexy." Then the woman put her head down and kept mopping.

The group was still moving, so Mary Catherine had no choice but to keep walking. "Did you see that?" she whispered to Marcus.

"What?" He looked behind them and back at her.

"That woman. She was mopping the floor." Mary Catherine held up the letter. "She handed me this. Said it was for Lexy."

Marcus looked back again. "There's no one there."

"She was just —" Mary Catherine turned around and stopped for a second. "Where is she? She handed me the note like five seconds ago."

"Maybe she stepped into a closet. You know, to put the mop away."

Mary Catherine started walking again, backward, and then turned around. Lexy was a ways ahead of them. "That's so weird." She gave Marcus a puzzled look. "She looked familiar, too."

They reached the first checkpoint. None of them had been allowed to bring in phones or purses or anything else. Now they were checked again and Mary Catherine produced the letter. "This is a letter for our participant. From her mother."

The prison guard took the letter, opened it, and read it. He shrugged. "Fine." He nodded to Mary Catherine as he handed it back. "Put it in your pocket. Anyone asks you tell them Sikes said it was okay."

"Thank you, sir."

Mary Catherine could only imagine what Lexy's mother might've written to her. How she had gotten the letter to the orderly and how the orderly had known to get it to Mary Catherine made no sense at all.

When they reached Marcus's Hummer back in the parking lot, Mary Catherine did what she'd wanted to do all day. She hugged Lexy for a long time. "I'm sorry. About all that."

Lexy resisted the hug. "I didn't know . . . my mama was gonna be there. Someone shoulda told me."

"We didn't know either." Marcus stood on her other side. "I'm sorry, too. Today was brutal."

"Yeah." Lexy slid past them and climbed into the backseat of the SUV.

They were on the freeway before the girl spoke again. "What happened to the boy?"

Her tone was softer than before. "The one Dwayne shot?"

"He's still in the hospital." Marcus looked in the rearview mirror. "He's in bad shape. Everyone's praying for him."

Lexy started crying again. Mary Catherine could hear her. Even through her tears, she managed to speak. "Can . . . we pray for him? Right now? Please."

"We can." Mary Catherine turned around best she could in her seat.

"Father, we've asked You before, but now we come to You again with Lexy. Lord, please give Jalen a miracle. Please wake him up and by Your divine touch, would You please heal his brain? Let him talk to his mama again and let him live the way he did before. We know it's a lot, God, but You can walk on water. You can calm the seas with a whisper." Her voice was raw with emotion. "We believe You can do this. In Jesus' name, amen."

Through her tears, Lexy managed two simple words. "Thank you."

In the front seat, Mary Catherine doubted the girl was used to saying *thank you*. The Last Time In program was working, like the training promised. But Mary Catherine had wondered if anything would pierce the darkness that surrounded Lexy Jones.

Until now.

Mary Catherine waited until they were fifteen minutes from home before she pulled out the letter. "Your mama wrote you something. She had someone give it to me before we left."

At first Lexy didn't seem like she was going to let them know she cared. She didn't respond for five minutes. Then she muttered, "What's the letter say?"

"You can read it."

"No." Lexy hesitated. "How 'bout you read it? I'm not that good at letters."

It occurred to Mary Catherine at the same time it must've occurred to Marcus. Lexy couldn't read. At least not very many words. Otherwise she never would've wanted two people she still didn't know well to read the letter from her mother.

Before Mary Catherine opened it, she looked back at Lexy. "Has your mother written you before?"

"Never." She raised her chin. "I hafta hear it to believe it."

"Okay." Mary Catherine unfolded the piece of paper and started at the beginning. "Here it is. 'Dear Lexy, this janitor lady is helping me write this to you.' " Mary Catherine felt her heart react. The cycle of drugs and violence and illiteracy felt almost hopeless. " 'I'm so sorry for today. That wasn't me in there. It was me acting. All I wanted to do when I saw you was run up and take you in my arms.' " Mary Catherine blinked back tears. " 'The way I used to do when you were little.' "

Marcus put his hand on Mary Catherine's shoulder, silently lending his support.

"Keep reading." Lexy didn't sound as hard as before. "Please."

Mary Catherine worked to find her voice. " 'I made so many mistakes, Lexy. I never should've gotten involved with that man. I wouldn't be here if I could've said no. Instead I've spent every day since they locked me up sitting here and missing you. I think about what you must look like and how big you must be getting. I think about you in school making better choices than me.' "

Tears ran down Mary Catherine's cheeks. She wiped them before they could fall on the letter. "You're with your grandma and I know she's a God-fearing woman. So I believe you can find the right way, Lexy. The way I missed out on. The right way is with God, baby.' " Mary Catherine blinked so she could see. " 'I said I'd do the program today on one condition. If I could work with you. Because you see, baby, in those minutes even though I was yelling at you, I was near you. I could see your eyes and your face. The face I've missed so much.' "

Mary Catherine lowered the letter. She looked at Marcus and shook her head. "I can't," she whispered. "It's too sad."

Lexy leaned up as far as the seat belt would allow. "Is that all?"

Marcus gave her shoulder the slightest squeeze. He mouthed the words *You can do it,* neither of them wanting Lexy to know how difficult the moment was for Mary Catherine.

"No. There's more." She sniffed and lifted the letter again. " 'So please forgive me. I never wanted to yell at you. I wish I could see you every day, baby, but not in here. Not like this.' " Mary Catherine wiped her eyes again. " 'I keep a picture in my mind, Lexy. You and me when you were six years old. Kindergarten graduation. Grandma took our picture. All I want to do every day is go back to that time and do life over again. I'd learn how to be a better reader and writer, and I'd be there for you at night-time, to read to you and teach you how to sound out words. I'd make sure you and I were safe, away from the gangs and shootings. And I'd spend every day showing you how much I love you.' "

From the backseat, Mary Catherine could hear Lexy sniffling.

She had to finish. She wiped her tears once more. " 'But, Lexy, baby, I can't go back. We don't get to do life over again. So, baby, please just know that everything today was an act. It wasn't me. It was my way of keeping you out of here. And that's the only way I have left to love you. My precious daughter. I just wish I could've hugged you before you left. I love you always. Every day. Even from here. Love, your mama.' "

If Mary Catherine hadn't felt drained after the prison tour, she definitely felt it now. She folded the letter and handed it to Lexy. "I'm sorry. I wish you and your mama could've had this moment together. Away from everyone else."

Lexy took the letter. "Thank you. For reading it." She pressed the letter to her chest and looked out the window. Like she was seeing all the way back to the time when she was six years old. Her kindergarten graduation.

There was no room in the car for music or conversation. Not after that. Mary Catherine sank low in her seat and again Marcus reached out and took her hand. He'd been wonderful all day, attentive to her and Lexy, and always aware whenever the situation

323

felt too intense. He had taken her hand or put his arm around her a number of times today.

She appreciated all of it. Especially now. He ran his thumb along her hand and kept driving. Mary Catherine thought about the woman's letter, and the miracle it was that the janitor woman had found them before they left. Especially considering it was the only letter her mother had ever written to her.

All her life Mary Catherine had been aware of people less fortunate than her. While her parents dined at the country club, she would go with her youth group friends to serve dinner at the Nashville Rescue Mission. Her parents would vacation at Atlantis in the Bahamas, but when they started taking two or three trips there each year, Mary Catherine opted for mission trips to Africa and Guatemala instead.

Still, never in that time had she thought about this segment of life. The people behind bars. How desperate and defeating to wake up every day in those small cells. And then to know that the extent of your freedom involved the common space on the other side of the cold metal bars.

More than that, Mary Catherine had never thought about the families those prisoners had left behind. Yes, they all had done something to deserve punishment. Crimes against people and society. There was a reason they were in prison.

But what about Lexy? What had she done wrong? Her daddy was dead before her third birthday, and her mom was serving time before she stepped foot in first grade. No wonder the pattern of crime and punishment continued in the inner city. Kids had no one else to follow. Mary Catherine closed her eyes. *Lord, please let this program work for Lexy. I'll do everything I can — as long as I can. But we can't do this without Your help.*

They dropped Lexy off ten minutes later, and again Mary Catherine hugged her. "We'll be back to pick you up on Tuesday at six." She searched Lexy's eyes. "Okay?"

"Okay." For the first time since Mary Catherine had met the girl, she didn't look defiant. She looked lost and broken. The letter from her mother was still clutched tight in her hand. "Maybe someday . . . you can read me the letter again."

"I'd like that."

Lexy walked inside without looking back.

"What a day." Marcus held the car door open for Mary Catherine.

"So hard." On the way back to her apartment, they didn't say much. But once more Marcus held her hand. As if there was no way to get through a day like this without physical support. As she showered that night and turned in early, she thought about her heart. Something she hadn't thought about all day. So what if she didn't have much time left to make a difference? Her life mattered today. It had mattered for Lexy.

Right now that was enough.

Jag sat near Jalen's hospital bed. It was Tuesday afternoon and they'd been keeping watch over the child for nearly three days straight. He was off his breathing tube, but he still hadn't woken up. Today, though, something was different. Jag could sense a breakthrough.

Something about the aroma of prayer that had made its way to heaven. That had to be it. Orlon had told him and Aspyn before the mission began. Keep praying. Make sure everyone is praying.

There were times Jag wondered what people thought about prayer. Most humans didn't understand it. They thought God was a genie, someone to beg favors off . . . or a Father to turn to when things went wrong.

But that wasn't prayer at all.

Praying was simply talking to God. Of

course, the Lord loved hearing from His people. Whether they were believers or not. When Marcus Dillinger asked his Twitter followers to pray, it started a tidal wave of sweet requests directed straight to heaven.

It wasn't that a child like Jalen needed so many voices praying on his behalf. God heard the desperate prayer of a single voice in a dark room. But sometimes something happened that caused the world to sit up and take notice. A time when miracles could sway a generation to believe in God.

Miracles amidst tragedies.

And in that way, God would be glorified. Which wasn't always easy for people on earth to see or understand.

"Do you feel it?" Jag looked at Aspyn. This mission had kept them busier than either of them had ever imagined. "Something's happening with the boy."

"Yes." Aspyn held out her hands. "It's God's energy. It's all around us."

"It'll be any moment now." Jag hovered closer to the boy. "Come on, Jalen . . . Jesus, breathe life into him. Please, Jesus. We need You now. Here. Please."

Aspyn was praying too, and there in the chair beside the bed, Shamika had never stopped praying. Even when she doubted, she kept seeking God's help. Never stopped believing.

Suddenly the boy made the slightest coughing sound.

Jag could hear the celebration starting in heaven. The other angels cheering as they watched. "Come on. Wake up, boy." Jag held his hands over the child's heart. "We feel You working, God. Be glorified through Jalen."

And with that the boy began to sputter. His mother was on her feet instantly. "Jalen! Jalen, it's Mama. I'm here, baby. Wake up, Jalen." She began to cry, her voice desperate to see another sign of life from her son.

Again Jalen coughed and his eyes began to blink. They didn't open. It would take a few minutes. But he was coming to. That much was certain. "Nurse!" Shamika ran to the door and yelled into the hallway. "Please! Someone come here! My baby is waking up."

The miracle was unfolding. Jag felt the sense of deep wonder and awe, the feeling that never grew old. When death was denied the last word.

If Jesus were standing here, He'd be crying. Jag was sure. This was the reason He'd died on the cross. So that what was dead might live again.

"Jalen! Baby, I'm here." Shamika hurried

back to her son's bed and put her hand alongside his face. Her hands trembled, and her voice was unsteady with the weight of her emotion. She kissed her son's cheek and took hold of his hand. "I've missed you so much, Jalen. Please . . . open your eyes, baby." She whispered low near his cheek. "Come back to me, sweet boy. I want to see you smile again. God, please bring him back to me." She brought his hand to her lips and kissed it. "Jalen . . . Mama's here!"

Again the boy tried to blink his eyes open, and this time his eyelids opened just a hint. Slowly his lips parted. He peered at Shamika. "Mama? I'm hungry!"

"Okay, baby. We'll get you something to eat." Then without hesitating, Shamika did what most humans forgot to do in a moment like this.

She fell to her knees. "Jesus, You did this! You gave me my boy back. Thank You, Lord. Thank You." With words and tears she continued to give praise to Jesus, the One who had brought her son back to life, the One from whom all good things flowed.

Including this.

26

Marcus wasn't sure what he had expected from the first group meeting with the girls, but he had never imagined this. They met at six o'clock that Tuesday in a classroom at the police station — one of the requirements. Tyler and Sami sat with Alicia, the small blond girl, and Marcus and Mary Catherine sat with Lexy.

Just the six of them.

But the topics that had come up made Marcus glad for the training. On the surface the girls looked very young. Too young to be in trouble. But they were sadly wise beyond their years. Today's focus was on the difference between love and abuse.

Since they were allowed to discuss God in the group meeting — as long as the participants were willing, and they were — Marcus started the meeting with God's definition of love. He read it straight from 1 Corinthians 13 in his Bible.

" 'Love is patient; love is kind.' " Marcus looked up at the two girls. They seemed despondent. Like they weren't listening at all. He kept reading. " 'Love isn't envious, doesn't boast, brag, or strut about. There's no arrogance in love; it's never rude, crude, or indecent — it's not self-absorbed. Love isn't easily upset.' "

Lexy was the first to roll her eyes. Marcus stopped reading and waited for her to speak. Finally she tossed her hands up. "Okay." Hurt filled her tone. "You want to talk about 'love isn't rude'? Dwayne's rude all the time." She looked at Alicia at the other side of the table. "That's how guys are, right?"

"Definitely." The girl fidgeted, twisting her fingers together. Clearly uncomfortable. "Love always means someone's angry."

For the next half hour they talked about how for these girls love felt the exact opposite of how it was described in the Bible. Lexy announced that last week Dwayne had threatened to kill her.

"See, Lexy?" Mary Catherine's voice was kind. "That's what we're talking about today. Dwayne has harmed you emotionally and physically. That's not love."

Marcus loved watching Mary Catherine in this setting. It was like she was made for this role. She looked past Lexy's exterior hardness and spoke to the girl's heart. Now that their time together was winding down, both girls had opened up a little.

Lexy talked about the guys she'd had before Dwayne, and Alicia talked about her current boyfriend. Though Alicia's crimes involved theft, her relationships had apparently been equally bad for her. Marcus's heart hurt for the young girls. It would take more than ninety minutes to teach them that abuse was not the same as love.

But they had made more progress than Marcus dreamed.

It was like Officer Kent had told them at the first day of training. These kids were starving for someone to invest in them, to care enough to listen and give guidance. Sure, they'd throw up ten-foot walls at the beginning. They might do that at every meeting. But eventually they'd talk, and then there were only two rules for the volunteers.

Listen. And don't act shocked.

Which was hard, Marcus had to admit. Where were the people who were supposed to care for these girls and cherish them? Because of neglect or lack of supervision or bad patterns, their lives had been destined for violence and abuse, crime and even prison.

Today's meeting, though, proved there was hope. The girls were talking and they were listening. That was a better start than he had expected for their first gathering.

When the meeting was over, they took the girls to Dairy Queen. Part of the program was introducing normal moments, where the girls could be kids. Marcus couldn't believe how easily the girls laughed and enjoyed themselves. A different environment changed everything.

They were about to leave when Mary Catherine's phone rang. She stepped away to answer it and almost at the same time her eyes lit up. "He is! That's amazing!" She put her hand to her mouth and shook her head. "Shamika, I can't believe that. Yes, I'll tell them." Her eyes shone with unshed tears, her smile filling her face. "It's a miracle for sure."

The call ended and she motioned the others close. Lexy and her new friend came closer, clearly interested. "What happened?" Lexy was the first to ask.

"Jalen's awake! He's talking to his mama."

"That's amazing." Marcus came to Mary Catherine first, and then Sami and Tyler did the same. They formed a circle, their arms around each other.

"I can't believe it." Sami's eyes welled with tears. "This is the best news."

Marcus felt his knees shaking. "He wasn't supposed to live."

"I know." Mary Catherine's eyes shone with joy. "Now they think his brain will be fine!"

"Wow . . . thank God!" Marcus whispered the words. He loved that they were all together when the news came in. His Twitter followers were still spreading the word, still getting people all over the world to pray for the boy.

"Should we go there?" Sami sounded hopeful. "I'd love to see him."

"Maybe tomorrow. Shamika said the doctors are doing tests." Mary Catherine opened up the circle, her eyes on Lexy and Alicia, who were standing awkwardly a few feet away.

"We can all go together." Tyler sounded thrilled. "I've seen God do a lot of things, but this is at the top of the list."

Marcus put his arm around Mary Catherine's shoulders. Their friendship was more comfortable now. So much of what they'd been through together had been intense. He wanted to be there for her, to be available in the highs and lows.

And this was one of the highest highs of all.

Only then did Marcus notice Lexy. The girl had her hands over her face, her back turned to them. He watched her walk slowly outside, like she was in a trance, and sit at one of the tables. Again she buried her face in her hands, her shoulders shaking.

"What's up?" Marcus looked at Mary Catherine.

A knowing look came into her pretty green eyes. "I think I know." She motioned for him to follow her. "Come on. Let's go talk."

Tyler and Sami stayed inside with Alicia. Marcus led the way, opening the door for Mary Catherine as they joined Lexy at the table. Mary Catherine sat next to her and put her hand on the girl's back. "Sweetie, what's wrong?"

Lexy was sobbing. Marcus realized the great changes happening in the girl. She had been so hard when Mary Catherine first met her. But at the prison tour and again today, her heart was plain for all of them to see. She still had miles to go if the journey was to make a difference. But these moments of opening up with her emotions were another beautiful answer to their prayers.

After a minute, Lexy lifted her head. Her

335

eyes were red, her face wet. "Nothing."

Marcus was confused. "Nothing's wrong?"

"No." She sniffed, and another few sobs came over her. "I told God if He was real, then He needed to save that . . . that little boy." She shook her head. "I didn't believe He could do it." She covered her face with one hand this time. "So He must be real." She looked at them again. "God must be real."

There was a stinging in Marcus's eyes as he watched the scene. Mary Catherine slid closer to the girl and put her arm around her back. "That's right. He is real. And He loves you, Lexy. More than you could understand."

"I thought I'd pick something really hard." She wiped her cheeks with the backs of her hands. "Something only God could do. If there was a God." The sobs were still coming. "But . . . but if there's a God, then why would He love me after . . . after all the things I've done?"

They had so far to go. Marcus drew a deep breath. "Lexy, we all have things we shouldn't have done. God wants us to be sorry for that and tell Him. Then, well, we can have a fresh start. A new life."

"For me?" The hardness flashed in her eyes again. "In my neighborhood? It'll take

336

more than that where I come from."

"Maybe there's another way." Marcus refused to feel defeated. "There's always another way with God."

Lexy thought about that and slowly she nodded. A smile lifted the corners of her lips and she turned to Mary Catherine. "When you go see the boy tomorrow . . . can I go?"

Mary Catherine shared a quick look with Marcus. There might be legal reasons why Lexy shouldn't go to the hospital. After all, she'd been in the car with Dwayne when the shot was fired. Mary Catherine moved closer to Lexy and looked intently into her eyes. "I'll see what I can do."

"I know . . . you probably think the mama wouldn't want me." She sniffed. "All I wanna do is tell 'em I'm sorry."

"Okay." Mary Catherine was beyond kind. "I'll talk to them. I'm sure they'll be so glad you're sorry. And that you were praying."

Lexy nodded again. "I need to get home. I told my grandma I wouldn't be late."

Tyler and Sami and Alicia came out then and said their goodbyes. "I have to work early tomorrow." Sami made a face. "I'm thinking about quitting. Finding a job that really matters." She and Tyler shared a smile. "We'll see! Mary Catherine is rubbing off on me."

Marcus and Mary Catherine took Lexy home, too, and the minute they were back in the car alone, Marcus felt his heart soar. "You have time for dinner? We could pick something up and take it to my house?"

It looked like Mary Catherine might say no, find some reason why they couldn't spend another few hours together. But then she found her best teasing smile. "I could cook."

"Organic, no sugar, no bread." Marcus laughed. "Or . . . we could get pizza?"

Mary Catherine pressed her shoulder into the seat. "Seriously. I'll make you almond chicken. It'll be better than pizza. Promise!"

"Actually, that sounds pretty amazing."

They went to Whole Foods near his house and picked up the ingredients. Then they worked together in the kitchen. "You be my sous chef. How's that sound?"

"It sounds like a girl's name." He washed his hands. "But if you have to call me Sue to pull off this meal, go ahead." His computer was on a desk at the edge of the kitchen. He turned on Pandora and found a piano station.

Mary Catherine was trying to explain that the word *sous* meant he was her assistant for the night. "Just think." She grinned as she handed him an onion and a bell pepper. "You might fall in love with organic cooking. The way I did. This night could change your life."

She turned to the sink and Marcus stood there, just watching her.

He had never met anyone like her, the way she didn't care what people thought of her, the way she grabbed onto life like every day might be her last. He smiled. Yes, he might fall in love, and no question this night could change his life. But if that happened it would have nothing to do with the cooking.

The chicken was in a colander and Mary Catherine was separating the pieces. She looked over her shoulder. "Hey. You're supposed to be mincing those."

"Mincing." He found a knife and a cutting board. "I know cutting and slicing. I believe you were going to give me a demonstration on mincing. Wasn't that it?"

She moved to the adjacent sink, washed her hands, and dried them on a clean towel. "Okay." She came to him, her eyes sparkling. Night had fallen and it was just the two of them in the house. "Step aside."

He did, but not too far. The smell of her perfume filled his senses and made him wish they were more than a couple of friends making dinner together. She took the teaching seriously. "Mincing is smaller, neater." She cut a slice of the onion and then, using small movements, she turned the slice into tiny squares no bigger than the head of an eraser.

"Looks like a lot of work." Marcus laughed. "You sure we can't just slice them?"

"It's not hard. Here." She handed him the knife. "You try it."

He was utterly aware of her presence, the way their arms touched, the movement of her hands. He took the knife and gave it a try. The work was tedious, but he managed it.

"Perfect!" She leaned closer, moving the pile of minced onions to the side. "You got it?"

He wanted to take her in his arms and dance across the kitchen, forget about the onions and everything. Everything but her. Instead he did a slight bow. "Glad it meets your approval, Miss."

She giggled at him. "You sure you weren't raised in the South?"

"I wish." He held her eyes. "Maybe I would've met you sooner."

His words seemed to touch her deeply. Her laughter softened and she smiled at him. "I would've liked that."

"Me, too." He looked at the onions. "Better get cooking."

When it came time to prepare the chicken, Mary Catherine made a mixture with almond flour and spices. She dipped each small boneless chicken piece into a bowl of almond milk and then coated it with the almond flour. In the pan, she melted coconut oil and fried the chicken in that.

"Uh, can I just say . . ." Marcus hadn't smelled something so good in months. "You can cook dinner at my house anytime."

"Told you it would change your life." She kept the teasing tone. Probably because it was safe and fun, given her determination that she didn't want more than a friendship.

Marcus didn't care. He only wanted to be with her. The teasing was fun for him, too. He sautéed the minced vegetables along with sliced zucchini and they ate out on his deck. The night was unseasonably warm. Still seventy-five when they sat down to eat.

"It's beautiful here." Mary Catherine looked out over Silver Lake. "Sami told me about the view."

"You need to come over more often." The meal was perfect. But it was nothing to how wonderful it felt sitting here with her, outside of training or prisons or anything to do with the youth center. It reminded him of that first walk. Before the shooting.

"So the Wayne family lives around the corner?" Mary Catherine grinned at him. "No wonder you're so close with them."

"Rhonda loved you. She really wants to get to know you better."

"I'd like that."

"By the way." Marcus held up a bite of the almond chicken. "You've sold me. Organic cooking definitely just changed my life." He chuckled. "Seriously, I had no idea it would be this good."

"Food the way God made it actually tastes better. That was one of the things I had to learn."

"So you really don't eat sugar or bread? Like ever?"

Mary Catherine laughed. "You make it sound like a punishment."

"I guess I can't imagine." He took another bite. "Tell me you didn't want ice cream earlier."

"Sure, it tastes good. But I didn't want it." She raised her brow. "Sugar causes disease. Diabetes. Dementia." She gave him a silly look. "And yes. I do eat pizza once in a while. I'm not perfect."

He stared at her, studying her. Memorizing her high cheekbones and the shine in her eyes. "Awfully close."

She smiled. "You're too kind."

"Just honest."

They finished their meal, and the whole time their conversation was easy and fun. Marcus could feel himself falling into her gravity, but he didn't care. The sensation was mesmerizing. Together they carried the dishes in and Mary Catherine looked back at him. "When will Tyler be home?"

"I think he and Sami went to the movies." He pulled his phone from his pocket and checked the time. "Probably not for another hour."

Mary Catherine nodded. They worked rinsing their plates and scrubbing pans. The whole time Marcus tried to think of a reason to make her stay. It was just after nine o'clock. "You don't work tomorrow, right?" He gave her a hopeful look.

"I don't. The studio's closed every other Wednesday." She dried her hands on the towel.

"Can you stay? For a little while?"

"Well . . ." She seemed to struggle with the idea. But then she smiled and slipped her hands in the back pockets of her jeans. "I noticed your pool table."

She was constantly surprising him. "You play?"

"Play?" She cocked her chin. "I thought

about going pro. Decided it would take too much time."

The air between them was electric. Marcus was grateful for the distraction of a pool game. "Well, then . . . rack 'em up."

Halfway through the first game, Marcus started to laugh. "I thought you were kidding. About going pro."

"Never." She feigned an innocent look. "I never tease, Marcus. Not ever."

"Not about pool. That much is for sure." She was three balls ahead of him. "You could win a fortune at this. How'd you learn?"

"Played with my dad." Mary Catherine held her cue stick at her side and smiled. "It was the way we connected."

Marcus shook his head. "The man taught you well."

They played two games, and she won them both. "I could suggest best of five. But I'm afraid that would become best of seven at this rate."

Her laughter mixed with the piano music drifting through the house. "Maybe something less competitive."

"I have backgammon." He nodded toward a shelf in the family room. "Nobody touches me at backgammon."

"Next time." She smiled. "I should go."

"It's early." He didn't break eye contact with her. "Let's step out back again. The stars are probably just perfect." He reached for her hand and hesitated, drawn to her in a way he could barely fight. But she had made herself clear at the beach. He couldn't push for more. "Come on." He walked with her outside and they took up their spots at the railing, staring at the lake.

"You were right." She lifted her face to the sky. "The stars are gorgeous."

"I don't come out here often enough. You can feel God on nights like this."

"Mmmm. I like how you said that." She put her head on his shoulder. "You're right. I can feel Him, too."

Marcus was losing the fight. Why would she put her head on his shoulder if she only wanted to be friends? He slipped his arm around her waist and they stayed that way, the music falling all around them.

A buzzing came from Mary Catherine's phone. "Sorry." She pulled it from her pocket. "I'll turn it off."

But before she did, she looked at the message. "It's from Shamika." Mary Catherine adjusted the brightness so she could read it. "She says Jalen is doing even better." A soft gasp came from her. "The doctors think he'll make a full recovery!" She texted back as quickly as her fingers could move. "Amazing!" She turned her phone off and slid it back into her pocket.

Then, as if it were the most natural thing, she hugged him, impulsively linking her arms easily around the back of his neck. "I can't believe it. So much has happened. So many highs and lows. I mean, only God." Her laugh was part surprise, part relief.

Marcus slipped his arms around her waist. "I wondered how I'd go on. At the youth center." He spoke near her face. "If the boy never woke up."

The hug was meant as a celebration. One of those extreme highs they'd shared over the last week. Except after a few seconds, neither of them seemed to want to let go. She rested her head on his shoulder again. The song was something instrumental by Chicago.

He leaned back, searching her eyes. "Wanna dance?"

"I'm not very good at it." Her voice fell to a whisper as they started to sway.

"I doubt that." He held her close and led her slowly across the deck. Never mind that they were outside. The magic of the moment made him feel drunk with joy. Was this really happening? They were dancing under the stars and Mary Catherine wasn't fighting him?

"You, on the other hand . . ." She tilted her face to his. "You're quite the dancer."

"Took it for a year in college." He laughed. "Coach thought it would give the pitchers better balance."

"Did it?"

He looked at the sky and then back at her. "It gave me this."

"Well then." She didn't look away. "I guess it was worth it."

The song was ending, and Marcus could barely breathe. They were back at the railing and he slowed their movement, stopped their swaying. "Mary Catherine." He swallowed. He didn't know what to say. He only wanted this feeling to last forever.

She put her head on his chest again. "I'm sorry."

"No." He gently lifted her chin so she would look at him. "Don't be sorry."

Her eyes told him whatever was happening between them, she was feeling it, too. "I can't . . . I'm not . . ."

"Shhh." He took her face in his hands. It was too late to stop, too late to do anything but kiss her. The way he had wanted to kiss her since their walk that night. Slowly he brought his face to hers. Their lips touched and the feeling was light and passion and desperation, all at the same time.

She didn't fight him, didn't try to pull away. Instead she returned his kiss, working her hand up his neck to the back of his head. Marcus was consumed by her, taken by her in a way that affected his entire being. She moved him, body and soul. He drew back, checking her eyes. "You okay?"

"I need to go." Her lips were still parted, her breathing faster than before. "Marcus . . . I want this." She hung her head and when she looked up the sadness in her eyes was greater than the heat a few seconds ago. "I can't. I'm sorry." She leaned up and kissed him again, slowly, deliberately. But it was a goodbye kiss.

Marcus could feel the difference.

She stepped back. "Take me home. Please."

He shouldn't have kissed her. Marcus reached for her hand. "I'm sorry. I should've waited."

"No." She shook her head. "It's not you. It's me. I can't . . . explain it." She allowed him to hold her hand as they walked in and got her things.

On the drive, disappointment greater than the breadth of the sky washed over him. What was wrong with her? When they reached her apartment, Marcus killed the engine and turned to her. "Is it me? You're not attracted to me?"

A single laugh escaped her and she let her head fall back. "Are you serious?" She looked at him, her cheeks slightly redder than before. "I can't even think around you." She took his hand and looked deep into his eyes. "You make me feel . . . like I've never felt."

"So . . ." Hope shot through Marcus. "Maybe we need to take things slower. Stay with Tyler and Sami so" — he laughed — "you know, we don't wind up dancing under the stars."

The laughter left her and she looked at her hands for a long few seconds. "It's not that." She angled her face and turned her eyes to him once more. "Please, Marcus. Trust me."

He wanted to argue, but there wasn't room. She had left him no choice. He climbed out, helped her from her side of the car, and walked with her up to the door. When he hugged her, she let herself linger. But she eased back before either of them might think about another kiss. "Thank you." She smiled, her eyes as sincere as summer. "I had the best night ever."

"Me, too." He wanted to stop time and make her explain things. How could she slip into her apartment without helping him understand? If they both felt this, then how come . . . ?

Her smile was marked with longing. "Bye."

"Bye."

He waited until she shut the door before turning around and heading back to his car. In all his life he'd never felt like this. The way she made him feel. And since she was as drawn to him as he was to her, he had no idea what the problem was or why she wouldn't tell him. He knew only one thing.

He wouldn't give up until she did.

27

Except for their group meetings at the police station on Thursday and a hangout with Tyler and Sami Saturday night, Mary Catherine did a good job of avoiding Marcus the rest of the week.

She had no choice.

Her doctor appointment was that Monday morning and as she signed in at the office, she knew her hurting heart had nothing to do with her health. The night at Marcus's house had been the best. Mary Catherine had told him the truth.

The pull Marcus Dillinger had on her was beyond anything she had ever experienced. She had replayed that night a thousand times and always she was sure. There was nothing she would've done differently. He made her laugh and feel, and in his presence all of life was good and right and whole.

By the time they stepped out on the deck

after the pool games, Mary Catherine didn't care about her damaged heart or the time she didn't have. She had that night. It was all she could think about.

The nurse stepped out and called her name. "The doctor will see you first. We'll do paperwork and blood tests later. Before you leave."

"Yes, ma'am." She followed the woman to a familiar room, changed into a hospital gown, and waited.

A few minutes later Dr. Cohen stepped inside.

"Mary Catherine." He shook her hand. His face was masked in shadows. "I'm sorry about all this." He raised his brow and gave a single shake of his head. "It took me by surprise." He pulled up a chair and sat down, facing her. "A heart transplant is always a possibility for anyone with your condition. But I really thought you'd only need a valve."

The Internet had given Mary Catherine ample time to research. "I wrote down a few questions." She pulled her phone from her purse. "Is that okay?"

"Of course." He crossed his arms, waiting.

She opened her notes app and started at the top. " 'Why not a valve transplant first?

It wouldn't be as invasive, and it could buy us more time.' " She looked at Dr. Cohen. "Right?"

"Well . . ." He angled his head one way and then the other, as if he were weighing the possibility. "I had a patient last year. Tried to replace his aortic valve and his ascending aorta — exactly the surgery you would need in that scenario." He gave a sad shake of his head. "Young guy. Just twenty years old. Suffered a heart attack during the procedure, which created more damage. He had to be resuscitated nine times before we finished operating."

The doctor explained that the surgery did such damage to the young man's heart, he was suddenly rushed to the top of the transplant list. "Thankfully, he got his heart. He's doing well."

Mary Catherine hung onto those last few words. "A person with a heart transplant can do well?"

"Yes." Caution sounded in his tone. "There are nearly two hundred thousand patients waiting for a heart. Conditions have to be just right."

"But if . . ."

"It's a long road, but yes. We know of heart transplant patients who are still alive twenty, twenty-five years after surgery. It's rare but possible."

Possible.

For the first time since the call from the doctor's office a week ago, Mary Catherine didn't feel like she was falling. The blackness that sucked her hope and light and energy cracked and she could see blue sky again. "I . . . guess I didn't know that."

"It doesn't always work that way. If a patient gets a heart . . ." His brow raised again. "*If* . . . well, then, sometimes the patient is sickly for the next few years and then we lose them. Their bodies can reject the organ or vice versa. Lots can go wrong."

"Dr. Cohen." Mary Catherine smiled. "You should know me better than that. I'm not a lots-can-go-wrong kind of girl. I believe in the most rare possibilities." They'd been over this before. "Remember?"

"Yes." The doctor smiled, patient. "Because that's where God works best."

"Exactly." She tried not to think about Marcus. "I had made a plan not to fall in love. Given the situation." Her smile took some effort. "But from what you just told me, there's still hope."

"For love?" The doctor had a fond way of looking at her. As if she were his daughter.

"For life. To really live."

"Your situation is complicated, Mary

Catherine. I don't want to give you false hope."

"Hope can never be false. It's the product of faith, the substance of things not seen." She exhaled and tried to settle down. "I didn't know heart transplant people could live that long. That's all."

"I'm afraid I have more, Mary Catherine."

She blinked and sank a little into the examination table. "Okay."

Dr. Cohen opened a notebook and went over her tests in detail. Her situation was much worse than he had expected. Worse than Mary Catherine had known.

"You'll start feeling symptoms soon. Tiredness, shortness of breath." He peered at her, sterner than before. "You need to curb the things that give you an adrenaline rush. I know that'll be hard."

Mary Catherine stared at the man and then let her gaze fall to a spot on the floor. "Adrenaline rush?" She muttered the words and then looked at him again. Her whole life was an adrenaline rush. "Like . . . skydiving?"

"That, obviously. But boogie boarding . . . sprinting . . . competitive games. Anything that makes your heart work too hard."

The darkness was back. "You're asking me to quit living?"

"No." He sighed and closed the notebook. "Mary Catherine, I'm asking you to take it easy. Be serious about this. Until we can find you a heart."

She nodded, but inside she was falling . . . falling the same as before. "And you think it'll be at least six months before I'll be on the list?"

"Yes." He frowned. "I'm so sorry. You'll need to talk once a week with a counselor about what's too much activity now and what's appropriate health and wellness care as you near your time on the list. We have a myriad of blood tests for you today and . . ."

Mary Catherine couldn't hear him. He was still talking, still telling her all that was required of her and how her life would change while she waited to be placed on the list. Something about the time being sped up if her next series of heart tests in a few months were significantly worse than they were now. All Mary Catherine could think about was adrenaline, and the fact that it had been hurting her heart.

The very thing that made her feel alive was taking years off her life.

Dr. Cohen was explaining something else, something about how though she wasn't quite sick enough to be on the list, she was getting there quickly. But Mary Catherine was picturing the children on her refrigerator, the ones she sponsored. What if she didn't get a transplant? Or what if she got one and it didn't take? She would never have another time like now to go to Africa, to live there and move among the people and love them the way she had always dreamed.

She couldn't have Marcus, that much was certain.

At least she could have this. "Dr. Cohen." She must've interrupted him because he looked like he was caught midsentence. "I'm sorry. I have to tell you something."

"I understand this is difficult." His patience remained. "What is it?"

"I'm moving to Africa. In a month." She couldn't pose the idea as a question. He'd never let her go. "I'll be living in Uganda for six months." She was aware she sounded a bit intense. She softened her tone some. "I . . . thought you should know."

"Mary Catherine, you can't move to Uganda. Not when we're trying to get you on the transplant list."

"You're doing the tests today, right? Any additional tests can be done there. They have a hospital. We can have the results sent to you."

Dr. Cohen looked caught off guard. "That

would be . . . well, it would be highly unconventional. You'd have to return at a moment's notice. The minute we could get you officially on the transplant list."

"I understand." A surge of elation rushed through her. Her damaged heart had cost her so much, but it wouldn't cost her this. She would leave California as soon as possible. Spend a week with each of her parents and then fly to Uganda. She was connected with a ministry there, and they were always looking for volunteers. If she had it her way, she would spend the next six months building a new orphanage. Something that would serve the people for decades.

Even if she couldn't.

"I have to tell you, Mary Catherine, I completely recommend against a move to Uganda. With your heart this way."

"I have no symptoms. I feel wonderful." She thought about dancing with Marcus the other night. "Better than wonderful. If I'm going to move to Uganda I should do it now. Before I start to feel . . . whatever you said."

Again he looked stumped. "How quickly can a person get home from Uganda? That's what I want you to find out. You'd need a couple days' travel at least." He removed his glasses and massaged his brow. "I'm not sure that would get you here quickly enough."

"I won't wait that long. If I start to feel sick, I'll come home."

"You understand that this goes against the advice on adrenaline?" Dr. Cohen set his notebook on the counter beside him. "I ask you to keep things calm, and you tell me you're moving to Uganda."

"It's a calm place, Dr. Cohen. Really." She grinned. "No amusement parks, no skydiving. Very simple."

"Let's get through your blood tests and paperwork." He stood and pulled his stethoscope to his ears. "Let me take a listen." He moved around behind her and pressed the base to her back. "Breathe."

Mary Catherine filled her lungs.

"Again."

She did as he asked. He spent several minutes listening to her heart through her back, and then through her chest. When he was finished he exhaled, like someone not willing to keep fighting. "No more than six months. You got that?"

"Yes, sir." Mary Catherine felt the exhilaration surging in her veins. It wasn't the kind of joy she'd known the other night in Marcus's arms. But it was something better, given the circumstances.

It was a plan.

She could check one more thing off her dream list and maybe while she was busy working with kids and babies in Africa she would get better. Stranger things had happened, right? Look at little Jalen.

The doctor left her to get dressed. She could hardly believe it was going to happen. Sure, her doctor was reluctant. But still he had cleared her to go to Africa. Her favorite nurse drew her blood that day. Sally Hudson. Sally was small and pretty with blue eyes and a warm smile. She was quick with a kind word or a Bible verse.

Usually when Mary Catherine needed it most.

"Hey, honey." Sally sounded subdued as she led Mary Catherine to a chair in the lab. "I heard about your tests."

"I still don't believe it." She held out her arm so Sally could reach her vein. "I keep thinking there has to be a mistake."

"Well, don't you go believing everything a doctor says." Sally put a stretchy band around Mary Catherine's upper arm as she felt around for the vein. "In 2001 I was diagnosed with leukemia. No one in my family was a match."

She inserted the needle in such a way that Mary Catherine didn't feel a thing. Sally smiled at her. "Doctors told me I didn't stand a chance without a bone marrow transplant. So I did the only thing I could do. I cried out to Jesus." The nurse focused on the blood draw. "Changed my whole life."

Mary Catherine appreciated the story. "You look super healthy."

"A few years later they found a donor. Perfect stranger. Perfect match." She finished filling three vials with Mary Catherine's blood. "Only God has the number of your days."

"I believe that."

"You have one chance to write the story of your life. Make it a bestseller." Sally put a piece of cotton and a bandage over Mary Catherine's arm on the place where the needle had been. "Look at this." She took a framed photo from the desk behind her. "This is my family. My daughter Angie had us all meet in Ohio for a family reunion. That's me and my husband. Our four kids and ten grandkids. That was the day we had our annual candy-making." Sally had never looked happier. "If I listened to every awful thing a doctor told me, I would never have prayed for a miracle."

Mary Catherine held onto Sally Hudson's words long after she left the office. But as she drove home through heavy traffic she let her mind drift. She was no longer stuck on an LA freeway. In her mind, she was on Marcus's back deck, dancing beneath the stars, feeling the amazing attraction and lost in his arms. *Stop,* she told herself. There was no point thinking like that.

She would go to Africa and she would believe the trip might even be good for her. She would watch for symptoms and head back if her blood work or tests or pain level changed. She had to go. The trip would give her the one thing she desperately needed, the one thing she had to figure out before she changed her mind.

How to say goodbye to Marcus Dillinger.

Jag waited at the door of the examination office, Aspyn at his side. They were both stunned. "I didn't see this coming."

"How could we have?" Aspyn looked ready to fight, ready to take action. Only this time there was nothing to act against. They could do nothing about this problem.

Because it was inside Mary Catherine's chest.

"The enemy will stop at nothing." Anger filled Jag's heart. Illness was part of a fallen world, the handiwork of the darkest forces on earth. "There has to be something we can do."

They had known Mary Catherine had a heart condition. That she would need a valve transplant in a few years. Not a big deal, they figured.

But this . . .

"We have to find a reason for her to stay." Aspyn's eyes blazed. "We need to ask Orlon."

"And pray for wisdom." Jag was in his element here in LA. But a heart condition? One that threatened to take Mary Catherine's life in less than a year? "It will take all of heaven pulling together."

They watched as Dr. Cohen typed his notes, filling out a report on his visit with Mary Catherine. The man sat alone in his office. He looked deeply defeated. A call came in and he answered it.

Jag and Aspyn listened intently.

"I told her I consulted with you and that we all agree." The doctor stared out the window. "No . . . I didn't tell her that." He paused. "It's such an unusual case. She isn't sick enough for a transplant today. But six months from now . . . you're right. It might be too late." He released a tired sigh. "She's in serious trouble." He waited. "Yes, I know. I tried to tell her."

"It's worse than we think." Jag's voice was distant.

"There's nothing more we can do." Aspyn's tone was broken. "It will have to be another Angels Walking team. Months from now."

"In Africa?" Jag's frustration nearly overwhelmed him. "We have to think of a way to keep her here, in Los Angeles. With Marcus."

It was a dilemma they'd battled for the past week. Finding ways to keep Mary Catherine and Marcus together. Jag's mind raced, still every time an idea came to him the impossibility was greater. Especially now that Mary Catherine was determined to leave.

Aspyn was right. They seemed out of options.

They moved to the waiting room, where Mary Catherine was filling out a stack of paperwork. Jag felt the heaviness in the room, the deep discouragement coming from Mary Catherine. *It's okay, dear girl,* he wanted to tell her. *Jesus isn't finished with you.* This Angels Walking mission might be nearly over.

But they hadn't lost yet. The greater battle was still at stake. Jag forced himself to hold on to that truth.

Even if the next stage of the war took them to the opposite ends of the earth.

28

Marcus could feel her slipping away. He picked Mary Catherine up each Tuesday and Thursday for the meetings with Lexy at the police station, but no matter what he suggested, she wouldn't spend time with him. Not alone.

Tyler and Sami were talking with Alicia, while Marcus, Mary Catherine, and Lexy listened. The program had been incredibly beneficial for both girls. At least it seemed that way. They hadn't had a run-in with the law, and every week they opened up a little more.

Lexy planned to be homeschooled by her grandmother for the next few years and get a job. She didn't know what the future held, but she was finished with the WestKnights. She had made that decision two weeks ago. Even sent texts to everyone in the gang. She got some pushback, but nothing like what she expected.

Sadly, there were plenty of girls ready to ride shotgun with guys from a gang.

The conversation now was about future plans, what Alicia would do in the coming months while the school year played out. Marcus tried to listen, but he struggled to focus. Mary Catherine was sitting beside him. He could feel the way she moved, sense the way she loved these lost girls.

She consumed him. There was nothing he could do to change the fact.

He let his mind drift. The two of them never talked about what had happened between them that night at his house, and he didn't push for answers. When they said goodbye he could see the pain in her eyes, the same pain that stayed with him whenever they were apart. It was insane to think that he hadn't figured out what a treasure she was until the beginning of January.

Now it was the first Thursday in February, the last meeting at the police station with the girls. Tomorrow morning Marcus and Tyler would leave for Glendale, Arizona. Spring training would begin Saturday. And then he wouldn't see her for two months.

For some reason, Marcus had the sense he didn't have long with Mary Catherine. Maybe because he was leaving tomorrow. But it was more than that. He couldn't quite get his mind around the feeling. Yet still it was there. No matter how hard he tried or how much he prayed, he couldn't find his way back to that moment with her in his arms, under the stars on his deck.

Marcus had thought of a hundred scenarios. Reasons she wasn't willing to think about dating him. Plausible possibilities for why she wouldn't talk to him about it. Some days he figured there must be something going on back in Nashville, something she had to make right before she could move on. Maybe it was someone her parents wanted her to marry.

Or maybe that was it. Her parents. Maybe they wouldn't approve of her dating a biracial guy. Whenever that thought crossed his mind, Marcus always dismissed it. If race had been an issue, she would've said something by now.

There were times when he thought maybe she had something physically wrong with her. Like she couldn't have kids or she was allergic to baseball diamonds. Maybe she'd suffered some traumatic event as a child and she wasn't able to form lasting connections with people. That was a legit disorder, right?

Marcus shifted in his seat, his eyes on Alicia, who was still talking.

Whatever the reason, there was no denying it. The feeling was there each time they were together. And lately she had kept her distance again, the way she had when they first started hanging out.

A few days ago after the meeting with the girls, Marcus and Mary Catherine took Lexy to the youth center. The new director was doing a great job. His work meant that Marcus could stop by when he wanted to, pay for pizza each week, and still get on with baseball. For now that was a more realistic setup.

That night they had played a pickup game of basketball with some of the teens who were there. When it was over he and Mary Catherine had high-fived. But when he tried to hold her hand, she eased away from him. "Gotta get water!" she had told him.

Sure, she had been out of breath. But that wasn't why she left so quickly.

Marcus tried to stay in the moment. Alicia was done talking. She smiled at Tyler and then at Sami. "Is it okay if . . . I still meet with you? Like once a month or something?" She looked uncomfortable for the first time that afternoon. "I think I might really need that."

Involvement in the program after the first four weeks was optional. But all of them were willing to help. At least they'd agreed on that at the beginning.

Tyler stroked his chin, clearly trying to find an answer for the girl. "Marcus and I leave in the morning for a few months." He looked at Sami.

"I'll be here." Sami reached over and patted Alicia's hand. "We can definitely meet."

"Me, too?" Lexy looked from Sami to Mary Catherine. "Could we maybe all meet?"

"I want to." Mary Catherine was quick with her answer. "But I'm not sure about my schedule."

Sami smiled. "I can promise you girls this. I'll be available for both of you. Once or twice a month at least. But let's talk and text more than that."

Marcus sat back in his seat and looked at Mary Catherine. Something had just happened, but he couldn't figure out what. Why wasn't Mary Catherine saying anything? How come she didn't offer to meet with the girls? He met her eyes, but she looked away. A sick feeling started in his stomach and quickly moved to his heart.

Just like he thought, she was pulling away. Not just from him, but from all of them. Whatever else happened, he had to get to the bottom of this. Figure out what was wrong and why she was distancing herself.

By tomorrow it would be too late to sort out what was happening, to hear what was going on in her heart. So that left just one option.

He would have to find out tonight.

Mary Catherine couldn't look Marcus in the eyes. They were all four going out to dinner after the final meeting with the girls. She had already told Sami her plans to move to Africa. She would tell the guys tonight. At the same time.

The session ended, and Officer Charlie Kent joined them along with a few new volunteers. Mary Catherine recognized one of the women as Aspyn, the neighbor who had pushed Marcus out of the way the night of the shooting at the youth center. Mary Catherine and the woman exchanged a smile.

Officer Kent asked the four of them to talk about how they thought the program had gone, and then finally he turned to the girls. "Would either of you like to tell our new volunteers about the difference this time has made?"

Mary Catherine didn't expect either of them to say anything. They'd come miles since a month ago. But that didn't mean they would share here. But even as she was telling herself the reasons Lexy wouldn't talk, the girl raised her hand. "I'd like to say something."

Lexy sat up straighter. Something else she wouldn't have done at the beginning of the program. "Before, I just always assumed I'd be in prison one day." Her eyes looked tender. "Like my mama." She turned to Marcus and then Mary Catherine. "I didn't know I had a choice. But now I know I got someone who cares about me. I don't need to hang with the guys, risking prison and getting killed. I belong somewhere else now."

Moments like this Mary Catherine wondered if she was making the right decision. Maybe she was supposed to stay in Los Angeles and help Lexy. She could stay out of Marcus Dillinger's way and keep from falling in love with him. And never — no matter what — have a night like the one at his house. If she could do that, she could stay.

But she would miss her one chance at Africa.

When Officer Kent was finished, the group dispersed. Aspyn walked up to Mary Catherine. "Remember me? From the youth center that night."

"Of course." Mary Catherine would never

forget. Marcus was alive today because of this woman.

"I wondered if you heard about the latest situation. The kids on the street are talking about the program." Aspyn smiled. She put her hand on Mary Catherine's. "You've done a wonderful job."

"Thank you." Looking into the woman's eyes was like looking into the ocean. They were that light, that complex.

"Anyway" — Aspyn glanced at the door — "there's another dozen girls ready to go through what Lexy did. But we only have a handful of volunteers." Aspyn gave Mary Catherine a single sheet of paper. "This describes the need." She smiled. "I told Officer Kent I'd ask you to stay on. You and Sami. The city really needs you."

Mary Catherine looked at Marcus across the room. He was talking to Tyler, his long legs and filled-out shoulders reminding her of what it felt like to be in his embrace. She looked back at Aspyn. "I'm afraid I may not be staying in Los Angeles." She took the piece of paper. "I'll keep it in mind, though."

"Okay." Aspyn didn't move. She looked deep into Mary Catherine's eyes. "Just remember . . . you don't have to go halfway around the world to find a place to help out. The need is very great right here." She smiled again and then slipped her purse onto her shoulder and headed for the door.

For a few seconds Mary Catherine wondered how Aspyn knew. How was that possible? Had she somehow talked to Sami? Or was she just guessing, assuming Mary Catherine might be leaving for some sort of mission work?

The woman had to still be just outside. Mary Catherine hurried to the door to call after her, but the parking lot was mostly empty. Just a few cars, nothing and no one else. She took a few steps out the door and looked to the left and then to the right. The woman had already driven away.

But her message remained.

It was a message Mary Catherine would keep with her. So that she would know there was a place for her here. If she was ever healthy enough to come back and take on work like this again. For now, she didn't dare dream of a time like that. She looked at Marcus again and felt the now-familiar hurt. No, she would stay in Uganda until she was sick enough to need a heart. Then she'd come back.

Not a day sooner.

Marcus made reservations at Gladstones in Malibu. A bit of a drive, but not bad considering the beautiful winter night. The moon was full, so he requested a table by the window. They arrived a few minutes early and found the place nearly empty.

Exactly as Marcus hoped it would be.

With his and Tyler's flight to Arizona set for the morning, anything that needed to be said had to be said now. Tonight. They took their table and chatted about the Last Time In program while they ordered and waited for their food. Only then did Sami look at Tyler and Marcus and finally Mary Catherine.

"I have an announcement." She folded her hands and smiled. "I can't believe I did this, but I quit my job!"

"What?" Mary Catherine lived with her, and she apparently hadn't heard anything about this. She laughed softly. "And you say I'm impulsive."

"I know. You changed me." Sami laughed, too. "I didn't make up my mind till today at work. I decided my time had to be worth more than handling public relations for businesses and movie stars." She grinned at Marcus. "So I took the marketing and community affairs job at the youth center. I'll mostly work from home, but I'll be there a few days a week."

Tyler looked hesitant about her decision.

"I told her it was too dangerous. It's one thing to meet with the girls at the police station. But the youth center . . ." He took Sami's hand and paused for a moment. His smile started in his eyes as he looked at her. "I'm happy for you, Sami. And I'm proud of you." He turned to the others. "She told me it was something Mary Catherine would do."

Marcus sat next to Mary Catherine across from the other two. Mary Catherine was about to say something, he could sense that much. But he had the worst feeling that whatever it was, he didn't want to hear it.

Then just when he wasn't sure he could take another moment of her pulling away from him, beneath the table Marcus felt Mary Catherine reach for his hand. She didn't let go. "Sami, you'll be perfect. The community is ready for change. I really believe that."

"After working with the Last Time In program, I figured I had to make a change." Sami smiled at Mary Catherine. "Because you have to live your life, right?"

"Right." Mary Catherine gave Marcus's hand a slight squeeze. "Speaking of which . . ." Her smile looked weak. "I have an announcement, too."

Only Sami didn't seem surprised. She

simply turned approving eyes toward her friend and waited.

Mary Catherine looked at Sami and then Tyler. "I'm moving to Africa. I'll leave here in the middle of the month to spend a few weeks with my parents in Nashville. Then I'm off to Uganda."

Marcus released her hand. He turned to her, but she wouldn't look at him, wouldn't face him. He worked to keep his tone even. "What . . . brought this on?"

"I've been planning it." Finally she turned to him. Her eyes begged him to understand. "It's something I've always dreamed of doing. I just got clearance a few days ago."

Clearance? Marcus felt like he was going to be sick. He wanted to take Mary Catherine down to the beach and hear the real story, the reasons she would've chosen to leave. Especially now, when she was making such an impact with Lexy. When she had admitted feelings for him. He struggled to keep his tone even. "What do you mean, clearance?"

"I've been in contact with a ministry in Uganda. They need someone to coordinate the building of a new orphanage." Again her smile didn't reach her eyes. "We figured it out this week." She tried to sound upbeat, but she was definitely failing. "I'm their girl."

There was nothing Marcus could say. Any conversation about the issue would have to happen later, when they were alone. If they were alone. Tyler and Sami made small talk about Africa and how Tyler had always wanted to take a mission trip there. Maybe one day they would all go.

The banter did nothing to ease the devastation Marcus was feeling. Halfway through dinner he thought of another question. "How long will you live there?"

"That's the good news." She hadn't tried to take his hand again. "Only six months. I should be able to make sure the orphanage is built and established in that time."

Marcus did the math. Six months meant she'd be back sometime in August or September. Just when baseball season would be wrapping up. Was this why she hadn't wanted a relationship? Because she knew that behind the scenes she was working to move to Uganda?

In some ways the idea was better than the other scenarios Marcus had imagined. He'd be busy pitching and traveling. He was frustrated she hadn't told him sooner, but six months away didn't have to be the end of things between them. They could talk and

Skype, right?

He felt bad for pulling his hand away. He reached for hers and she willingly let him. This time he slid his fingers between hers. The way they'd never held hands before. She smiled at him, a sad sort of smile, and again her eyes said more than her words could. At least here.

"Everything will be so different tomorrow." Tyler put his arm around Sami's shoulders. "Sami told me she might make a trip to Arizona halfway through spring training." He smiled at Mary Catherine. "She hoped maybe you'd come with her."

"Yeah." Mary Catherine frowned. "She told me that earlier today. I would have. If the move to Uganda hadn't come through."

Marcus wished she'd quit calling it a move. She was taking a trip. Nothing more. He wasn't going to let her go, not until she told him she didn't care about him.

A somberness hung over the table as they finished eating. Tyler was right. Come tomorrow everything would be different. But Marcus wasn't finished with tonight. He would drive her home and they would finish this conversation later. She didn't have to be afraid of being gone for six months. He would've waited much longer than that.

He could hardly wait to tell her.

29

Mary Catherine was quiet on the drive back to her apartment. Halfway there, Marcus asked if she could come back to his house. So they could talk about her trip.

"I really can't." They weren't holding hands this time. "I have to work tomorrow."

Marcus didn't respond.

She hated this, hated the look in his eyes. He didn't understand, and she couldn't blame him. The trip to Uganda worked in her favor. Her leaving meant she had one reason why it wasn't an option to give in to their feelings. Their lives were going in different directions.

They were both quiet until they reached the apartment. She wanted to talk to him. This was the last time they'd see each other for a long time. Maybe forever — depending on how things went with her heart. She couldn't let him leave here upset with her.

"Walk me up?"

"That's all? Just walk you up and say goodnight and that's it?" He wasn't angry, just confused. She could see that much in his eyes. She understood. The chemistry between them, the attraction and pull — it was undeniable. They had so much in common. She prayed God would give her the words to help them both understand.

"Sami's out with Tyler." Mary Catherine smiled at him as they reached her apartment door. "Come in. Please."

He looked relieved. The truth was, neither of them were willing to say goodbye yet. Once they were inside they sat together on the sofa. The lights in the room were dim — perfect for the farewell ahead.

The space between them felt like an ocean. Marcus pulled one leg up so he could face her. "Why didn't you tell me?"

"I wasn't sure." Mary Catherine didn't want to hurt him. She had never meant to get involved so quickly. "I mean, I always talked about Africa."

"Not moving there." His tone wasn't antagonistic. He only wanted to make sense of what was happening.

"It . . . came together quickly."

Marcus exhaled and for a minute he looked away, looked at the apartment and the photos on the walls. "You've never asked me inside before."

"I wanted to." He was dissolving her defenses again. "I just . . . I didn't want either of us to get hurt."

"That's what this is about?" He reached for her hand and again she let him take it. "I'm not worried about getting hurt. What I feel when I'm with you . . . it goes all the way to my soul."

Mary Catherine nodded. "I know." She eased her fingers between his. "It's that way for me, too. With you."

"So what's six months? You miss baseball season, big deal."

"I don't want to miss it. I want to be at every game." She paused. "I watched you pitch that World Series win from right here."

He looked in her eyes, to the places only he had ever seen. "I wish I'd known you then."

"Me, too." She ran her thumb over his hand. "I've thought about this. How we've gotten so close so fast." She tried to smile, but it didn't touch the sadness in the air between them. "I think it was all the tragedy. The shooting. Jalen. Lexy. Even the program."

"And our faith." He looked like he wanted to slide closer to her. But he kept his distance. "Your most beautiful crazy amazing faith made me take a harder look at God. The Bible. One day after we were together I drove out to Dodger Stadium and gave my life to the Lord. It was the day before I was baptized."

"Mmm. I didn't know." It was another reason why the connection between them was so strong. What they shared was more than physical and emotional attraction. It was spiritual. If only she had more time.

Marcus didn't look away. "What did Aspyn tell you today?"

"She said the program needs more volunteers. She was hoping I'd stay on for another round."

"See . . . that's what I don't get." He leaned his shoulder into the sofa and looked at her. As if maybe the answers were in her eyes.

She loved the way his pale blue sweater made his eyes look even lighter. The connection between them was so strong it breathed life into her. At least it felt that way.

"I wish . . ." His voice was thick with emotion. "I wish you would let me love you, Mary Catherine."

Tears clouded her view. She had known tonight would be difficult, but she hadn't expected this. All she wanted was to be in his arms again, kissing him under the stars as if she had ten thousand more nights like this.

She didn't want him to see her cry. Without saying a word, she stood and walked to the window. She leaned on the frame and looked at the dark sky. Through the glare of the streetlight she couldn't see a single star.

There was no need to turn around. She could feel him coming to her, the way she always felt his presence when he was near. He slid his arms around her shoulders and pulled her to him. "That makes you sad? That I want to love you?"

With all her being she wanted to stay facing the window, to keep from turning into his embrace. But she could no more stop herself than she could tell herself not to breathe. Or her heart not to beat.

"Marcus." She turned and faced him and nothing else in all the world mattered. "It makes me sad because you can't."

He didn't want to fight with her. That much was evident in his eyes. They were deep and afraid and full of the most incredible love. All at the same time. He nodded. "Okay." For a moment it looked like they might kiss. Because neither of them was strong enough to resist this kind of pull. He ran his thumb softly over her cheekbone.

"I'll wait then. Till we're both back here. When the season's over and you've had your time in Africa."

A quiet terror ran through her veins. She wasn't getting through to him. If he waited for her, things would only be worse. He would be devastated when he learned the truth. And that wasn't fair. Her health was her problem. "That's just it." She searched for the next words. "I might not come back, Marcus. I might stay in Nashville."

A new sort of fear filled his expression. "You can't do that." He worked his fingers back into her hair. "Please. Tell me you'll come back here."

"Sometimes . . . it just can't work." She thought about telling him the whole truth . . . or lying to him, convincing him she wasn't interested. But he would never believe her. Not when she was seconds away from changing her mind about Africa. That was the effect he had on her. She put her hand on his chest. If only her heart were as strong as his. Her eyes searched to the deepest places in his soul. "Can you understand that?"

"No." He held her closer, and for a few seconds he brushed the side of his face against hers. "I won't understand that. I'll wait for you. And if you don't come back here, Mary Catherine" — he looked into her eyes again — "I'll find you."

There was no fighting her feelings. Love fell like autumn leaves around her, filling her heart and soul and senses. She lifted her face to his as easily as if they'd loved each other all their lives. The kiss started slowly, desperately. But the passion came quickly and made Mary Catherine feel things she'd never felt. She understood how easily two people could fall.

Even the air around her felt like something from a dream. Like all her life had led to this one single moment. She kissed him again. "I'm sorry."

"Don't be." He kissed her jaw and her cheekbone. "What if God made us for such a time as this? To be together?"

"I can't." She was drowning. If she didn't step back from him now, she might say things she'd regret, make promises she could never keep. She was breathing hard. They both were. She put her hands on his shoulders to steady herself. "Could you . . . could you be my friend? While I'm gone?"

The muscles in his jaw tensed. For a long time he thought about her question. Mary Catherine knew why. Marcus didn't want to be just her friend. She didn't want that either. But it was all she could offer him.

Finally he nodded. "Yes." His wanting her was still in his eyes, the way she was sure it was still in hers. "If it means staying in touch with you. Sharing my heart with you. Then, yes." He pulled her close again, and this time they shared a hug. Nothing more. He ran his hand over the back of her head. "I'll be your friend, Mary Catherine. If that's what you want."

The moment was ending — Mary Catherine could sense it. She took a half step back and looked at him one last time, memorizing his face. "If . . ." Tears filled her eyes and she had to blink to see him clearly. "If I was going to love someone . . . it would be you."

She put her hands on either side of his face and one last time she kissed him. The feeling was different than just a moment ago. Because this time — once again — the kiss meant goodbye. "I always said I could only love a guy who was real." She smiled. "Remember? When you said you wanted real?"

He nodded, never breaking eye contact with her. "I meant you. I told you you're the most rare kind of real."

"You, too. I mean it, Marcus." She pressed her fingers beneath her eyes. "I've never met a man like you. And for what it's worth . . .

it nearly kills me . . . to say goodbye."

He didn't understand. She could see that in his expression, in the depth of his heart. But she'd said all she could say. He mustn't know about her heart. She wouldn't tell him. This night would not turn into an hour of pity, of worrying about her and convincing her not to leave. She had to go to Africa. The move was the one right thing she could do in the little time she had left.

She walked with him to the door and stepped outside with him. He hugged her one last time. "I'll email you. I'll text and call. Whatever way I can get to you." He smiled, but tears glistened in his eyes, too. "I'll be the best friend you ever had."

The sound that came from her was more cry than laugh. "I believe it." She allowed herself to get lost in his eyes one last time. This was what she had prayed for, what she had hoped for. That he wouldn't leave here upset or angry. She placed her hand against his cheek. "Thank you."

There was no need to explain. Marcus was clearly willing himself to understand.

He kissed her forehead, and then he stepped back and held up his hand. "Bye, Mary Catherine."

"Bye."

The distance between them hurt more

with every step he took. She wondered what could possibly be worse. A love that might only last a year . . . or feeling the pain of watching him go?

She stood there until he drove off and then she didn't try to stop the tears. Her empty arms ached from missing him. And he hadn't been gone five minutes. She lifted her face to the sky. "I don't like to ask why, God." She hugged herself, the tears still streaming down her face. "There's a reason you gave me this heart. I know."

A wave of exhaustion came over her. She leaned against the apartment door and the sobs began to come. Quiet, full-body sobs. She was going to be okay. This was the life God had given her. Soon she would begin to feel symptoms of her failing heart. She would feel tired and short of breath and she would know the end was near.

Whether they found a heart for her or not.

When that happened she would let herself relive this night again and again, replaying it from her place in a cold hospital room. And she would feel once more what it felt like for just an hour to be loved. Really loved. And when the time came to leave this place for heaven, she would do so with a full and healed heart. Because she would know at least this much.

She had spared Marcus Dillinger the pain of loving her.

Marcus couldn't stop the tears.

He brushed at them, angry and unsure of everything. Why couldn't she believe him? He would wait for her. Six months . . . six years. Whatever it took. He didn't want to love anyone but her.

But if she wanted his friendship, he would give her that. It was his only hope, and probably more than she'd planned on offering him. Whatever the reason.

Instead of going home that night he went by Coach's house. He needed to talk in the worst way. He pulled up in front of the Waynes' and texted him. *You home?*

The response came quickly. *Sure. What's up?*

I'm out front. Can you come here?

The porch light was on in less than a minute, and Coach Wayne stepped out in shorts and a sweatshirt. He walked to the SUV and slid into the passenger seat. "Marcus."

"Coach."

He looked concerned. "You okay?"

Marcus couldn't remember anyone seeing him cry. He kept his composure. "I'm in love with Mary Catherine."

Coach Wayne visibly relaxed. He smiled. "That's a good thing, right?"

"No." Marcus wasn't sure how to explain the situation. He was still trying to understand it himself. "I mean, she doesn't want me. Or she doesn't want love." He looked straight ahead, but all he could see was her face, her green eyes. "She told me she only wants to be friends."

"Hmmm." His smile faded. "I didn't know."

"She's moving to Uganda." Marcus looked at his coach again. "For six months."

"I knew that. She talked to Rhonda about it."

Marcus wished he could've heard that conversation. Hopefully Rhonda Wayne tried to talk Mary Catherine into staying. Not that it mattered now. She was leaving. Her mind was made up.

"She said I could keep in touch with her . . . while she's gone."

"But you want more than friendship."

"Yes." Marcus kept a rope around his emotions. He needed answers, not pity. "What do you think? Can I be her friend and still . . . pursue her?"

"I think so. Ultimately the One who knows best is God." Coach Wayne gave him a pat on his knee. "If she's part of the plans

He has for you, then yes. Chase that girl, Marcus. You'll know when it's time to let her go. If that time comes."

Marcus nodded. He liked how Coach said that. There was only one other thing he wanted to do. "Would you pray with me?"

"Of course." Coach Wayne kept his hand on Marcus's knee. "Father, You know how we men need to chase. Give Marcus the ability to do both — love and chase — even in the form of a friendship. At least until You make Your plans for his life clear. Keep Mary Catherine safe and grow the connection between her and Marcus according to Your will. Thank You, God, ahead of time. We trust You in all this. In Jesus' name, amen."

"Amen." Marcus felt a little better. "Thanks."

"You got it. We can talk more on the plane if you want." He opened the car door. "See you in the morning."

Marcus drove home, his heart still heavy. He had no idea when he'd see Mary Catherine again. He was back to baseball for now.

Back to chasing sunsets.

He thought about Shelly and how he hadn't known whether he had pursued her or she had pursued him. The idea sounded ridiculous now. But then, he had never known what it meant to want to pursue a girl until Mary Catherine.

If God would allow him to chase after her, he would do so every day, with all his heart. He would pray for her and check in on her often. She wanted his friendship, so there would be good days ahead. Times when they would text and laugh and tease. Times when they would share their hearts and fears and hopes and dreams. Even from different continents. And not for one day would he think about giving up on her.

Not unless God Himself made that clear.

Tyler Ames made the drive to Sami's grandparents' house early the next morning. Two hours before the flight to Arizona. There was something he had to ask them, something that couldn't wait.

Her grandfather opened the door. It was only seven thirty, but already the older man was dressed in a stylish dark gray suit, ready for the next power meeting. "Tyler." He opened the door and Tyler stepped inside. The man looked slightly bothered. "How've you been?"

"Well, thank you." He shook the man's hand. "You?"

"We'd like to see our granddaughter more

often." He softened a bit. "Of course, we've been at our San Francisco home." He chuckled, but he made no attempt to invite Tyler into the house. "We've only been back a week."

"She told me she's planning to come by. Maybe tonight."

"Perfect." Mr. Dawson studied him. "You look good, Tyler. Coaching now, isn't that right?"

"Yes, sir. It's going better than I hoped." Tyler needed to get the question out. If he didn't get back on the road soon he'd miss his ten o'clock flight. "Anyway, I came because Sami and I have gotten very close."

The man remained unmoving. As if he had no idea what was coming.

"We share the same faith, same dreams and goals." Tyler could feel sweat on his palms. He would probably be one of the few guys in history turned down at this phase of "the ask." He put the thought out of his head. "Anyway, before I leave for Arizona this morning, I wanted to ask you."

Mr. Dawson blinked. "Ask me what, young man?"

"For Sami's hand in marriage. I want to marry her, sir." Regardless of what happened next, Tyler felt a rush of joy. Just saying the words left his heart practically bursting.

Tyler really wasn't sure what Sami's grandfather was going to do next. For several seconds he only stood there, like he was either in shock or thinking of a way to tell Tyler no.

But then his expression changed and his eyes grew damp. "Tyler." He hesitated. "I believe I owe you an apology."

"Sir?"

"You see . . ." His chin quivered and he shook his head, clearly trying to find the words. "When you left Samantha . . . she was never the same." He put his hand on Tyler's shoulder. "I vowed you would never break her heart again." He allowed the hint of a smile. "Can you promise me that, Tyler? That you'll never break her heart again?"

Tyler gave the man a hug, the kind a father and son might share at a reunion. "Yes, sir. With everything I am, I promise you."

Mr. Dawson stepped back and this time his smile stretched across his face. "Well, then. My answer is yes. You have my blessing."

Sami's grandmother joined them. "What's this?" She was wiping her hands on a dish towel. When she saw Tyler she stopped short. "Hello, Tyler. Is everything okay?"

"Yes, ma'am." He was one step closer to marrying Sami. The whole world was okay. "I asked your husband's permission to marry Sami." He hesitated. "Samantha."

"And I said yes." Mr. Dawson put his arm around his wife. "Looks like we'll be hosting a wedding!"

Sami's grandma hugged him. "We're very proud of you, Tyler. Of the man you've become. I'm sure Samantha will be very happy."

"Any idea when you'll ask her?" Mr. Dawson crossed his arms.

"Soon. If I can pull my ideas together." Tyler grinned. He'd never felt so sure of anything. "I have spring training first. But sometime after that."

He wrapped up the conversation, got back in his car, and headed to the airport. They wouldn't have much money, not at first, anyway. His salary with the Dodgers was still entry level. And now she'd taken the job at the youth center. The pay was half what she'd made at the PR firm. But none of that mattered.

There was nothing but sunshine and happy days ahead.

He was about to ask Sami Dawson to marry him.

EPILOGUE

Angel Town Meeting — Heaven

Orlon felt the same concern as everyone on his team. The mission had taken a very difficult turn. The baby who was supposed to be born in time might never be born. Their greatest goal was definitely in jeopardy. Like everything else good and true and right on earth.

The angels entered the room, their faces somber, serious. Usually at the end of an Angels Walking mission there would be cause to celebrate, reason to know they had succeeded.

Not this time.

When every angel was accounted for, Orlon moved to the front of the room. "I'd like Jag and Aspyn to join me."

The Angels Walking team moved to their places beside him. "I want to make one thing clear." Orlon's voice was strong, resolute. "You did not fail this mission."

Jag set his jaw, his face slightly raised. If any angel needed this talk, he did.

Orlon continued. "Jag . . . you and Aspyn were the perfect angels for this mission. Just as we all agreed before you left. You were given several tasks, and you succeeded in each one of them." He ran through the list. "Most of all, you kept Marcus Dillinger alive and saw that his would-be killer was placed behind bars."

Jag put his arm around Aspyn. The two of them looked down for a few seconds, as if they were remembering the intensity of their time on earth.

"I can't remember a recent Angels Walking mission with so much danger, where so many lives were at stake." Orlon looked at the other angels. "We watched and we prayed. And now we will give thanks to God for His miraculous intervention and for the success of the work done by Jag and Aspyn."

This was one of Orlon's favorite parts of being an angel. Listening to the applause break out through the room, the soft utterances of Jesus' name and the praise meant to glorify God alone.

When the noise settled down, Orlon took a deep breath. "Any questions?"

An angel in the front row raised his hand.

"Did you ever see Ryan Williams? The little boy you saved the last time you went on an Angels Walking mission?"

Orlon could tell by the look on Jag's face that the meeting hadn't occurred. He put his hand on Jag's shoulder. "The boy is a police officer. Just out of the academy."

Deep concern filled Jag's eyes. "I . . . I didn't know."

"Yes." Orlon looked to the angel who had asked the question. "Ryan may be a part of another mission. We'll have to see."

"I'd . . . like to watch when that happens." Jag's tone was proof that the long ago failed mission still stayed with him. "If that's okay."

"Definitely."

Other questions came. Concerns about how Jag was able to control his anger. Orlon was curious about that, too.

"Very simply, I didn't control it. I felt everything a human feels and in light of the little boy being shot, I wanted to kill. The desire ran through my veins." Jag looked at Orlon. "I'm being honest."

"We know." Orlon was grateful for the way things had turned out. "The question was, how did you find control?"

"The name of Jesus. Lexy shouted Jesus' name, and the anger left me. All in a rush. I

401

belong to Him. I couldn't think about acting on my own after that."

Orlon felt a sense of pride over Jag's actions. Many angels in the room would've struggled with the same challenge. It was another reason why it was so important to choose the right angels for each mission.

Angels Walking always came with risks.

This one more than most.

Jag and Aspyn were dismissed back to their places among the others.

The unknown ahead was their greatest problem now. Orlon faced the angels and straightened to his full height. "We must talk about what's next." He hesitated. "The main concern now is Mary Catherine."

He let that sink in. "She will go to Africa, and she will get sick. The next stage of our mission will be nearly impossible. There will be very great heartache." Michael had confirmed that much. Orlon looked at their faces. "You are heaven's most prepared angels. Experts in matters of the heart. But we will need two very experienced angels next time around."

The meeting was dismissed and Orlon spoke to Jag as he left the room. "I'm proud of you. I know how hard this mission was. There wasn't an hour of rest."

"Thank you, sir." Jag ran his hand through

his blond hair. "I just wish we could've done something for Mary Catherine."

Orlon smiled. "You did."

"Sir?" Jag clearly didn't understand.

"You kept Marcus Dillinger alive."

With that Jag smiled and headed after the other angels. When the room was empty, Orlon got down on the golden floor and lay his face to the cool stones. For the next hour he talked to the Father, begging for wisdom and direction.

If they failed the next mission, there would be no going forward.

All of heaven and earth would pay the price.

Dear Reader Friend,

I promised you this time around I'd share my own angel encounter. Like all interactions with angels, I can't be sure I was really in the presence of a heavenly being. But I know this.

There's no other way for me to explain what happened.

It was 2007 and I was headed to Atlanta, Georgia, for the International Christian Retail Show. That year my book *Even Now* was up for book of the year — the first time a novel had been nominated. Before I left, my mom and dad drove to my house — just to say goodbye.

My dad, Ted Kingsbury, was especially emotional. "I wish I could be there," he told me. "I know you're going to win."

It was the same way with my dad ever since I was a little girl. He would read what I'd written and rave over it. From the time I was twelve he would tell me, "Someone has to be the next bestselling novelist, Karen . . . it might as well be you!"

All my life my dad believed in me, and that night before I left for Atlanta with my kids Kelsey and Tyler, my dad was convinced the big award would be mine.

The award show happened two nights later, and my dad's prediction came true.

Even Now was named book of the year. Back home my dad was so excited. He spent the next day talking to my mom and calling my husband, Don. "We need to throw Karen a party," he told them. "Let's think of something."

But the party was not to be.

That afternoon my dad suffered a massive heart attack. One minute he was talking with my mom, and the next he was out. Laid back in his recliner like he'd fallen into a deep sleep.

My nephew Andrew was thirteen at the time. He was the first to think something was wrong. He called 911 and an operator talked him through giving my father CPR for the next fourteen minutes. Keep in mind my dad was very heavy and he wasn't on a flat surface. He was in a recliner.

By the time paramedics arrived, my dad was blue and unresponsive. Andrew ran into the next room and started sobbing. He thought he'd done something wrong. He believed his grandpa's death would be on his shoulders.

The house was chaotic, the paramedics working feverishly on my dad. Ten minutes became fifteen and there was talk of calling in the time of death.

Suddenly a police officer rushed into the

house. He found my mother and pulled her aside in the next room. "Do you believe in Jesus?" he asked her.

"Yes!" she cried out. "Yes, we're believers."

With a peace-filled intensity, the man looked straight into my mom's eyes. "We're going to pray that God gives your husband life again." He pointed back to where young Andrew was still crying. "We're going to pray because otherwise that boy out there will spend the rest of his life thinking this was his fault."

And so the officer took hold of my mom's hands and he prayed. "Dear God, we ask that the power that raised Lazarus from the dead would breathe life into Ted Kingsbury this very minute. In Jesus' powerful name, amen."

The very second the officer said, "Amen," from the other room the head paramedic yelled, "We have a heartbeat!"

They were able to keep my dad alive all the way to the hospital, where he lived another six weeks in ICU. We had time to tell him everything we ever wanted to say. We laughed and remembered every wonderful memory and we prayed every possible prayer.

When he died, our family was at peace

and so was my dad.

Later my mom tried to find the officer who randomly came into the house to pray with her that day. She called the police station and asked the paramedics. No one had ever heard of the man.

We came to believe that the officer was an angel, sent in response to so many prayers being cried out on behalf of my dad. An angel, maybe, on an Angels Walking mission.

Now you know why I allowed Jag to be a police officer.

Keep a lookout this fall for book three in the *Angels Walking* series. Mary Catherine, Marcus, Tyler, and Sami have so much ahead. The Wayne family, too.

Until next time, keep your eyes open. God is working all around us. Sometimes it's just a matter of looking.

In His light and love,
Karen Kingsbury

P.S. Connect with me on Facebook or Twitter, @KarenKingsbury. If you found yourself changed while reading *Chasing Sunsets,* if you became closer to God or if you gave your life to Jesus for the first time, then drop me an email at Karen@ KarenKingsbury .com. Write "Life Changed" in the subject line. If you do, I'd love to send you a Scripture letter I put together. Also, if you are unable to afford a Bible, and if you are unable to borrow one from your church or a family member, I will send you one. Simply write "Bible" in the subject line of your email.

FOREVER IN FICTION

A special thanks to Angie Rhyne, who won the Forever in Fiction item at my One Chance Foundation auction in 2012. Angie chose to name her mother, Sally Hudson, as a character in this book. Sally is small with beautiful blue eyes that long ago gave her the nickname "Blue-Eyed Sally." She loves her family, including her husband, four children, and ten grandchildren. Her favorite vacations are the ones that take her back to Ohio to visit extended family. Sally loves reading and cooking — especially her annual "candy-making day" with her daughters and granddaughters. Beyond that, Sally found a faith in Jesus when she was first diagnosed with leukemia in 2001. She needed a bone marrow transplant, but no one in the family was a match, so Sally and her family prayed. A match was found and Sally received a lifesaving transplant. Years later she had the opportunity to meet her donor in what was an emotional reunion.

In *Chasing Sunsets,* Sally is a nurse at the doctor's office where Mary Catherine is a patient. In the book, Sally's story serves as an encouragement and allows Mary Catherine to believe that God is not finished with her just yet.

The One Chance Foundation is an organization that grants money to people at the end stage of adopting. For more information, please check my website —
KarenKingsbury.com.

READING GROUP GUIDE:
CHASING SUNSETS
KAREN KINGSBURY

Use these questions to go deeper into the story or to encourage discussion with your small groups.

1. Read Ephesians 6:12. According to this verse, what are our struggles against? Are they from this world? Explain.

2. Where did you most see the spiritual battle being waged while reading *Chasing Sunsets*?

3. Why was Jag concerned he was the wrong angel for this Angels Walking mission? What did you think about his past?

4. How can failing make us better equipped for today? Give an example from your life.

5. The term *chasing sunsets* is brought up early in the book by Marcus. What was that in reference to? Have you ever flown west

and thought that you were chasing the sunset? What else could that term mean? Discuss it.

6. Have you ever considered the possibility that angels might fail? Discuss what happened to Jag in his Angels Walking mission a decade ago. Do you think the Bible supports such an idea? Why or why not?

7. Read Genesis 19:11. According to this Bible verse, is it possible one duty of an angel is to fight men? How did this play out in *Chasing Sunsets*? Is it comforting to imagine angels fighting on your behalf? Explain.

8. In your opinion, what was the most intense part of this Angels Walking mission? Can you think of an intense time in your life when things took a miraculous turn? Talk about it.

9. What do you think of the idea that not all people can see angels when they're on earth? Talk about an angelic encounter you or someone you know may have had.

10. Hosea 12:2–4 tells a story of man overcoming an angel. How do you think

that could happen? Was Jag at risk of being defeated by Dwayne? Explain your thoughts.

11. Lexy had a very difficult life. Why do you think girls like Lexy are drawn to guys like Dwayne? Explain.

12. Do you know much about gang warfare? Are gangs a problem in your area? Talk about that. What is your city doing to stop gang violence?

13. Talk about Marcus Dillinger. How did he feel after a shooting erupted outside his new youth center? Where was he finally able to find real meaning? Give examples.

14. Marcus was baptized at the beach. If you were baptized, talk about the experience. If not, talk about a special time at the beach. Why do you think we are drawn to the water?

15. The Wayne family has an open-door type of home, always welcoming people into their lives. Do you know anyone like that? What do families like that teach you? Why?

16. The Waynes also had a home church service every Sunday. Have you heard of

house churches? What is your experience with church?

17. Early in the book, Mary Catherine learned that her heart was in trouble. At that point, she took a new position on ever falling in love. Explain how she felt. Do you agree with her? Why or why not?

18. Have you ever watched a documentary on the Scared Straight program? What are your thoughts about that type of tactic with at-risk kids? Talk about the Last Time In program. How was it different from a traditional Scared Straight program?

19. Do you agree with the idea of volunteers acting as advocates for at-risk kids? Share personal examples.

20. Mary Catherine talked often about moving to Africa. Have you ever dreamed of doing something like that? Share your stories.

ABOUT THE AUTHOR

#1 *New York Times* bestselling novelist Karen Kingsbury is America's favorite inspirational storyteller, with almost 25 million copies of her award-winning books in print. Her last dozen books have topped bestseller charts and many of her novels are under development as major motion pictures. Karen lives in Tennessee with her husband Don and their five sons, three of whom are adopted from Haiti. Their actress daughter Kelsey is married to Christian recording artist Kyle Kupecky. You can find out more about Karen, her books, and her appearance schedule at www.KarenKingsbury .com.

The employees of Thorndike Press hope you have enjoyed this Large Print book. All our Thorndike, Wheeler, and Kennebec Large Print titles are designed for easy reading, and all our books are made to last. Other Thorndike Press Large Print books are available at your library, through selected bookstores, or directly from us.

For information about titles, please call:
  (800) 223-1244

or visit our Web site at:
  http://gale.cengage.com/thorndike

To share your comments, please write:
  Publisher
  Thorndike Press
  10 Water St., Suite 310
  Waterville, ME 04901